W9-BYF-719

# When Darkness Falls

## Tales of San Antonio Ghosts and Hauntings

### Docia Schultz Williams

**Republic of Texas Press**

Library of Congress Cataloging-in-Publication Data

Williams, Docia Schultz.
  When darkness falls : tales of San Antonio ghosts and hauntings  /
  Docia Schultz Williams.
      p.     cm.
  Includes bibliographical references and index.
  ISBN 1-55622-536-9 (pbk.)
  1. Ghosts—Texas—San Antonio     2. Ghost stories—Texas—San Antonio.
  3. Haunted places—Texas—San Antonio.    I. Title.
  GR110.T5W56    1997
  398.25`09764'35101—dc21                       97-9192
                                            CIP

Copyright © 1997, Docia Schultz Williams

All Rights Reserved

Republic of Texas Press is an imprint of Wordware Publishing, Inc.

No part of this book may be reproduced in any form or by any means
without permission in writing from Wordware Publishing, Inc.

Printed in the United States of America

ISBN 1-55622-536-9
10 9 8 7 6 5 4 3 2
9704

All inquiries for volume purchases of this book should be addressed to
Wordware Publishing, Inc., at 2320 Los Rios Boulevard, Plano, Texas 75074.
Telephone inquiries may be made by calling:

(972) 423-0090

# Contents

## Chapter 1
## Haunted Hotels and Inns

## Chapter 2
## Food, Service, and Spirits: Haunted
## Eating Establishments

## Chapter 3
## Phantoms in Public Places

## Chapter 4
## School Spirits, Public and Parochial

# Contents

# Acknowledgments

First, I am very grateful to all the people who shared their time and their stories with me. Without them, there would have been no book. I have tried to mention each one in the section titled "Sources."

I must give my special thanks to Brandy Davis of Bed and Breakfast Hosts of San Antonio and South Texas, who did a fantastic job finding ghost stories among San Antonio's many fine bed and breakfast inns; to John Leal, former Bexar County archivist, for his assistance and historical information; and to John Igo, Professor of English, San Antonio College, for his stories and special information.

Sam Nesmith, military historian and psychic, and his lovely wife, Nancy, have long been friends and special advisors to me. Sam has helped me to more fully understand the world of the supernatural, and he and his friend Robert Thiege, to whom I am also indebted, spent many hours with me, visiting some of the more difficult-to-explain haunted sites. I am extremely grateful to them.

Managing editor Mary Elizabeth Goldman and publicist Sharon Bogard of Republic of Texas Press deserve a big thank-you for their encouragement and continuing faith in me.

I am, admittedly, a computer illiterate. Without my dear husband and helpmate, Roy Williams, who spent many hours at the computer to help me whip this manuscript into proper shape for publication, I would never have completed this project. After working with me on four books he has never wavered in encouraging me to "write another one!" My love and thanks, Roy.

# Introduction

On a recent trip to the British Isles, one of the true haunting grounds of the world, I quizzed numerous innkeepers, guides, castle guards, and bookshop clerks as to the probability of ghostly inhabitants being in their particular bailiwicks. Most of the time I received affirmative answers! I found also that numerous books have been written about these hauntings and ghosts, and I purchased enough of them to make my hand-baggage pretty unwieldy by the time my twenty-one-day odyssey ended.

What most interested, and also surprised me, was that the British couldn't seem to own up to having any modern-day ghosts. I was told about medieval ghosts, Georgian ghosts, Roman ghosts, Druid spirits, and Victorian ghosts. There were tales of lords and ladies, kings and queens (many of whom were beheaded!), knights, tragic Scottish clansmen, soldiers and statesmen and other assorted nobility, most of whom have rested in their crypts for hundreds of years. But no one admitted knowing about any recent hauntings.

Not so with San Antonio! No, indeed! Our city boasts of ghosts and wraiths of all sizes, descriptions, and ages. Some of these spirit beings have not long rested in the solitude of their graves, while others may have been departed from their earthly labors for many years.

Maybe we can't boast of history as tumultuous as that of the Tower of London or the haunted Palace of Holyrood in Edinburgh, but our hauntings are just as fascinating, and because I actually know a lot of people who cohabit with residents of the spirit world, I personally find our present-day

San Antonio spirits, novices though they might appear to be to the British, just as interesting and intriguing as Great Britain's famous habitue of castles and haunted manor houses.

This work is the fourth book I have written in as many years. I guess I have been cast into the role of super reporter of Texas's spooks and spirits. It's become a habit to look for these strange lost creatures everywhere I go. I enjoy researching, interviewing, and writing about the subject because so much is still out there beyond our comprehension.

In the course of writing my books dealing with the supernatural, I have run into numerous people eager to share their experiences with me. Here in San Antonio I give a lot of talks and programs for clubs, conventions, schools, and various organizations. Often at the conclusion of my talks people come up to me, wanting to share a story or a personal experience they might have had. But then, when I set up an interview, they back off, becoming reticent and sometimes almost paranoid when they realize their names and their stories might actually appear in print. They insist on their names being changed, locations not to be mentioned, descriptions of houses to be disguised, until finally, in their quest for total anonymity, their stories have become so changed they are scarcely recognizable. Many times, I have found the stories I wanted to tell have become sufficiently altered that I have been forced to abandon them entirely. This is an on-going frustration, one I presume I probably share with other writers.

Wherever allowed, and whenever possible, I have named names and places, and reasons why it is believed that some of these hauntings take place. The stories are all based on actual events, and I have made every effort possible to check out the authenticity of each story and the veracity of each storyteller. The people I have interviewed are normal, intelligent, sincere individuals who just happen to have had some very unusual experiences in the realm of the supernatural.

Ghosts, which is what this book is all about, seem to be the souls, or spirits, of people who have died and do not yet realize they are no longer living. Often these people were the victims of sudden, traumatic, tragic deaths. They just weren't prepared to go! They have not stepped over into the "light," that peaceful world of eternal rest, and they keep returning to the places where either they died or conversely, where they were happiest when they were alive.

I have been told that a haunting results when there are constant repetitions of the same ghosts doing the same things, almost as if the same movie was being shown on a screen over and over again. These particular ghosts seem to come back on anniversaries of events more often than not. Then, there are the spirits who never are able to manifest themselves to the point where their apparitions are actually seen. They are the shy types, who are content to make their presence known by just making noises. Their footsteps are heard, they open and close doors and windows, turn lights, television sets, or radios on and off, cause the pages of a book to turn, a rocking chair to move, or a curtain to flutter when there is no breeze. The more active types can be quite mischievous, making things move about, causing objects to fly across rooms, and hiding things from the living owners. These naughty spirits are called poltergeists.

I have not put these stories into print with the object of convincing the reader there are such things as ghosts or spirits. I am only a storyteller, a chronicler of experiences related to me by reliable witnesses. My intention is to enlighten and hopefully, to entertain.

Many writers have tried to explain the phenomena over the years. Way back in 1778 the English writer Samuel Johnson penned these words: "It is undecided whether or not there has ever been an instance of the spirit of any person appearing after death. All argument is against it, but all belief is for it."

Personally, I believe it.

# Author's Note

It was in 1992 that I coauthored *Spirits of San Antonio and South Texas* with former newspaperwoman Reneta Byrne. It has been widely accepted by lovers of ghost stories!

Many people contacted me after that book's publication and told me stories about places in San Antonio I did not realize were haunted. It appeared to me that there was enough material for a second San Antonio book. I just needed to do some interviewing, compiling, investigating, and organizing to get it done. This book is the result of over two years of research. Even so, I am quite sure some good stories have eluded me.

Because many of you who have purchased this new collection of San Antonio ghost stories already have *Spirits of San Antonio* on your bookshelves, I have referred to some of the stories in that volume when I have received updated information, since hauntings seem to be an ongoing thing. If you don't already own *Spirits of San Antonio*, I believe you would enjoy referring to that book as you read this one. It will soon become evident to you as it has to me that San Antonio, Texas, is certainly one of America's most haunted cities. But then, I am not at all surprised. San Antonio is such an interesting and fascinating place in which to live, a lot of folks just don't want to leave it when it's their time to go; so those *Spirits of San Antonio* just keep returning, and it's most often *When Darkness Falls*.

Hauntingly yours,

Docia Schultz Williams

# A Glossary of Ghostly Terms

In studying the spirit world I have come to realize there are many types of ghosts and hauntings. Sometimes the terminology causes confusion, so here is a listing of a few of the terms used in referring to the supernatural in this book. Definitions are from *Webster's New World Dictionary of the American Language.*

Apparition: A ghost or phantom, anything that appears unexpectedly or strangely.

Ghost: The supposed disembodied spirit of a dead person, appearing as a pale shadowy apparition. (Author's note: They can also be very solid in appearance, just like a live human being.)

Haunted: To recur repeatedly; a place often visited, supposedly frequented by ghosts.

Phantom: An apparition or specter.

Poltergeist: A ghost held responsible for mysterious noisy disturbances.

Specter: A ghost or apparition.

Spirit: A supernatural being as a ghost or angel; not corporeal (which means of a material nature).

Spook: A ghost (colloquialism often used at Halloween).

Supernatural: Not explainable by known natural forces or laws; specifically of or involving God or ghosts, spirits, etc.

## WHEN DARKNESS FALLS

*When darkness falls, the night-bird calls*
*And the moon glows full in the sky,*
*Out they creep, from where they sleep*
*They're the souls that will not die.*
*Silently they reappear*
*Lightly treading as they roam*
*Through time and space, back to the place*
*They consider their rightful home.*
*Sometimes you'll clearly see them;*
*Fleeting shadows on the walls*
*And sometimes, you'll only hear them*
*As they come, when darkness falls.*

Docia Schultz Williams

# CHAPTER 1

# HAUNTED HOTELS AND INNS

## HAUNTED HALLWAYS

*Hotels, like houses, can haunted be. . .*
*By ghosts one can both hear and see.*
*In inns and charming dining places*
*Spirits dwell in the hidden spaces.*
*At one, there's a wraith that walks the hall*
*And one, there's banging on the wall.*
*In one, a shadow, dark and scary*
*Enough to make a traveler wary!*
*Candles move, and lights go out,*
*When 'ere the spirits are about.*
*So when you stop to spend the night,*
*Perhaps you'd best leave on the light!*

Docia Williams

# All Sorts of Hostelries

The dowager queens of San Antonio hoteldom are the Menger, the Gunter, the Crowne Plaza St. Anthony, and the Crockett. These hotels bear the distinction of being San Antonio's oldest hostelries.

The Menger, located on historic Alamo Plaza, opened its doors to the public on February 2, 1859. This was just twenty years after the Battle of the Alamo! It has never closed.

The St. Anthony, named for the city's patron saint, opened on January 4, 1909, at the corner of Travis and Navarro Streets. It was the first air-conditioned hotel in America. Just a few months later, and just a block away, the Gunter, now known as the Camberley Gunter, opened its doors on November 20, 1909. At that time the 301-room, eight-story hotel was the largest building to have been constructed in San Antonio.

The Crockett, named for the heroic David, celebrated the laying of its cornerstone by the builders, the Independent Order of Odd Fellows, on April 26, 1909. This hotel is located right behind the Alamo and across Crockett Street from the Menger.

All of these hotels are beautiful, comfortable, and still extremely popular with visitors to San Antonio. And, or so it seems, all of them are haunted!

This old city also boasts many beautiful and spacious homes over a century old. Many owners have converted their too-large-for-a-small-family residences into charming bed and breakfast inns. In doing so, they have served a dual purpose: to provide visitors to the city with an interesting alternative to larger, more impersonal hotels and motels, and to provide a source of income to the owners to offset the ever-rising costs of maintaining such large and expensive-to-operate residences.

I am indebted to the managements of the Menger, Gunter, Crockett, and St. Anthony for letting me use their stories. I am also grateful to Brandy Davis, of the Bed and Breakfast Hosts of San Antonio, for finding so many inns for me that have spirits in residence. Of course, I am also indebted to the individual innkeepers for sharing their stories with me.

I have tried to describe the various properties and what they offer to visitors to our city while at the same time writing about their various and sundry spirits. To enjoy your own stay in one of these lovely bed and breakfast inns, call Bed and Breakfast Hosts of San Antonio and South Texas at (210) 824-8036 and they will be happy to put you in touch with the inn of your choice.

# The Marvelous, Mysterious Menger

The old Menger Hotel, a beautiful hostelry situated on Alamo Plaza, has long been the venue of history in the making, and mystery for the taking! Built in 1859 by German immigrant William Menger and his wife, Mary Guenther Menger, the old hotel has been the scene of many a gala ball, extravagant reception, and candlelit dinner party. Generations of debutantes have been presented to local society in its grand ballroom. The hotel has seen life whirl by, with vignettes of pathos and tragedy sometimes mixed in with all the glamour, glitter, and excitement it has known.

Menger Hotel

Many famous people have made the hotel their homes away from home. Captain Richard King always stayed at the hotel during his frequent visits to San Antonio from his famous South Texas ranch. On one visit he took very ill. His personal physician told him he wouldn't live much longer. He spent the last months of his life in his suite (now named the King Ranch suite) saying good-bye to his friends and getting his affairs in order. When he passed away in August of 1885 his funeral was conducted in the original lobby.

Writers O. Henry and Sidney Lanier penned some of their famous works while staying at the Menger. The beauteous Lillie Langtry stayed there, as did Sarah Bernhard, Anna Held, and more recently, the golden voiced Beverly Sills. Gutzon Borglum, the creator of the Mount Rushmore monument, once maintained a studio at the Menger.

Teddy Roosevelt, Presidents Taft, McKinley, Eisenhower, and Nixon all stayed at the hotel at one time or another. There's a photo of Harry Truman in the lobby, too, taken during one of his visits.

Financial titans Cornelius Vanderbilt and Hamilton Fish signed the guest registers as well. Can you believe these fabulously wealthy New York millionaires came to Texas to sign up with "Teddy's Boys," the famous Rough Riders, in 1898?

While traveling through the country on a lecture tour, the ultra flamboyant, totally outrageous Oscar Wilde stopped over at the Menger in 1882. Now don't you know the Texas cattlemen who often gathered at the bar to culminate a cattle deal must have been astounded by the appearance of Wilde, clad in a lace-frilled black velvet frock, knee-length trousers tucked into scarlet stockings, and slippers buckled in silver, as he strolled around the patio sipping spiked lemonade while smoking exceedingly long foreign cigarettes? It must have been more fun just to see him than to hear his lectures!

Roy Rogers and Dale Evans (How many Saturday afternoons did I spend my allowance money watching Roy and Dale gallop across the silver screen, when I was a little girl!)

spent so much time at the Menger there is a suite named for them.

Along with all these famous people staying there, there were several suicides and other deaths. All this activity naturally stirs up ghostly visitations. In *Spirits of San Antonio* I wrote at length about the appearance of Captain King's ghost. There was also a rather lengthy accounting of Salie White's demise and subsequent appearances. Salie was a chambermaid, murdered by her common-law husband, Henry Wheeler. She often appears in the corridors of the old section of the hotel where she once cleaned rooms for the wealthy guests at the Menger.

Like a reel of film unrolls to reveal a fast-moving motion picture, so time itself continues to move on, ever faster, revealing more mysterious manifestations at the Menger. The spring of 1996 had quite a rash of them, many of which centered around the old Menger Bar. Why this was such an active period, I couldn't say. Then I spoke with Robert Thiege, a psychic friend, who seemed not at all surprised. He explained that he believed there would be more and more activity as the time approached 1998, the hundredth anniversary of the recruitment of the famous Rough Riders. It was at the Menger Bar that Teddy Roosevelt, then a cavalry colonel stationed at Fort Sam Houston, held "court," luring a lot of Texas cowboys into the cavalry by buying them full mugs of Mr. Menger's famous beer. Robert thinks there are a lot of old vibes from that colorful era still holding out at the bar.

For those who may not know, the bar is a replica of the House of Lords' Pub in London, and while it bears the date of 1859 on its door, the bar itself was placed in the hotel in 1887. The manager then was Hermann Kampmann. He sent an architect to England to examine the pub and duplicate it as closely as possible. The bar, which at first was located facing Alamo Plaza, was moved to its present location on Crockett Street in 1949. Prior to its relocation, there had been a livery stable located there for the convenience of the Menger guests.

When the Spanish-American War of 1898 broke out, Teddy Roosevelt was given the monumental task of recruiting, training, and leading a cavalry unit which would go to Cuba to fight in that engagement. There wasn't much time. Teddy figured if he could get some cowboys, already skilled in horsemanship, into his unit, he'd be ahead of the game. Their favorite hangout was Alamo Plaza, and Mr. Menger's Bar, which served great brew. Teddy decided he'd play host, and when the cowboys had had just enough beer to feel mellow, he'd move in for the kill! The slightly tipsy cowhands were easy prey for the clever colonel. They signed up for the cavalry before they knew what had hit them! The locals called this rough and ready bunch the Rough Riders. Some San Antonians called them "Teddy's Terrors," too!

The dark cherry wood paneled barroom, with its charming little balcony and big mirrored bar, has been a busy place of late! I first received an inkling that there might be something new going on at that location which might be worth investigating from a friend who lives up in North Texas. Cindy Shioleno, from Kennedale, had participated in one of my *Spirits of San Antonio* tours last fall and thought I would be interested to know that she had been back to San Antonio and had stayed at the Menger. She was told about a custodian who had a strange encounter at the bar. She also told me that while she was in her fifth floor room, she had felt a strong presence of someone, or something, there. Several times she suddenly smelled the unmistakable aroma of cigar smoke in the no-smoking room. The smell would come and go and was most noticeable in the early morning hours.

I decided to see what I could find out about the recent manifestations, and called upon several staff members, who were most cooperative in telling me what they could.

Mr. Ernest Malacara, assistant manager, has been at the Menger for many years, and we have become good friends. He knows every employee and every nook and cranny of the hotel. He was very helpful when I wrote the story that appeared in *Spirits of San Antonio*. Yvonne Saucedo, night manager, was equally cooperative in telling me what she knew about the custodian's experience that Cindy Shioleno had referred to. This is what happened:

On a recent (April) night, one of the custodians at the hotel had gone to clean up the bar. It was actually in the wee hours of the morning, when both patrons and bartenders had called it a night. The young janitor, a husky man of about six feet, three inches in height, was the kind of fellow you'd want on your side in a fight. He looked like he wouldn't be scared of the bogeyman himself.

That night he'd opened the inside double doors to the Menger Bar and put on the door stop to hold them open so he could wheel his cart of cleaning supplies down the center aisle of the barroom. He started getting his cleaning equipment organized and just happened to glance towards the bar over to his right. He noticed one of the bar stools was on the floor. All the others had been placed, as was customary, upside down on the bar to facilitate cleaning of the floor. A glance to the end of the bar revealed a man, dressed in what the custodian later described as an old-fashioned military uniform, suddenly had materialized! He sat on the end bar stool and beckoned with his index finger to the startled janitor.

Realizing the man had suddenly appeared and was definitely an other-worldly being, the young man hastily headed for the open doors. But something was wrong! The double doors had slammed shut. And they were locked! It took a few minutes for the shaken janitor to gather his wits, yell, and make enough noise to attract the attention of someone to come and get him out of the locked barroom. The unusual guest still sat upon the bar stool.

Mr. Malacara told me the young custodian was just about hysterical. Yvonne Saucedo was on duty at the front desk in her capacity as night manager that night. She had been chatting with one of the night security guards. The pair were startled to see the custodian, breathing hard and visibly shaken, come stumbling into the lobby. He headed for one of the lobby chairs, where he slumped into the seat. Yvonne feared he might be having a heart attack. The terrified young man was gasping for breath and shaking violently. He managed to blurt out, "I I think, I think I must have seen a ghost. . . . " Because he seemed to be in shock and was as white as a sheet, Mrs. Saucedo called 911. In only a few minutes the EMS crew arrived and escorted the man to a nearby clinic for observation.

Later that night, Yvonne and the security guard went into the bar and looked all around. She said they must have stayed there for at least half an hour, hoping for a reappearance of the ghost, but the strange spirit did not make another appearance.

Incidentally, the custodian has never come back to his job at the Menger!

Mr. Malacara said there had been a couple of other incidents connected with the bar. Another night employee was in the bar after midnight, in fact, it was around 1:30 a.m, when he happened to glance up to the balcony area. He noticed a man, dressed in what appeared to be a dark gray suit and wearing a little hat. He just sat there for a few minutes at the railing on the side closest to the Alamo. The surprised custodian ran out to summon another staff member. When the men returned to the bar a few minutes later, the apparition had completely disappeared, and he did not return.

Just a short time back (this would have been around September of 1996) a couple who remained until closing time in the famous bar were preparing to leave. The woman stood in the center of the bar, and her husband was standing slightly off to one side. He saw a man enter the bar and start towards his wife. He stepped in front of the man since he seemed to be purposely approaching the woman, and the astonished couple both were shocked to see the man vanish in front of their eyes!

Rodney Miller, a hotel staff member who works in the valet parking area, told me he understood that one night recently all the glasses in the bar began to tremble and shake, and this was witnessed by several hotel guests.

There's bound to be a reason for so much activity at the Menger Bar. It may be, as Robert Thiege believes, just because it's getting closer to the time that the "Rough Riders" were recruited there, almost a hundred years ago. Robert thinks the figure the young custodian saw at the bar might have been a Rough Rider, or even Teddy himself, since the figure was beckoning to him. I might mention another possible explanation. The bar was first located in the original portion of the building, over by Blum Street, and was moved to its present location in this century. It's a well-known fact that the U.S. Army had a headquarters located at the Alamo at one time, and it was they who added the famous "apron" to the facade. The building was also used as a police headquarters back in the late 1800s. Perhaps the figure that appeared to the custodian was a military officer stationed at the Alamo compound, or even a constable assigned to the building when it had become the police headquarters. Then, of course, there was once a livery stable located where the Menger Bar is now located. It had been placed there for the convenience of the hotel guests, before the age of automobiles. It was an 1800s version of the hotel's current modern parking garage! The figure seen in the bar could have been a military man who hung out at the livery stable. Who knows? It's all interesting, and highly speculative. Probably any of these theories could be applied. That's half the fun of researching these stories: trying to arrive at a plausible explanation.

Mr. Malacara also volunteered several other unusual things that have happened at the hotel. One evening as he stood at the front desk chatting with three young men who work at the hotel, all four men noticed one of the front doors as it suddenly swung open. Only nobody came in! These doors are very heavy, made of brass and beveled glass, and they just don't blow open. Anyway, there was no wind that night. The doors aren't on the outside of the building, either. They are located in a covered and protected entryway. There's just no possible way of explaining why one of these big, heavy doors opened that evening, to admit no one at all.

Then the hotel executive went on to tell me that one of the women who operates a gift shop off the main lobby reported she actually witnessed a display of little shot glasses she had just placed on the counter get up and move, by themselves, from the left to the right side of the counter. They were lifted, moved, and set down by invisible hands as the astounded woman watched.

As we were talking, Mr. Malacara remembered other notable events that I hadn't covered in my first book's story on the Menger. He recalled an incident that took place several years ago when a hotel guest saw a male figure appear just before she stepped into an elevator on the top floor one evening. She had just pushed the elevator button and chanced to glance over to her left. She distinctly saw the figure of a man dressed in strange-looking clothing, wearing a jacket with big puffed sleeves, and a funny peaked hat, definitely not an ordinary 1990s sort of attire. It sounds a little like someone from the Spanish period of our city's history to me. The woman was visibly shaken when she came down to the lobby and reported what she had seen.

Then, I was also told that several years back, a gentleman who was checking out of the hotel questioned some items on his hotel bill. There were a number of telephone calls billed to his room, and he hadn't made any calls at all. Then, he noticed that the phone number he had supposedly called, and which appeared on the room charge, was his mother's old telephone number. But, she had been dead for ten years! One of my psychic friends read this as a signal that the mother's spirit was somehow trying to reach her son.

Yvonne Saucedo told me many of the waitresses who work at the hotel during early morning hours have seen a spirit they refer to as "Mr. Preston." This is the figure of an old man they've seen sitting on a bench in the patio. He always wears a top hat and a dapper dress suit of the late 1800s era.

One morning recently, when I was in the hotel with David Garcia, from Fox TV National News Service, and his cameraman, we had a brief visit with Ernest Malacara before going on into the dining room for breakfast. When we came back through the lobby, a visibly startled Malacara told us he had just had an "experience." It seemed he and Tom Brady, the hotel's chief of security, were walking down the corridor that leads to the hotel parking garage when they both happened to glance through the glass door to the executive offices and saw a man sitting in the office. They'd passed the door, when they looked at each other and said, "now who was that?" They knew the offices had not yet opened for the day. They back-tracked and looked into the office, and the man they had just seen had completely disappeared!

Another hotel executive, Gil Navarro, an assistant man-ager, told me recently when he was up in the older section of the hotel, standing outside of room 205, he distinctly felt someone pass by him very closely, actually brushing his shoulder. He whirled around to see who, or what, had collided with him, saying, "pardon me," at the same time. But, of course, no one was there. There had not been enough time for whoever it was to have totally disappeared. When ghosts at the Menger are mentioned, Navarro doesn't laugh. Like many other staff members, he just takes them for granted as being hotel fixtures.

I am sure by the time this manuscript goes to the publish-er, other interesting incidents will have transpired at the Menger. That's the way it is when one is writing about ghosts. They don't seem to slow down. I am sure that spirits from San Antonio's bygone days will continue to find this gracious hotel with its charming Victorian furnishings a lovely place to visit. There's absolutely nothing to fear about these spirits who frequent the old hotel. An occasional manifestation just adds a spicy note of mystery to the elegant inn, another fascinating facet to that precious gem that so beautifully adorns Alamo Plaza!

# Spirits at the St. Anthony

One of the stately hotels known as the "grand old ladies" of San Antonio is the elegant Crowne Plaza St. Anthony, located on Travis Street between Navarro and Jefferson Streets, facing onto the shady square known as Travis Park. Built in 1909, the hotel was designed to offer comfortable lodgings to cattlemen and their families, the discriminating traveler, and visiting tourists.

F.M. Swearingen, a former manager of the Hot Wells Resort Hotel, first thought of the idea of building the hotel. He was financed by two prominent cattlemen, B.L. Naylor and A.H. Jones. Jones later served as mayor of San Antonio. He died in 1913 while still in office.

Today's hotel has been greatly enlarged but has lost none of its early charm. It is beautifully furnished with fine antiques and cut crystal chandeliers. The walls are decorated with fine tapestries, original oil paintings, and nineteenth-century French mirrors. The hotel was the first to have electric eye entrance doors, to provide drive-in garage registration facilities, as well as the first auto lobby. The garage permitted guests to drive their cars in and take an elevator directly to their floor to change clothes before entering the main lobby, often referred to as "Peacock Alley." All the china and glassware in the hotel bore the crest of the establishment. The modern kitchen was located at the basement level and boasted such state-of-the-art accoutrements as mechanical dishwashers and potato peelers!

Built during the days before integration, there were two dining rooms provided for the guests' servants, one for white and one for black servants. Now I wouldn't know of anybody even traveling with servants! Times have indeed changed!

In 1959 the St. Anthony Club was founded. It was one of America's finest dinner clubs and drew its members from around the world. Known as "the" nightclub of the Southwest, it was rated third in the nation. Every week it boasted one of the top bands in the country. The big band sound was broadcast live nightly from the club to radio fans all around the country. The membership was only of the upper echelon. Sadly, today it no longer exists. The rooms once used for gala dinners and balls are now offered as dining facilities for conventions and such. Having been members for several years, my husband and I sadly miss the gracious atmosphere, flawless service, and wonderful dance music that the club once offered. Its beautiful mural walls, reminding one of enchanting Mediterranean balconies, have been replaced with more conservative wall coverings.

Unlike the Menger, where the identities of the spirits in residence are pretty well known, it seems that no one really knows who the St. Anthony's spirits might be. There are no clear-cut stories of sightings of identifiable apparitions, but there are enough stories that have come filtering down from various hotel employees to leave little doubt in anyone's mind that the hotel hosts its share of ghostly guests.

Mark Eakin, one of the bellmen, who admits to being sensitive to the presence of other-worldly spirits, says he has often felt a presence in the basement-level male employee's locker room. He told me as he is putting away his belongings he hears sounds of someone washing up in the lavatory area, but when he takes a look to see who it is, there's never anyone there. He has seen strange shadowy outlines and generally has a feeling he is not alone. He also said that when he is called to deliver the newspapers on the tenth floor level he always feels as if he is being followed. He added that he knows the doors that open out onto the old former roof garden, where San Antonians used to dance on summer nights, have been known to open up all by themselves!

A front desk employee, who requested not to be named, said once a couple checked into their room, and soon afterwards they came right back down to the registration desk and asked to be checked out! They said the room assigned to them was already occupied. When they unlocked the door they saw a man and a woman sitting in the room, drinking cocktails. They were quite upset to find their room was already taken. An immediate and thorough check by the hotel staff revealed that the room was empty, and there were no empty glasses scattered about to indicate a drinking party had just taken place. One staff member confided that several times people have just checked out because something in their rooms spooked them! We were told by a hotel executive that recently a woman thought someone got in the bed in her room. She hurriedly checked out. The executive thinks the spirits may be upset because the hotel is undergoing a lot of renovations just now, and we all know that situation often causes unrest among the ghostly population.

Warren Andrews, another hotel bellman, says that he has heard the sound of footsteps following him as he walks on some of the upper floors. They sound as if the walker is wearing old-fashioned galoshes, as they squeak and squish as they stride along. He has turned around to find nobody there, but he usually gets a really cold feeling just as he stops. Also, he has heard the lavatory faucet turned on or the shower running in the men's locker room, just as his friend and fellow bellman, Mark Eakin, reported.

Mark also told me he had heard of a ghostly lady in a red dress, but he has never personally seen her. A couple of ladies who worked in the sales department in the executive office section up on the mezzanine have seen ghostly feet! Cindy Waters, who used to work in sales, and Jet Garcia both told me they had seen them. Housekeeper Manuela Espinosa also reported she had seen the dark-stockinged legs with slim ankles clad in black old-fashioned pumps in the first stall of the mezzanine level ladies' powder room. The lady never comes out. Her feet and legs eventually just disappear. No one seemed to have a clue what might cause the phantom feet to appear. I promised Cindy I would try and bring a psychic to check out that facility. More about that later.

I also spoke at length with two security guards. I questioned them if they'd seen or heard anything unusual that might be construed as a ghost or spirit. They did not laugh at me. One man mentioned that when he made his usual rounds on an unoccupied floor, he heard television sounds coming from rooms he knew were unoccupied. He opened the rooms to check, and the TV would suddenly turn off. As soon as he closed the door and started to walk away, the noise would start up again.

Warren Andrews told me that one of the room clerks told him that he had seen a tall man, clad in dark clothing, with a decidedly Lincolnesque look to both his dress and stature, get off the elevator. The minute the man stepped out, he disappeared!

Al Langston, one of the security staff and a former ranger at the Alamo, is a levelheaded and trustworthy individual whom I have known for some time. I believe Al when he says he thinks the Anacacho Ballroom is haunted. Once when he was there alone, checking the room for security, he both saw and heard a deadbolt lock fall into place. And the same night, he heard a kick against a closed door, and of course, no one was there. He said a cold chill went up his spine, and he is convinced he was in the presence of some unknown entity that night.

After hearing so many things from a number of staff members, I contacted Sam Nesmith and Robert Thiege. They agreed to go "ghost hunting" on a night when the moon was full, always a favorable time to seek out the spirits. Sue Baker, former sales director, and Shari Thorn, the executive secretary to the general manager, Mr. Peter Ells, were our hostesses. Our party consisted of Sam and his wife, Nancy; Robert and his wife, Joie; my husband, Roy, and myself. As we trooped around the hotel, we also picked up housekeeper

Manuela Espinosa, who had been alerted to our coming and had agreed to accompany us.

Sam and Robert said that their late evening visit to the mezzanine's powder room was definitely a "first" for them. Both psychics picked up the image of the woman to whom the mysterious black-clad phantom feet belonged. They both "saw" the same image, an elderly gray-haired woman wearing a tailored black suit. They said she was wearing a little round black hat with a veil. After she entered the stall she was stricken with a terrible chest pain and was terrified she was going to die. She finally was able to make her way out and into the hallway where her son was waiting for her. He called an ambulance. Sam and Robert say they think the woman's name was either Claire or Clara. She was taken to a hospital, and recovered, but later died from a stroke. Sam told us that this was such a frightening and traumatic experience for her that the energy remained and the scene periodically repeats itself.

One strange thing happened while seven of us were in the powder room: Sam, Robert, Joie, Sue, Shari, Manuela, and me. We were suddenly assailed by the fragrance of a very sweet perfume. We all smelled it. Then it went away just as suddenly as it had come.

Although we had been told that there had been a number of manifestations, including the rather frequent appearance of a gentleman wearing a tuxedo coming into the laundry room and housekeeping department, the night we paid our visit to the basement level of the hotel, nothing was discovered in that area by the psychics. Manuela told us she had once seen a male figure in the housekeeping section, and he disappeared even as she watched him. And one early morning she had seen a woman in a white uniform in the inner corridor which connects the two main hallways that run the length of the basement. Of medium build, the figure had dark hair. She had not seen the face as the woman was walking away from her. Sam and Robert located this entity in the corridor, and she communicated to them that her name was Anita. She was an Hispanic employee who loved the hotel where she had worked in the 1950s, and because she was so happy there she frequently returns. She communicated to Sam that she wanted to know what all of us were doing there. Sam told her we were just visiting and she need not let our presence disturb her. He also told her she was not bound to the place and was free to move on to the light if she so desired.

We also visited the once-lovely roof garden. Quiet, dark, and deserted though it now is, it still retains some vestiges of its former beauty. The moon was full and the stars were out. A soft breeze caressed our faces as we strolled in the moonlight. We could imagine how glamorous and romantic it must have been as couples swayed to the sounds of music that drifted out over the dark, quiet streets of San Antonio. The heyday of the garden nightclub was during the World War II years. The big band sound was in. Music was romantic then, and so was the setting. Doubtless, in this atmosphere, many proposals were made, and probably many tender and sad good-byes were said as the military men prepared to go overseas to fight for their country, leaving their sweethearts and wives behind. Much of this poignancy seems to linger there. Sam felt the strong presence of a young woman wearing a white ballgown. He said the spirit was in a storage or service room behind the bandstand, probably where service people brought up food and drink from the kitchens below. Sam said she seemed very sad. Her sweetheart had brought her to the roof garden to dance on his last leave before shipping out. He never returned. Now her sad little spirit comes back to linger where she had once been young and happy and in love.

We also visited an unoccupied guest suite where Sue and Shari said various activities had been reported. The door between the bedroom and the living room of the suite is said to often slam by itself, and unusual noises have been heard in the bedroom. Sam and Robert picked up that a honeymoon couple sometimes return to where they spent such a happy, romantic time at the hotel. They just want their privacy! That's why the door shuts by itself. Sam told them they don't have to stay there any longer, but they seem quite content where they are. We didn't ask Sam any further details about the activities that take place in that suite!

If it hadn't been well past midnight, we might have stayed even longer, since we had not had the chance to visit all the known "haunts" in the grand hotel.

A short time after our late night visit to the hotel, a guest had an unusual experience which she shared with me. Karen Martin, of Odessa, New York, called me from the hotel to see if I had any openings on my Halloween week *Spirits of San Antonio* tour. I was able to accommodate her, and I picked her up at the hotel and drove her to the restaurant where we joined the other tour participants. In the course of the evening I told Karen that I had collected several interesting stories about the hotel where she was staying, and they would appear in my latest book. I mentioned that the tenth floor seemed to be the most "populated" area as far as ghosts were concerned. Karen said, "Oh dear, that's the floor where I am staying."

Shortly after Karen returned to New York she wrote a note to me saying that night, and the next one as well (this would have been October 28 and 29), she had a very strange experience. At precisely 5:45 a.m. on Monday, the 28th, she heard a loud "whacking or snapping" sound against the door to her room. It was loud enough to wake her from a sound sleep. She rushed to the door to see what had caused the sound at that early hour of the morning. She stuck her head out of the door and saw that no one was in sight. But she heard a succession of "whacks" as whatever it was hit each door all the way down the hallway. People rushed to their doors just as Karen had done, to see what had made the sounds.

Karen went on to say the same thing happened the next day, at 6:15 a.m. Again, all the doors were hit by a snapping or whacking noise, which Karen likened to a bullwhip or heavy leather belt being snapped against the doors.

I telephoned Karen after I received her note to see if she could recall anything else. No, that was it, and she said it was not only disturbing, but strange and puzzling as well. She said it added a final exclamation point to her Halloween week visit to San Antonio!

I called Shari Thorn to tell her about Karen's experience, since she had so recently escorted me and my psychic friends around on our ghost-hunting venture. She told me that recently Mr. Peter Ells, the general manager of the Crowne Plaza St. Anthony, his head housekeeper, and one of the resident engineers were making a routine inspection up on the sixth floor of the hotel. As they stood talking in the stairwell, the engineer was whistling a little tune. Then he stopped whistling. Just then something whistled right back at him! All three looked at each other and said, "What was that?" They all clearly heard the unseen whistler. Shari said Mr. Ells had been skeptical of the ghost stories about the hotel until he had this experience. Now he has begun to believe there really might be some spirits in his fine old hotel!

The St. Anthony, which has been a home away from home to many famous people, celebrities from all walks of life, politicians, military leaders, stage and screen stars, and outstanding athletes, has seen it all in its long lifespan. Since 1909 it has been the scene of many grand balls, receptions, banquets, and wedding parties. It is still one of the most elegant and splendid hotels in South Texas. No wonder some former guests and employees just couldn't bear to leave it permanently! Frankly, I find just knowing that this fine old hotel is among the haunted places in San Antonio adds another fascinating dimension to an already wonderful place. But its elegance, beauty, tradition, and Continental ambiance, combined with a gracious staff always eager to please, is what makes it truly unique!

# Ghosts at the Glorious Gunter

The Camberley Gunter Hotel, built in 1909, occupies the corner of Houston and St. Mary's Streets. It has always been the site of a hotel since 1837 when the Settlement Inn was built on that location just a year after the Battle of the Alamo. There have been numerous buildings, with numerous owners, on that land since. I wrote a lot about the history of the famous old hotel in *Spirits of San Antonio* and I don't want to be repetitious. Suffice it to say, the hotel, which has enjoyed a colorful and illustrious past, is also well known for its ghosts. In fact, one of San Antonio's most famous unsolved murders took place there on February 8, 1965, and some people feel this led to at least some of the hauntings on the property.

Several times since the publication of *Spirits of San Antonio*, I've been at the Gunter with TV crews and news reporters doing interviews for various "spirited specials." *The Eyes of Texas, a* Houston based project, local stations KENS and KMOL, and several other out-of-town companies have filmed at the Gunter. Various staff members have been interviewed about their ghostly encounters.

The *Express News* ran an article on November 20, 1994, which was written by staff writer Becky Whetstone Schmidt. It was called *San Antonio Haunts*, and Schmidt quoted a visit she'd had with Christina Richards:

> Christina Richards, who works in accounting at the hotel, had hotel guests tell her they saw ghosts when she worked at the front desk. But she thought

they were just making up stories to avoid paying their bill.

Until she saw one herself.

"I saw something that crossed from one side to the other side," said Richards. "So I turned to look and somebody crossed through the wall, and through yet another wall. She had on a long white dress."

Gunter Hotel

Schmidt had a psychic, Irma Latham, come in to investigate. She soon connected to a female spirit named Ingrid, a woman who died around the turn of the century. Rather avant-garde for her day, she loved wine and smoking, and she enjoyed roaming around downtown San Antonio, within about a three-block radius of the Gunter. But the hotel was her favorite headquarters. Later, several other psychics saw Ingrid, and they also came up with another Gunter spirit. This one is named Peggy, and she's a flapper from about the 1920s Prohibition era. She and Ingrid do not get along. Perhaps they don't want to share the same turf!

Former sales manager Lydia Fischer and I enjoyed a visit over lunch recently. We had previously met when Fischer was interviewed for one of the TV specials in which I was a participant. A strikingly attractive and business-like young woman, Fischer is not the sort of person to make up wild stories. But she is convinced she saw Ingrid (or someone who matched her description) as she made her rounds on one of the upper floors. She saw this lady, clad in a long white dress, going down the hall, sort of floating from room to room, sometimes going through the walls and coming out again. The figure had long black hair, upswept on the sides, and down long in the back, rather like the belle epoch style worn at the turn of the century. She said to herself, "Am I seeing what I think I am seeing, or what?"

Unfortunately, Lydia doesn't recall the floor on which she saw the apparition.

Now, as previously mentioned, the police still don't have all the answers to the 1965 murder in room 636. It is believed that not only a shooting, but a butchering took place on that cold February morning. But call it a strange twist of fate, just a few months ago, Gil Lopez, the general manager, received a strange envelope in the mail. It was a post office envelope bearing no return address. The envelope was addressed to the Gunter (not the Camberley Gunter) Hotel, and the zip code was the old, outdated one used back in 1965. Inside the envelope was an old room key, the key to room 636! This was a regular old-fashioned key, like the hotel used back then, not the credit-card-like plastic openers used today. No one has been able to figure out who might have mailed the key, or why!

When Liz Wiggins, a former KENS reporter, did a special for Halloween at the Gunter in 1995, she took Kathleen Bittner, a local psychic, Kathleen's husband, and a couple of KENS news photographers, and the group spent the night in room 636. The psychic found a lot of vibes and supposedly saw a re-enactment of the heinous murder that took place there. Although no one had told her, Bittner announced the room was different from how it looked in 1965. She was right! After the room was completely cleaned and refurbished, the murder room divided into two much smaller rooms.

The building just adjacent to the hotel, the Travis Convention Center, may have a few stray spirits of its own. Or maybe, they are Gunter visitor spirits. Vivienne Zamora, on the staff at the Center, which is housed in the old Frost Brothers Department Store building, says she definitely believes there are spirits in that building. Strange noises, footsteps, etc. have been reported by employees at various times. Once Viv and another employee working late in the evening saw a chair move several feet all by itself in one of the meeting rooms! Vivienne is an old friend of mine, and she is just not the sort of person to make up stories.

Old hotels seems to have lives of their own. And this one, the Camberley Gunter, has quite a bit of mystery to add to its highly interesting and illustrious history. The food is great, the rooms are charming, and as far as we know, there are still some watchful spirits there to keep you company!

# A Shy Spirit at the Crockett

The historic Crockett Hotel is located behind the Alamo on a piece of property that once was used as farmland. Later, the grounds of what is now the Crockett's site were part of the bloody battlefield at the March 6, 1836 Battle of the Alamo. During the night before the battle, it is said that hundreds of Mexican troops moved into the general area where the tree-shaded patio and hotel swimming pool are located today. There they lay in wait, ready to attack the greatly outnumbered Texans at dawn.

In 1874 a prosperous French-born merchant, Augustese Honore Grenet, purchased the property and opened a general merchandise store on the site. Then in 1887 the land was sold to G.B. Davis as part of a judgment for the estate of Grenet. The ownership changed three more times until it was sold to the International Order of Odd Fellows on January 30, 1907. In 1909 the Order built a combination lodge hall and hotel. The first four floors served as a hotel, which brought income into the lodge coffers, while the fifth and sixth floors were used for lodge purposes. The Odd Fellows maintained ownership until 1978 when an investor from British Columbia bought the property.

In 1982 John Blocker, a San Antonio native, bought the property. John and his wife, Jenne, carefully renovated the building to be faithful to the plan of the original. Using photographs of the original structure, the architects uncovered original brickwork, windows, and storefront structures; cleaned and repaired trim and cornices; and restored the lobby to its original condition. In addition, a lovely atrium was

Crockett Hotel

constructed, guest rooms were added, and existing rooms were refurbished. As a result of this careful renovation, the hotel is listed on the *National Register of Historic Structures.*

Today the Crockett is a comfortable hotel with a relaxed, inviting atmosphere. It's also said to be haunted.

I was at a Convention and Visitors Bureau quarterly meeting for local people involved in tourism when my friend Peggy Moneyhun, who is the sales manager at the Crockett, said there had been some talk that the hotel might harbor a ghost. The figure of a man had been sighted in the executive offices section by several employees. This section is located in the modern two-storied section of the hotel which circles the patio and swimming pool.

Armed with this information, my husband and I visited the Crockett on a full moonlit night, May 31, 1996. We were accompanied by psychics Sam Nesmith and Robert Thiege and their wives. Our little party was cordially greeted by Ann Norris, the front desk manager, and her assistant, Terri Long. The staff of the executive section had all gone for the day, but Ann was happy to let us in. Dave Mora, the reservations manager, decided to tag along. He had actually seen the figure of a man clad in a dark blue jacket as he moved into the small kitchen area adjoining the boardroom. He vividly recalled the day he had come around the corner from the area where the offices are located and spied the figure of a sturdy man with dark brown hair as he moved into the kitchen. A quick check into that room revealed no one was there. No one! Yet Mora is convinced he saw the man quite clearly. He added that other hotel staff members had seen him at various times.

Sam and Robert found another spirit, a rather quiet one, that seems to like the inner office area occupied by Peggy Moneyhun. Both psychics picked up on this entity right away, and they believe that his energy will gradually get strong enough to actually materialize.

Dave Mora also mentioned that when he was in the office and the air conditioner was not running, on several occasions he heard people whispering. He couldn't make out the words, but it is evident that the sound he heard was whispered conversations.

Ann Norris told us she has, at various times, chanced to look up from her front desk vantage point across to the hotel section and has seen curtains moving in windows of rooms she knows are unoccupied. She also noted that many times she has watched, in utter amazement, as the hotel's electronic doors open and close by themselves as if unseen footsteps had suddenly crossed the threshold.

Norris volunteered the information that the building in which the executive offices are located was built in the 1960s when the hotel was expanded in anticipation of Hemisfair. Previously a bar had been located at the site. Sam Nesmith believes the figure that has been seen entering the kitchen area is the type of spirit that is involved in a psychic photographic impression, doing something he did a long time ago, paying no attention to what might be going on around him now. (Maybe he's just going into the bar for a cool brew!) Sam believes the same scene will continue to replay from time to time.

# Antebellum Elegance:
# The Oge House

It was a beautiful September morning when I kept my appointment with Sharrie Magatagen at her elegant home and bed and breakfast inn, the Oge House, at 209 Washington Street. It is located in the King William Historic District. The place is charming on the exterior. A broad veranda is at the top of a flight of stairs leading to the first floor reception area. The house is built along the lines of Southern plantation homes, and I believe in Natchez, at least, they refer to this style with a half-basement as a "raised cottage" or "planter's cottage" type of architecture.

When I first stepped inside I was instantly reminded of many of the fine antebellum homes I have visited on trips to Louisiana and Mississippi. Pat and Sharrie Magatagen, who purchased the house in 1991, have spared no effort or expense in furnishing the place to reflect the graciousness of a bygone era. The effect is a careful blending of French and English Chippendale style antique furnishings, exquisite Oriental carpets, delicate fine china and bric-a-brac in the china cupboards. It all goes together to create an atmosphere of gracious elegance. When you step inside the Oge House you are immediately transported to another era. You literally leave the twentieth century outside the wide fanlighted doorway!

The house, which is situated on a large landscaped lot, in its original state was a good example of pre-Civil War classical revival residential architecture. It is one of the few buildings of its type dating before the War Between the States to be found in San Antonio.

The Oge House

Sharrie had prepared a lot of historical data for me, detailed information about previous owners and the builders of the large stone and masonry house. It is believed to have been built sometime between 1857 and 1860 on land belonging to one Catherine Elder. Miss Elder married Newton A. Mitchell, an attorney, on February 12, 1857. As was customary in those days, with the marriage Mitchell inherited all his wife's property. It is not clear just when the house was actually built, but it was probably just after the marriage. The original building consisted of a basement and one story. In 1873 a writer, Augustus Koch, wrote in *Bird's Eye View* that the house was a one-story structure with a flat or low-pitched roof and a low parapet.

Catherine Elder Mitchell died sometime around 1862, and her husband passed away in 1864. There were no children born to the union, and Mitchell left no will or heirs. The property was finally divided up among Catherine's siblings. Her sister, Malvina Nelson, had the house repaired and used it as a rental property until she sold it to a woman named Eudora S. Abrahams for $5,600 in 1868. Abrahams kept the place only two years before selling it to Catherine Sampson, who may have been responsible for having the second story added to the structure. The records show that Mrs. Sampson paid Mrs. Abrahams $3,300 for the place in 1870 and then she sold it to Louis Oge for $7,000 in 1881, doubling the price she had paid for it. In view of the fact that other two-story houses in the area were valued in the six to seven thousand dollar price range at that time, it seems logical to assume the second story might have been added during Mrs. Sampson's ownership.

At any rate, the place was purchased by Mr. Louis Oge on August 29, 1881, for the sum of $7,000. The house is still called the Oge House after the colorful and outstanding citizen who owned it for many years.

Adolph Oge, a native of Alsace-Lorraine, brought his family to Texas with the Henri Castro colony in 1845. Louis was just a boy when he arrived in Texas, having been born in 1832. The Oges landed in New Orleans and then went to Galveston, then to Port Lavaca and finally traveled overland to Castroville, just west of San Antonio in Medina County. They apparently soon left there and moved to San Antonio. When Louis was only eighteen he joined the Texas Rangers, where he served in the company commanded by the famous Indian fighter and frontiersman Bigfoot Wallace. Young Oge saw service on the frontier, between San Antonio and the Rio Grande, where there were many confrontations with Lipan Apaches and Comanches. The Rangers were involved in constant conflict, and only strong men survived. Later, after he had served his tour of duty with the Rangers, Oge for a time worked as a mail carrier, riding the route between San Antonio and El Paso. He was one of seven men chosen to guard the mail stages against attacks by Indians and outlaws. He remained in this work for four years and repulsed many a dangerous attack during that time. Later he did similar work in New Mexico and Arizona. After that, he became a conduc-

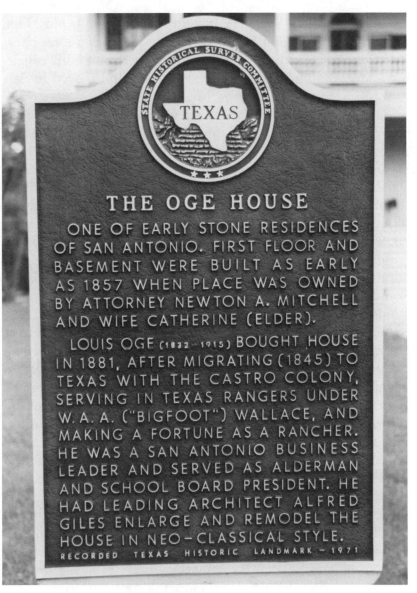

THE OGE HOUSE

ONE OF EARLY STONE RESIDENCES OF SAN ANTONIO. FIRST FLOOR AND BASEMENT WERE BUILT AS EARLY AS 1857 WHEN PLACE WAS OWNED BY ATTORNEY NEWTON A. MITCHELL AND WIFE CATHERINE (ELDER).

LOUIS OGE (1832-1915) BOUGHT HOUSE IN 1881, AFTER MIGRATING (1845) TO TEXAS WITH THE CASTRO COLONY, SERVING IN TEXAS RANGERS UNDER W. A. A. ("BIGFOOT") WALLACE, AND MAKING A FORTUNE AS A RANCHER. HE WAS A SAN ANTONIO BUSINESS LEADER AND SERVED AS ALDERMAN AND SCHOOL BOARD PRESIDENT. HE HAD LEADING ARCHITECT ALFRED GILES ENLARGE AND REMODEL THE HOUSE IN NEO-CLASSICAL STYLE.
RECORDED TEXAS HISTORIC LANDMARK — 1971

Historic Placque at The Oge House

tor, carrying the mail from Tuscon to Fort Yuma, Arizona, for the Butterfield Stage Company.

Finally, when he was twenty-eight years old, Oge returned to Texas and began ranching. He owned a ranch in Frio County. He built up a modest fortune through his ranching endeavors and finally retired in 1882 and moved to San Antonio.

Oge married Miss Elizabeth Newton, a native of Mississippi and the daughter of Reverend William C. Newton, a minister of the Methodist Episcopal Church South. The couple had four children: Josephine, George, Annie, and Frank. Oge bought the Washington Street house for his growing family when he came back to San Antonio in 1882 and hired the prominent architect Alfred Giles to enlarge and remodel the house. That 1882 remodeling included the addition of the handsome principal stairway, which is located in the right-hand wall of the central hall. This beautiful staircase has Romanesque foliate patterns and flutes, turned balusters, a molded handrail, and a decorative patterned stringer. The wood is imitation oak grained and is in an excellent state of preservation.

During his later years Oge purchased property in downtown San Antonio which became very valuable. He served as chairman of the San Antonio School Board and was one of the aldermen of the city during the Elmendorf administration. Oge died in 1915. His family remained in the house for many years. His widow lived there until 1942, indicating she was much younger than her husband. The house was purchased by Lowry Mays and converted to apartments, and numerous other owners followed.

The stone and masonry building is sturdy and has a permanent look. It has withstood floods and storms and numerous tenants. It is the magnificent result of the work of owners who have lovingly and painstakingly restored it.

From the time the Magatagens purchased the house in 1991 and started their refurbishing project, Sharrie sensed that "something" was there. Having never encountered any supernatural entities before, the aspiring innkeeper didn't quite know what to make of it when she saw images on the dark tile of the kitchen, and caught flashes of something, or someone, passing by through her peripheral vision. These rather unnerving experiences centered around the room now used as a kitchen, which at one time was Mrs. Oge's bedroom, the room in which she passed away.

An excellent cook who really enjoys spending time in her kitchen, Sharrie was puzzled as she stood over the stove preparing a favorite dish, when herbs and spices she was trying to season with were blown away, never being allowed to land in what she was cooking. The condiments landed at the side of the pot or pan, on the stove, or even on the floor. This happened over and over again, and Sharrie said it was not when there was a draft or an exhaust fan turned on. Something just didn't like spices and refused to let them go into the food being prepared in that kitchen!

Several guests who have stayed at the Oge House have told Sharrie that they were psychics. One, a local lady, told Sharrie she definitely felt a presence in her room but it was a happy, benevolent spirit. Another lady, whom Sharrie referred to as Sylvia, a well-known Austin clairvoyant, also told her more or less the same thing. Still another recent guest, who also professed to being a psychic, told Sharrie she had picked up on a little girl, about ten or twelve years old, who had drowned in the river. She apparently comes to the house pretty often. Of course, the house is right on the banks of the San Antonio River, which used to flood and get up into the grounds and even into the lower level of the house at times before the downtown floodgates were built. Sharrie has not been able to find any historical evidence to substantiate the psychic's remarks.

While Sharrie believes her live-in spirit is a male entity, all the psychics have identified it as a female. Most of the people who have mentioned sensing a presence to Sharrie have stayed in the Mathis Room, named for Sharrie's good friend, local philanthropist Walter Mathis.

Although Sharrie was a little frightened when she first moved into the house, she is no longer afraid. She just takes the presence for granted now. Since the place has become so well accepted as a bed and breakfast inn and is filled with people all the time, it has been a while since anything unusual has happened. This is normal. Most ghosts don't seem to like a lot of activity. Even the prankish behavior the Magatagens used to experience, like lights turning on and off all the time, has slowed down.

Sharrie told me that the descendants of Louis Oge frequently come back to stay in the home that meant so much to their great-grandparents. This is certainly a tribute to the way the Magatagens have maintained the house.

After all that Sharrie told me, I think the presence, be it male or female, is probably a former owner who just wanted to be sure that things were being properly looked after in the beloved old home. And when it observed what an absolutely fantastic job that Pat and Sharrie have done on the place, bringing it back to all its antebellum elegance and charm, it has probably just settled down, or gone on to peaceful rest. Frankly, if any spirits did want to continue hanging around, I wouldn't really blame them. They could never find a lovelier place to live out eternity!

For a real Deep South, pampered visit to San Antonio, call and make your reservation at the historic Oge House on the banks of the San Antonio River. Call (210) 223-2353 for reservations and information.

# A Gem on Cedar Street:
# The Gatlin Gasthaus

A story I wrote for *Spirits of San Antonio* was titled "The Ghost Who Liked Lavender." The tidy house, built in 1903 of late Victorian style, sits on a very narrow lot, and therefore the house is only one room wide. Its width is nineteen feet, and it extends back sixty feet to the rear. There's a spacious entry hall off the shady front porch, a formal front parlor, a formal dining room, and a combination kitchen-breakfast-sitting room on the lower floor. Three inviting bedrooms and a couple of attractive old-fashioned bathrooms are upstairs. Betty Gatlin, the owner, has converted her house into a cozy bed and breakfast inn which she calls the Gatlin Gasthaus. Located at 123 Cedar Street just off South Alamo in the King William Historic District, it's just a few steps away from a trolley stop, and Rosario's, one of San Antonio's favorite Mexican restaurants.

At the beginning of this century, the lady who lived next door to the property was widowed and found she was in need of a source of income. Back in 1903 women didn't do much but keep house and have babies. If they worked at all, they were probably seamstresses or schoolteachers. Since this lady was neither, she decided to build a little house which she could rent out on the narrow garden space that ran beside her large brick home. That's why Betty's house is so narrow!

There have been several interesting happenings at Betty's home-turned-guesthouse since I first met her and wrote about the place. For a time I used her house as a stopping place for my evening *Spirits of San Antonio* tours, much to the delight

Gatlin Gasthaus

of my tour guests. I would probably still be going there, but
an ordinance forbidding tour buses in the King William District prohibits me from doing this any longer.

Once, when we had a group there, including a TV crew
which was filming a Halloween special, one of the guests
picked up an antique etched brass vase filled with dried flowers. She wanted to look at the arrangement more closely to
see how Betty had placed the flowers. Suddenly, all the flowers started to vibrate violently! I saw it happen. The lady

holding the vase was probably in her late twenties, and she certainly wasn't afflicted with palsy! Something, we don't know what, made those flowers tremble!

Betty tells me that the lights go on and off all the time. She is used to that. But one night during the Christmas holidays her three daughters and their families had come home for a Christmas visit. All the family was seated around the big dining room table. The room was ablaze with candles. Betty has a collection of lovely antique crystal candleholders on her buffet. Each one was adorned with a lighted Christmas candle. The family members were reminiscing about happy Christmases past, when suddenly the locked front door blew open and a strong wind came through the entry hall into the dining room with a great whish!, blowing out all of the candles and knocking over but, oddly enough, not breaking any of the glass candleholders. Betty believes her late husband, John, was responsible. He didn't want to be left out of the family celebration!

Another time when the daughters were visiting, Betty said one daughter and her children had to get up early and leave to go home to Atlanta. Right after the alarm clock went off, the bedside lamp came on. Only no one turned it on, unless, of course, Betty's husband was there again, like the punctual military man he had always been, to see his daughter was up on time.

A gifted psychic, Liz Null, told Betty that her husband was definitely there a lot of the time, just looking after things and sort of protecting Betty. Strangely enough, he passed away soon after the couple moved into the house and restored it. Betty later learned that all the previous owners had moved in as couples and the women became widows soon afterwards.

Along with some really lovely antique furniture and quite a collection of fine restored old trunks (great for linen storage in an old house that doesn't have too many closets), Betty has used excellent taste in her selection of Victorian objects and color schemes. In fact, the house was featured on a recent Christmas historic homes tour!

When I asked Betty about what kind of breakfasts she serves her guests, the attractive brunette answered, "the works." She and her mother, who helps her run the inn, send their company away with a full Texas breakfast under their belts. A qualified tour guide as well, Betty can supply you with lots of historical facts and information about San Antonio. For reservations and information concerning her Gasthaus, call Betty Gatlin at (210) 223-6618.

# A Spirit Filled Chateau: The Terrell Castle

One of San Antonio's truly grand mansions is a magnificent limestone pile known as Terrell Castle, located at 950 East Grayson Street, facing Fort Sam Houston's beautiful Staff Post Road. The owners are a charming mother and daughter team, Katherine Poulis and Nancy Haley. The two purchased the thirty-two-room house, complete with turrets and towers, in 1986. They spent several years and a great deal of money and effort in restoring a building which was in a slowly deteriorating condition at the time of purchase. Almost every room, ceiling, and floor had to be completely restored and refinished in order to return the house to its former grandeur and elegance.

Edwin Holland Terrell, a lawyer and statesman who served as ambassador and plenipotentiary to Belgium under President Benjamin Harrison in the early 1890s, was greatly impressed with the castles and chateaux he had seen in Belgium and France. A wealthy man, Terrell commissioned the noted English architect Alfred Giles to supervise the building project for him. He sent Giles to Belgium to more or less duplicate the plans of a castle he admired, a home that would exemplify the elegant style of living enjoyed by wealthy Europeans of that era. Terrell had recently remarried. His second wife, a member of the influential Maverick family, was a widow with several children, and Terrell wanted to provide a lovely big house for his new bride and ready-made family!

Terrell Castle

The Terrell name, by the way, is well known in San Antonio and around the state of Texas. Both Terrell County and the city of Terrell, Texas, bear his name.

When Terrell commissioned the building of his fine home, he also selected a name for it. During his lifetime it was called Lambermont after a favorite business associate. When Terrell died in 1908, the house fell into the hands of a succession of owners. The name its current owners have bestowed upon it, Terrell Castle, seems most appropriate.

This grand home, which boasts over 12,000 square feet, nine fine fireplaces, many curved windows, galleried porches, and beautiful woodwork, is now a comfortable bed and breakfast inn managed by Nancy and her mother. It is also haunted.

Nancy says that often when she knows she is all alone in the house and is sitting in the downstairs den off the main entry hall she hears footsteps moving back and forth across the floor above her. It sounds like a woman's high-heeled shoes clicking across the hardwood floors, rather rapidly. This happens only when Nancy is alone, or when her mother is there but already asleep. I asked Nancy if she ever goes up-stairs to investigate. She says, "Who, me?" The sounds of the footsteps continue to the present time, and Nancy has grown quite used to hearing them, but she still has no inclination to go upstairs to find out who is doing the walking.

A couple of years ago a nice couple from San Angelo spent several days at the popular inn. The first two nights were spent in the Alfred Giles suite, named for the architect. The last night they were in San Antonio they had to move to another room because the Giles suite was already reserved. They moved up to the fourth floor room, which is decorated in red, white, and blue and is called the "Americana Room."

This was a friendly, outgoing couple, Nancy recalls. When they returned to West Texas, they wrote the innkeepers a let-ter. Besides saying they had enjoyed staying in the beautiful house, they also said they wanted to say some things they thought Nancy and her mother should know.

It seems while they were staying in the Giles suite they heard a crash in the middle of the night, which sounded exactly like the toilet seat had dropped down. They got up and checked the bathroom, but that wasn't the cause of the noise. Several more times that night, at about thirty-minute inter-vals, they were awakened by the same noise. They got very little sleep during their stay in the Giles suite.

Then, when they moved up to the fourth floor, they settled in for a comfortable night of watching television. They decided to move the small TV set from its perch atop a cabinet to a small coffee table which they moved to the foot of the bed, so they could lie in bed and view a movie.

First, the ceiling fan began to spin. All by itself! The switch was on the off position. It did this off and on during the whole evening. It would spin really rapidly. Then it would stop. Then it would start up again. They checked all the switches and just couldn't figure out what was causing it to do this. Then, in the middle of the movie, the TV set just up and jumped off the table, landing upside down on the floor, just as if it had been hurled off the table! They were really dumfounded!

The couple just wanted Nancy and Katherine to know that they had these strange experiences while guests at the inn and told them they just might want to check into things about the big house.

Recently, when I visited the Castle with a group on one of my nighttime *Spirits of San Antonio* tours, I took a psychic along. He was interested in the house and said it had one, possibly two, spirits, but they were friendly and harmless. Since Nancy has never been frightened by the sudden night noises she has heard, this must be true.

When Nancy recently mentioned to her two housekeepers she was having the ghost tour people in that night, they confided that they, too, have had their experiences. They had never mentioned this to Nancy before. Mostly they hear footsteps or glimpse someone passing by in the hallways outside the upstairs rooms as they go about their cleaning. At first, each woman thought it was the other housekeeper, but when they checked and found out that their counterpart was working downstairs and was definitely not the figure they'd seen walking in the hallways, they realized there was something "different" going on at Terrell Castle!

I asked Nancy if she knew any stories of deaths or violence associated with the mansion. She told me there was one story, an unsubstantiated rumor, really, that she had heard about the original building contractor that Giles had hired. She didn't know his name. It seems he was using a number of government workers on the project, on government time, and he had been found out. He is said to have plunged off one of the upper balconies during the construction of the house, rather than face the exposure of his wrongdoing.

Then Nancy told me that just a short time ago a lady came to the house one afternoon and asked Katherine if she could just see the old house where she had once lived. It seemed the place had been divided up into numerous little efficiency apartments for military families at Fort Sam Houston during World War II. This lady had lived in one of them.

The woman asked Katherine if the bloodstains were still on the floor at the foot of the stairs. Katherine didn't known what on earth the woman was talking about. The lady went on to say that while she was living there, a man and his fiancee were occupying a third-floor apartment. The soldier came home early from the Fort and found his sweetheart with another man. He was enraged! He supposedly killed the man and got into a terrible argument with the woman, which extended out into the hallway. He apparently struck the girl and then either pushed her, or she fell over the stair railing, plunging three stories below to her death. The lady said that there was a big ugly bloodstain on the floor for a long time. Nancy told me that all the parquet floors had been redone prior to their purchase of the place. Neither she nor her mother had ever heard of this incident.

At this writing, Nancy and Katherine have the Castle up for sale, antique furnishings and all. They have enjoyed their years there, but both women need a well-deserved rest. Running a bed and breakfast, especially one as large as Terrell Castle, is hard work!

In the meantime, if you're interested in spending the night in what has been described as one of Texas's most elegant bed and breakfast inns, or if you want to buy a piece of history, just call Nancy or Katherine at (210) 271-9145.

# Sounds of Music:
# The Chabot-Reed House

There are many beautiful homes, reminiscent of a more genteel era in our city's history, that are located in the King William Historic District. There are a number of such houses on Madison, dating from the late 1800s to the early 1900s. One of the loveliest homes in the neighborhood is the white limestone house at 403 Madison owned by Peter and Sister Reed. It is situated on a large, well-manicured corner lot punctuated by numerous venerable old shade trees.

On the day I visited the Chabot-Reed House, as it is now called, I met the charming mistress of the household, Sister Schodts Reed, for the first time, although we had previously had several telephone conversations. A warm and friendly woman, Sister Reed is the epitome of the modern lady of the '90s who enjoys having her own identity along with career and personal interests while still maintaining certain mannerisms of the gracious ladies of the Deep South. I found her to be a fascinating personality, and her home is absolutely stunning. Her collection of Santos and ecclesiastical artworks has been tastefully worked into the overall decor in the gracious home built by George Starks Chabot in 1876. Chabot came to San Antonio by way of England where he was born, and Mexico, where he first lived and worked for the British foreign service. When he moved to San Antonio, he prospered with a business located on Main Plaza where he served as a commission merchant dealing in wool, cotton, and hides.

Chabot's wife, Mary Van Derlip Chabot, was a civic-minded woman. She was one of the founders of the Protestant

Chabot-Reed House

Orphans' Home. She and her sister, Adelia Van Derlip Cresson, were great benefactors of the home. She was also well known in art circles in that time.

The Chabots had two sons, George A., and Charles J. Charles' son, Frederick Charles Chabot, became a well-respected and prolific writer. Sister showed me part of her private collection of Chabot first editions, including his well-known work *With the Makers of San Antonio*.

George Chabot died in 1902 at the age of 81, and Mary lived on in the house until her death in 1929. Other Chabot family members lived there until 1940, and during this period the place had been made into nine apartments. A similar fate had befallen many of the large old King William District homes.

Mrs. A.W. Bouquet bought the place in 1956 and used it as a rental property. In 1975 Walter Mathis purchased the place and a 1917 era apartment house next door to it, which he tore down in order to replace the orchard that was originally on the Chabot lot. This exposed the beautiful carriage house behind it which had been built by the Chabots as a part of their property. Mathis did quite a bit of restoration to the house, but it was not until the Reeds bought it in 1985 that it was fully restored to its former grandeur. The old stone carriage house fronted by a beautiful shady patio has been made into an inviting bed and breakfast inn for visitors seeking a tranquil and relaxing stay in San Antonio.

Sister told me about all the challenges involved in restoring an old house, and she showed me a number of "before" and "after" photographs. She employed Michael Hilger, an architect who specializes in historic restorations. She said it took a full contingent of workers and artisans a year and a half working full time to create the flawless oasis of elegance that greets the visitor fortunate enough to be received into the Chabot-Reed House today.

Although the house is cheerful, bright, and appealing, Sister says there have been incidents of ghosts, or spirits, existing in the house. It has been home to many people, not only the Chabot family and subsequent owners, but numerous renters of the small apartments into which it was divided. Along the way, who knows what might have happened there? Someone may have passed away, or there might have been domestic turmoils of one sort or another down through the years. This would certainly not be an uncommon supposition in a house over a century old.

Sister mentioned to me that a skilled cabinetmaker they had brought up from Laredo stayed at the house for a time while the restoration work was going on. He slept in an upstairs bedroom. He told the Reeds, "You've got ghosts in your house." He went on to say he had heard footsteps and all sorts of strange noises during his stay there.

Most of Sister's experiences of the other-worldly nature have centered around the library, which is situated to the left of the entry door on the first floor. For some reason that she cannot explain, whenever she has an "encounter," her daughter, Denise, who is married and only comes over to visit, is usually there in the house with Sister.

The first time Sister had an unusual experience it was around 10:30 or 11:00 at night. Peter had already gone upstairs to bed, but Sister was engrossed in reading a good book downstairs in her library. Suddenly she became aware of music playing. Thinking someone had left the television set turned on, she got up and walked across the room to the cabinet which encloses the television set. But when she opened the doors she found the set was turned off. She listened again. There was definitely music, and it sounded like an old victrola playing "speakeasy" music from the Roaring Twenties! And there was the undercurrent of talking, the typical babble one hears when a big party is going on. By now she was very puzzled and called out to her daughter, Denise, who was in another part of the big house. She said, "Come in here and sit down for a minute." Denise sat down on the couch by her mother and said, "Where's that music coming from?" So Sister knew she wasn't just hearing things! The two women went out of the room into the wide hallway. They heard nothing. Then they went out to the front porch that is adjacent to the library. Again, there was silence. The music and laughter and chatter were only discernible in the library.

Later on, Sister and Denise were downstairs together on another late evening. Denise' husband and Peter Reed were both upstairs already sound asleep. The mother and daughter started up the wide staircase walking side by side. Suddenly, both of them felt the presence of something coming up the stairs behind them. They looked at each other and then they both literally flew up the stairs as fast as their legs would carry them!

Several times since, Sister has heard the honky-tonk music from the era of the Black Bottom and the Charleston. And she also heard the laughter and garbled conversation of what must have been a whale of a party once held in the house. Now, for some unusual reason, imprinted in time, it sometimes replays the sounds of a special evening in the old Victorian mansion.

Sister told me she isn't afraid of ghosts. But she's curious, just as I am. Once when she was visiting her sister's husband's family home in Mobile, Alabama, she encountered a real ghost! Her hostess, Eleanor Benz, had already told her that the old house, which had once been a stagecoach stop, was reputed to be haunted. As they spoke, Sister was facing the door which led into the entrance hall. She had a clear view of the staircase from where she sat. Suddenly, she saw the figure of a young woman sort of floating down the stairs, with her full length skirt billowing and swirling around her feet. The figure was rather transparent, but still clearly discernible as a lovely young woman. She just came down the stairs, paused a moment in the doorway, and disappeared. Sister said she must have had a startled look on her face because her hostess remarked, "Oh, you saw her, didn't you?"

Sister Reed and her husband enjoy their lovely home and garden. They are actively involved in the family business, the Reed Candle Company, and in various altruistic endeavors in the community. In fact, Peter was chosen Rey Feo during Fiesta Week in 1993. For readers not acquainted with San Antonio's Fiesta royalty, this is a coveted honor that is bestowed upon a civic leader who is greatly involved in charitable works, usually involving underprivileged youth.

Sister, her real, legal name, by the way, is of an interesting ethnic mix. Her great-grandfather, Joseph Michael Schodts, came from Antwerp, Belgium, and settled first in Brownsville, Texas, where he prospered in the lumber business. The Belgian married a Mexican woman. And Sister's mother's family all came from Northern Italy. With that ethnic mix, no wonder Sister is such an attractive woman with classic features, dark hair, and the most expressive, big, beautiful brown eyes! Her taste is impeccable, and I think the ghosts had the right idea when they decided to visit the Reed household. The place really is the perfect place for a party!

To reserve a stay at the Chabot-Reed carriage-house-turned-inn, a call to 1-800-776-2424 will put you in touch with the hospitable Reeds.

# The Haunted Veranda Suite: The Royal Swan Inn

I first learned about the Royal Swan Inn from a neighboring innkeeper, Cliff Tice, who is the proprietor of the Yellow Rose Bed and Breakfast Inn. Cliff and his wife, Jennie, stayed for several weeks at the Royal Swan while their property across the street, purchased in what has been described as deplorable condition, was completely restored and renovated.

Tice told me they experienced numerous occurrences in their Veranda suite at the Royal Swan which were totally unnerving to say the least. Their bed shook violently, rocking back and forth. Once Jennie was bodily thrown from one side of the bed to the other, finally landing on top of her sleeping husband. Cliff told me the bed often shook as if they were experiencing an earthquake. This activity seems to be centered in the Veranda suite area, although other unusual occurrences have taken place in the house. After speaking to former owner Donna West, and the current owners, Curt and Helen Skredergard, I was so fascinated I made an appointment to go and visit the Royal Swan.

One early September morning I visited the lovely inn and met the hospitable owners. The place is kept in an immaculate state, and it is furnished in perfect taste for its period. Built in 1892 by San Antonio dentist Dr. Jabez Cain, the address is 236 Madison. The carriage stone at the curb bears Cain's name.

Wanting to know more of the history of this lovely old house, which has original stained glass in some of the windows, beautiful fireplaces, and paneling of loblolly pine, I

Royal Swan Inn

questioned the obviously proud owners. They were kind
enough to share a little brochure they have prepared, outlining the history of the inn, which I quote as follows:

> The houses at 234, 236, and 242 Madison are
> known as the Cain houses. Dr. Jabez Cain, dentist, is
> said to have built the first two of these houses and pur-
> chased the third one later. In 1890 Dr. Cain paid
> $1,800 for lot 9 and a half of lot 10, where the houses
> at 234 and 236 are located. In February, 1892, he
> secured a builder's lien for $3,100 and probably built
> the house at 236 then. This was his home until about
> 1900. For the next few years his address was listed as
> the Dullnig Building at the corner of Alamo and East
> Commerce Streets, where he had his office. His part-
> ner, Dr. James H. Graham, lived in the house for a
> short time. Later residents were for the most part
> renters.

During World War II, with the influx of military wives and a shortage of apartment space, this house was converted into apartments, as were many in the neighborhood. Following the war, there was a great move to the suburbs and the whole King William area went into decline as did many inner city neighborhoods all over America. Many of the fine old houses fell into disrepair at this time.

Fortunately, in the 1970s, when the River Walk was beginning to be developed, a few people began to recognize the potential of the King William Historic District. These people purchased and began to restore some of the old homes, and the neighborhood was on its way to becoming San Antonio's crown jewel.

The Cain house was purchased by Mr. and Mrs. Egon Jausch, who restored the facade and reduced the number of apartments to two. There were several owners over the following years, each of whom continued the restoration process of the house.

In 1993, the house was purchased by Doug and Donna West. After an eight-month renovation, the Royal Swan was opened for business as a bed and breakfast inn. In October, 1995, the present owners, Curt and Helen Skredergard, purchased the house and continue the bed and breakfast operation.

The Skredergards told me that during the year they've been there, they have had no real experiences of the supernatural sort. However, a guest confided to them as they sat chatting one recent Sunday morning, "You have a ghost up in the Veranda room, you know." The lady went on to say she had planned to sleep in the middle, or sitting room, area of the suite, on the comfortable daybed, while her husband was to take the queen-sized bed in the larger bedroom. But something, some unseen presence, made her so terribly uncomfortable she quickly moved in with her husband. Other guests have said they sometimes feel as if someone is sitting down

on the side of the bed, and they feel the weight of an uninvited
bed partner at times!

The Skredergard's housekeeper has had several brushes
with the live-in spirit, which incidentally, everyone thinks is
a woman. She has often reported the water faucets in rooms
turn themselves on and off, and a little radio in the downstairs front parlor turns on and off all the time, for no
apparent reason.

Donna West told me during her tenure as owner-inn-
keeper, her maid had a strange experience in the lovely blue
and white Veranda suite. The suite opens out onto a covered
porch, or veranda, which is invitingly furnished with wicker
furniture. It is especially popular with guests in the early
mornings or in cool evenings as a place to sit and sip coffee
and chat. Well, thinking all the guests had checked out, the
housekeeper had gone upstairs to tidy up the suite. She happened to glance out onto the porch and saw a young woman
sitting in one of the rockers. She had dark hair and looked like
she might be of Hispanic background. The maid said, "Oh,
pardon me," and the young woman rose from the chair. Has-
tening downstairs, the maid told Donna, "I am sorry, I didn't
know we still had a guest upstairs in the Veranda suite."
Assuring her that they didn't, Donna accompanied the maid
back upstairs. No one was there, but the chair on the porch
was still gently rocking, although there was absolutely no
breeze that day!

Donna went on to say that the ghost later appeared to
several guests. She always came to the Veranda suite about 3
a.m., and Donna said she usually appeared to guests who
seemed to be of Latin or Hispanic descent.

Mrs. West also said numerous guests told her that their
bed shook and rocked, sometimes quite violently, and often
the ceiling fans came on, going at full speed for a few minutes
and then turning off by themselves.

I recently spoke by telephone to Linda Baird of Altus,
Oklahoma. She and her sister-in-law, Carol Baird, of Houston,

get together as often as possible and enjoy mini-vacations together.

During the Labor Day weekend of 1995 the two ladies decided to visit San Antonio, and they checked into the Royal Swan for a couple of nights. They chose the blue and white Veranda suite. The first night passed uneventfully. The two ladies enjoyed a restful night's sleep. However, the second night was anything but restful, especially for Linda, who slept in the larger of the two rooms, in the old iron bedstead. At exactly 3 a.m. the bed started shaking enough to jar Linda wide awake. The intensity of the shaking increased until she had to hang on to the sides of the bed to keep from falling out. At the same time, she noted that the pictures were jumping around on the walls, and the closet door was banging open and then loudly closing. She said there were no curtains at the high, narrow casement windows and the moonlight was very bright so she could plainly see the movement of the pictures on the walls. At first she thought, "Goodness, we're having an earthquake!" But then she started to think, they don't have earthquakes in Texas! It was exactly as if a huge freight train were running right beneath her room, she said.

Linda told me it was a very hot weekend, and while there was an air-conditioning unit in the room, it didn't make it extra cool. But suddenly the atmosphere in the room dropped to an almost arctic-like temperature.

Although she heard the closet door banging and the pictures rattling on the walls while the bed thumped about, Carol, who occupied the daybed in the little sitting room adjacent to Linda's bedroom, didn't get up to check on what was going on in Linda's room. Both ladies said they felt like they'd been made immobile for that brief time!

When they spoke to the owner the next morning, she said a number of other guests had similar experiences when they stayed in that particular suite. It always happened at exactly 3 a.m. and the manifestations generally came to a dark-haired woman who was occupying that particular bed, alone.

However, the Tice's had told me that it happened often to them, as they both slept in the queen-sized bed.

If you don't mind the possibility of an interesting little spirit showing up, I think you'd really enjoy a stay at the beautifully appointed and immaculately kept Royal Swan. It beckons with pristine lace curtains at the front parlor windows and features a delicious full breakfast served in the lovely formal dining room or the sunny morning room. A call to the Skredergards at (210) 223-3776 will hold your reservation.

# The Spirit in the Tower: La Mariposa Inn

I had often passed the old house at the corner of South Alamo and Peralda Streets which form a confluence running into Adams Street, in the King William Historic District. Set behind a high wrought iron fence amid a tangle of shrubs and tall oaks, it is hard to see from the busy intersection. And that's just how the owner wants it to be, I later discovered.

Known as "La Mariposa," which is Spanish for "butterfly," the stucco house at 104 Adams is painted a soft terra-cotta. It has wide upper and lower front verandas and boasts floor-to-ceiling length louvered shutters, which were popular in the Deep South of the late 1800s. In fact, the house reminds me of an old planter's house I once visited near New Orleans. I was absolutely delighted to learn, through my friend and super-spirit-sleuth Brandy Davis, at the Bed and Breakfast Hosts of San Antonio, that there just might be a ghost story attached to the house, which is now a bed and breakfast inn. At last I might get to see the inside of a house I had long found fascinating! And so I called the owner, a very charming and extremely interesting young woman named Bitsy Gorman Wright, and arranged a meeting time.

Bitsy, a San Antonio native, spent a number of years away from her hometown. Much of that time was spent in Hollywood, where she participated in the production of films. She has a most eclectic background, having lived and traveled to many places all over the world, and the furnishings in her home-turned-inn reflect her taste. The place is a livable museum!

La Mariposa Inn

Because she cherishes her privacy, and because the inter-section in front of her house is so busy and noisy, she has purposely closed off entry from the front, and guests enter from the Adams Street side of the house into a large driveway-patio area, entering the house from the rear entrance. There are lots of native plants, many old-fashioned ones that are not often seen in today's gardens, like larkspurs and hollyhocks, growing in a tangled, informal effect. Bitsy said it reminded her of her grandmother's herb and flower garden. I felt the same way. My visit to the Mariposa was a nostalgia trip for me.

Bitsy Wright had prepared a couple of well-written pages about her house for me. So descriptive are they, of both the house and its history, and the ghost that once resided there, I am going to just quote her words, verbatim:

La Mariposa, a restored terra-cotta Italianate "villa," is graced with a Texas Victorian gingerbread front porch and crowned with a charming and intimate third story tower. It was soon known as Ingelke House. Benno Engelke, who was a jeweler, built the house in 1884 after he married Mary Elmendorf. It was also the lifetime residence of Miss Emily Netter, a niece of Mary's, who became San Antonio's first librarian. It was she who turned the house into five apartments.

The exciting interior of this grand house in the King William Historic District has been adapted and transformed by the owners, with the innovative and dynamic vision of architect Isaac Maxwell. Your hostess, Bitsy, who has returned to her native San Antonio after having been involved in film-making in Los Angeles (she met her husband in San Antonio on the set of the Sam Peckinpah movie *"The Getaway,"* in 1971), welcomes you into a serene, expansive space with eighteen-inches-thick limestone walls, twelve-foot ceilings, restored woodwork and beautiful old pine floors where you can enjoy your Continental breakfast.

An elegant stairwell with a velvety smooth Honduran mahogany handrail leads up the stairs past the leaded glass windows. The dramatic color scheme of the spacious guest bedroom enhances the exotic carved and gilded Indonesian wedding throne, which serves as a double bed. The private bath is enlivened by colorful folk art and toys, one wall covered with wonderful hand carved and painted alligators and lizards. An old-fashioned bathtub holds an invitation for a bubble bath by candlelight.

The third-story turret, made even more intimate by deep rich red walls and pyramidal wood ceiling, has twin beds. It was here that the spirit of the house first made its presence known, by the sounds of footfalls and the creaking of the narrow stairs leading up to it. The first person to stay in the house after Bitsy bought it, one of the carpenters, stayed there during the construction and renovation. He was so convinced that someone was coming up the stairs that he slept with a baseball bat by his side! One guest could feel a depression on the edge of the bed where she (it was felt to be a feminine spirit) sat down during the night. Nothing was seen, and nothing was moved by the ghost, and she appears to have left the house in 1989 when guests arriving for a New Year's Eve party sensed her passing them near the bottom of the main stairs. They felt her pass them on her way down as they were making their way up. Her presence has not been sensed again.

Frankly, I believe that the spirit of an earlier resident of the old house, satisfied that her old home was being well cared for and in loving hands, decided it was time for her to move on to a place of permanent peace and rest. She was a gentle spirit, and Bitsy was never frightened by her, only curious as to who she might have been in life.

I was fascinated by Bitsy's blending of old, new, modern and antique. There are rich fabrics from Turkey, hand carved Spanish furniture, that magnificent Indonesian wedding couch, unusual San Antonio handmade punched tin and copper lamps and wall panels, and an absolutely huge Oaxacan wooden Ferris wheel peopled with all sorts of interesting hand carved passengers. This fine piece of Mexican folk art was the gift of a well-traveled friend of Bitsy's.

For information and reservations at the Mariposa, you may call Bitsy Gorman Wright at (210) 225-7849. You will be charmed by the house and fascinated by its lovely owner!

# The Log Cabin Spirits:
# The Riverwalk Inn

When San Antonio businessman and entrepreneur Tracy Hammer learned a choice piece of riverfront property in the downtown area might be coming up for sale, he jumped at the chance to purchase it! Thus he launched a similar project to an endeavor he had developed in Fredericksburg, the Hill Country Bungalow, which is a bed and breakfast inn. The fachwerk house in the hill country town, which Hammer reconstructed, has been so well received that he felt a similar project would meet with the same success in San Antonio.

Hammer and his wife, Jan, traveled to Tennessee and Kentucky in search of old log cabins that might be up for sale. He showed me a photograph album filled with pictures of all sorts of cabins and barns, most of which were in ruinous condition. All were deserted, many had caved-in roofs, and underbrush was growing on the dirt floors of most of them. Some had been reduced to piles of old logs and rubble. The more old derelict cabins they were shown by the realtor during the fifteen-hour nonstop driving search they made, the more Tracy wanted to buy them all! He said he felt as if he and Jan had been sent on a mission to save the old cabins! He also added that the realtor probably thought the couple had lost their minds!

As a result of this buying trip, a huge shipment of log cabin parts, carefully numbered so they could be put together again in proper order, was soon on its way to San Antonio. It was a tremendously tedious and expensive undertaking.

The result, which one can see today at 329 Old Guilbeau Street, is an interesting log cabin structure in front, which contains the "common room," used for Continental breakfasts and various informal gatherings. Then, there is a larger structure, also in log cabin style, containing numerous guest rooms. This portion stretches back off the street towards the river. Some of the rooms in the structures boast old log walls and beams. The owners have searched the country, attending antiques shows and auctions in New England, Tennessee, and Kentucky, in search of primitive furnishings appropriate to the 1830s and '40s which is when most of the cabins were constructed.

These furnishings have been used to great advantage. Each room has a great deal of personality. There are old bedsteads, rugs, spreads and quilts, and interesting artwork on the walls. It's like a trip way back to the early pioneer days when settlers built similar cabins on their homestead claims.

Hammer told me that they found out, while on their cabin search in Tennessee and Kentucky, that the 1880s settlers were considered "country bumpkins" if they continued to live in log cabins, so many either tore down their old cabins or covered them with various types of sidings. Now, the status symbol for rural folk in those parts seems to be mobile homes scattered throughout the area.

When the Hammer's project was going full steam ahead, a carved name and date on a beam was found. It says "Clarence Peterson built this roof in 1842." They also found the initials "C.P." on one of the exterior log walls. Hammer and his property manager, Johnny Halpenny, said this main house is from Edmonton, Kentucky.

One prize possession, among the many items of furniture and accessories the Hammers purchased, is the portrait of a young woman. This was purchased in Massachusetts, and the builder has no idea who the lady was. For some reason, the name "Sarah" has popped into his head, and that is what she is called. Strangely enough, when they had just hired Olivia Rincon, their full-time housekeeper, one morning as she sat

at the antique harvest table chatting with Johnny, just getting acquainted, she glanced up at the portrait over the
fireplace and said, "I believe her name was Sarah."

Tracy and Johnny say they think a few spirits have clung
to the old logs of the cabin, or maybe to the portraits and furnishings. This is not uncommon. I have in my files several
stories of spirits who have attached themselves to their portraits or photographs.

There's one painting, a portrait of a middle-aged man
named Mr. Gilbo, that is in the inn. Hammer said the
antiques dealer also had the companion portrait of Mrs.
Gilbo, but she was such a homely woman they decided not to
buy her likeness. They think maybe Mr. Gilbo's spirit has
been angered that his wife's portrait was not purchased to be
brought along to Texas with his! She may have been beautiful
in his mind's eye.

When I recently visited the inn, I asked the two men,
Tracy and Johnny, what had happened to indicate to them the
place might be haunted. Both men were full of instances to
relate to me. Halpenny told me the TV in the common room
has repeatedly gone on and off by itself. He has slept in this
room several times and finds the room gets very cold, and he
usually wakes up with a start, having the distinct feeling
there is someone or something in the room with him. Doors
also close by themselves when there's no wind or drafts, and
footsteps are often heard on the steps connecting the common
room to the bedrooms upstairs. This is all in the "old Kentucky cabin" portion of the inn. Both men think the presence
is a female spirit.

However, a couple who were married in the inn and had a
small reception in the common room of the old Kentucky
cabin took a lot of photographs. They had really gotten into
the theme of being married in an old settler's cabin. The bride
and groom and all the guests wore Victorian dress, having
rented special costumes for the occasion. A year later the couple came back to the inn. They showed Halpenny a photo of
the reception where they cut the wedding cake. A man who

was not in the wedding party, dressed in old-fashioned clothing also appears in the photo. No one can identify him. Could it be Mr. Gilbo? Or a friend of Sarah's perhaps.

I was impressed with the country-right-in-the-middle-of-town atmosphere that the owners have created. It's a cozy, comfortable place. I'd like to while away a pleasant afternoon just sitting in one of the rocking chairs on the long shady porch overlooking the river!

While the Hammers insist a spirit inhabits the inn, I noted nothing negative, eerie, or depressing about the place. It must be a very warm and benevolent spirit.

For a step back in time, to the days when pioneers lived in log cabins, call manager Johnny Halpenny at (210) 212-8320 for information and reservations.

The Riverwalk Inn

# A Loving House: The
# Linden House Inn

In 1902 Judge Walter Linden built a comfortable two-story dwelling for his wife, Martha, and their only child, Mary Ann. It is located at 315 Howard Street in an area known as Tobin Hill, just south of the historic Monte Vista area. The house was well situated to the downtown area, not too far from the courthouse where the judge was professionally occupied.

The present owners of the two-story white house, now trimmed in pale pink and accented by upper and lower porches, are Cathy and Juan Diaz. The Diaz couple have lived in the house for the entire lifespan of their marriage. Juan bought the place from the Lutheran Church, which had received ownership of the house from the Linden estate in 1961. He lived there alone for five years. Then in 1966 he and Cathy were married. The Linden family and the Diaz family are the only people who have ever lived in the house.

It seems that Judge Linden passed away around 1926, and his wife, called "Miss Mattie" by her friends, survived him. She was never happy after his death, and they say she finally died of heartbreak. She just couldn't enjoy life without her life's partner. Mary Ann, the daughter, had been extremely close to both parents and was unable to think of remaining in the house where there were so many poignant memories of her beloved parents. That is why she gave the place to the Lutheran Church. Needing money more than they needed a house, the church sold the building, and that is how Juan Diaz came into its possession.

Cathy Diaz bade me welcome to the pleasant front parlor reception area of her comfortable home, which has been a bed and breakfast inn since 1989. She had a lot to tell me! She believes the house is haunted by the spirit of "Miss Mattie" Linden. To quote Cathy:

> Juan never encountered any happenings here, but I have had experiences that I cannot explain. For instance, every day at the same time in the afternoon, around 3:30 p.m. when I am sitting at my computer in the room I use for an office, I hear the stairway squeaking, as if someone is coming down the stairs. Now this happens EVERY afternoon at the same time! After looking into this with my neighbor, Miss Ella Stump, who is now deceased, I found out Mrs. Linden used to come down the stairs every afternoon at 3:30 p.m. and go next door to have tea with Miss Stump. They did this for years.

Cathy went on to tell me that Miss Stump was a good friend of hers, and a lovely neighbor. She told Cathy quite a bit about the Lindens, but Cathy now regrets she did not ask more about the family and the house before her elderly neighbor passed away in 1990.

Cathy did tell me an interesting story about an old syca- more tree stump that had once been in the backyard. Juan wanted to remove the stump, but it was too much for him to do alone. He hired a couple of strong young men to come and help him remove it. It was a big job and it took the men most of the day to pull the stump out. Once they removed the stump, the earth around it started to sort of cave in. One of the workers commented he thought there had been a well or something there. They started cautiously digging around the opening in the ground and soon uncovered a metal object. After some more digging, they discovered it to be a large tin bucket, covered with a lid and bound up with ropes. At once fascinated by their discovery and fearful of what might be disclosed once the bucket was opened, Juan gingerly pried the lid open. There, wrapped in yellowed newspapers dated 1926, was an artificial leg, clad in a leather boot with a thick, raised sole. Evidently when Judge Linden died, he was not buried with his peg leg. Because it was such a part of him, his distraught widow must have had it interred in the backyard of the home they had shared for so many years and then planted the sycamore tree over the "gravesite" of the wooden limb.

When Cathy's daughter, Jo Ann, was born in February of 1970, she came home from the hospital about four days after giving birth. On a cold night she got up for the baby's 2 a.m. feeding. Juan was sleeping soundly. As Cathy walked to the back of the house to the kitchen, she distinctly felt something go past her in the darkness. It was an eerie feeling, and she said she felt cold air pass her with a swishing sound. She called to Juan to wake him up, but she says he doesn't believe in ghosts as she does, and he just told her to go feed the baby and go back to sleep.

In 1989 Cathy and Juan decided to convert their home to a bed and breakfast inn. Their daughter was grown and gone and they didn't need all that space. Juan, a plumber by trade, built some attractive bathrooms upstairs so each of the four guest rooms could have a private bathroom. Three of the rooms have their own verandas as well, furnished with inviting Victorian wicker furniture.

On the very day the house was officially inaugurated as a bed and breakfast and the first guests were expected to arrive shortly, they had a strange visitor. An elderly lady of eighty or so years drove up in an old white Cadillac chauffeured by a black maid servant dressed in an old-fashioned black uniform accented by a starched white apron and frilled cap. The woman, who was small of stature and dressed all in white, walked with a cane. She had to be helped up the steps by both Juan Diaz and her servant. She introduced herself as Mary Ann Linden Stumberg, the only daughter of Judge and Mrs. Linden. She explained she wanted to see the old house where she had spent such a happy childhood and wondered if they would permit her to see her old room. Cathy recalled telling her the stairs were steep, but the woman assured her she would be careful and insisted on going upstairs. Thinking back, Cathy said the maid never said a word and did not even sit down, nor did she accompany her mistress upstairs. She just stared in a rather expressionless manner, almost zombie-like. Cathy showed the elderly lady around the upper floor, proudly showing off Juan's new bathrooms and the pretty new wallpaper she had selected to give each room a distinct and separate color scheme. Mrs. Stumberg told Cathy she loved the wallpapers and commented that she just couldn't believe what they had done with the house.

The visit was quite brief. The elderly lady said she must go, and just before she departed, she said, "I wish you all a lot of luck. And remember, there was always a lot of love in this house." Just before the woman left she gave a card with an Austin address and phone number to Cathy.

Shortly after the surprise visit, when her first guests had come and gone, Cathy wrote a note to Mrs. Stumberg thanking her for dropping by and telling her she would like to learn more about the history of the house. She was shocked when her letter was returned with the notation, "addressee deceased." She mentioned the visit and her returned letter to Miss Stump, next door. Her neighbor was shocked. "My dear," she said, "Mary Ann Linden couldn't have come to see you. Why, she has been dead for years."

Cathy said although she and Juan saw the elderly lady, her maid, and the old white Cadillac that day in 1989, they now have to believe that they were visited by the spirit of a deceased Mary Ann Linden Stumberg. But the maid? The Cadillac? Were they phantoms as well? What do you think?

Cathy Diaz took me on a tour of the house to see the inviting guest rooms that are available for visitors. Each is attractively decorated in a different color scheme, and each one is immaculately clean. The yellow room, featuring sunflowers in the printed spread, was Judge Linden's favorite room where he studied his law books and often stayed awake

far into the night to prepare his briefs. Cathy says she sometimes senses his presence in the room, but it is a friendly
feeling, and she is not at all frightened.

While Cathy fully believes the spirits of the Linden family
members still cling to the house, she says, "I'm convinced they
are good spirits. They just don't want to let go of their home!"

If you'd like to visit the Linden Diaz home and enjoy a
restful night with thoughtful hosts (and it's just a block from
the Main Avenue Luby's Cafeteria!), a call to (210) 224-8902
can secure your reservation.

The Linden House Inn

# Haunted Historical Landmark: The Bullis House Inn

The beautiful white mansion which stands at the corner of Grayson and Pierce Street, just across from Fort Sam Houston, boasts a fascinating history. Construction began in 1906, and the house was completed down to the last detail almost three years later, in 1909, when its owner, Brigadier General John Lapham Bullis, moved in. Unfortunately, Bullis was only able to enjoy a couple of years in his fine home before he died in 1911. Perhaps the old general was in ill health when he built his house, or maybe he was just the type of person who liked to plan ahead. At any rate, I was told that the reason the huge front door is so much wider than ordinary doors was because the general planned it that way. He wanted to be sure it would be wide enough to admit his coffin, flanked by pallbearers on either side, when he was brought home to lie in state in one of the big front parlors. And, I was told, that's where he did lie in state, for a whole week, in fact!

Today the mansion is a spacious bed and breakfast inn, owned by Steve and Alma Cross, and ably managed by Michael J. Tease. And, it's said, the old house just may have a resident spirit or two who come around from time to time.

General Bullis enjoyed a colorful military career. A Union officer during the Civil War, he ended up in Texas during the Reconstruction period, where he served with considerable distinction under the famous Colonel Ranald McKenzie at Fort Clark, near present-day Brackettville. While at the fort, Bullis was promoted and given his own detachment as a

The Bullis House Inn

reward for his valiant service during a raid on a hostile band
of Indians camped across the Mexican border.

While the old Indian fighter was known to be a tough
officer, he is said to have treated his men fairly, and he was
respected and well liked. He later served as an Indian agent
in New Mexico and Arkansas before he was transferred, with
the rank of major, to Fort Sam Houston.

After his retirement, Bullis moved into the big white mansion he had built just across the street from the fort. His
family lived on there after his death, until they finally sold it
in 1949 to another famous general, Jonathan Wainwright.
General Wainwright commanded Fort Sam Houston after his
return from a Japanese prison camp in World War II. Known
as the hero of Corregidor, Wainwright survived the infamous
Bataan death march and became the highest ranking military officer to be incarcerated in a prison camp during the
war. Although Wainwright purchased the Bullis house, for
some reason he decided not to live there. He preferred a

smaller house, which he named "Fiddler's Green" on Elizabeth Road, in Terrill Hills.

After 1949 the house was leased to various insurance companies for office space. Then for a time it was a child care
center. In 1983 its present owners bought it, renovated and
restored it. A popular bed and breakfast inn today, its spacious parlors and dining room are frequent choices of San
Antonio brides for wedding receptions as well. It is a Texas
Historic Landmark.

Manager Michael Tease says he's only had one brush with
the resident spirit at the inn. A few months back, a very
excited guest arrived at the front desk with an unlikely story.
He told Tease he had been coming down the back stairs when
suddenly he'd been blocked, for several minutes, by some sort
of invisible barrier. It was like he was pushing against a rope
or barricade. He literally was unable to continue his progress
down the steps. He was absolutely astounded by this. Tease,
not quite believing what the gentleman had told him, went
right away to the back staircase and started going up. Suddenly, his upward movement was stopped. He could not
proceed up the stairs. Something was holding him back, some
invisible resistance that kept him from moving forward. It was
like some sort of barrier had been erected across the stairs.
The stubborn resistance which impeded his progress lasted
only a few minutes, but both Tease and the guest were totally
baffled by the strange experience.

Tease told me that was his only experience with anything
supernatural, but he knew Alma Cross had some strange
experiences, and he felt sure she would be willing to share
them with me. I finally was able to reach the busy owner, and
we enjoyed a nice visit. Mrs. Cross told me for the first three
years that they had the house, she and Steve lived downstairs
while they worked to restore the place. When their work was
completed, they began to rent out the upstairs portion as a
bed and breakfast. They don't reside there now, but Alma is
frequently on the premises.

One evening soon after they purchased the Bullis House Inn, the couple was upstairs working, when they suddenly heard loud men's voices involved in what sounded like a heated argument. The sounds came from downstairs in the vicinity of the entrance foyer. Knowing they were supposed to be alone in the place, they hurried to the staircase and yelled down, "Hey, what's going on down there?" Then they rushed down to see for themselves. But there was no one there. The front door was locked. They looked all over the big house, even going down into the basement. They found absolutely nothing.

Alma said Steve, an engineer, is pretty much of a skeptic where ghosts are concerned. But that night he heard the voices. He searched the house. He started to believe!

Once, when Alma's mother was visiting the couple, she was sleeping in a downstairs bedroom. Alma occupied the next room, now used as the inn manager's office. At 3 a.m. Alma suddenly awoke with a start, and in the moonlight she could plainly see the figure of an Indian man standing by her bed. She saw his face, his long black hair tied back with a bandanna around the forehead, and his body down to about the waistline. About the same time she saw the figure, her mother let out a blood-curdling scream! Still in a daze over having seen the Indian form, Alma leaped from her bed and dashed into her mother's room. She asked her mother why she had screamed, and her mother told her she had the most awful nightmare, about an Indian man standing right by her bed. The women each described to the other what they'd just seen, and the figure had looked just the same to them both. Alma said they decided to go to the kitchen and make some hot chocolate to try and settle their nerves.

Alma said she had never thought much about the types of dress of the different Indian tribes that once lived in the area, but the more she got to thinking about it, the man she saw that night looked like an Apache. And General Bullis was instrumental in capturing the most famous Apache of them all, the Chiracahua head man, Geronimo! Maybe that's why the spirit of an Apache brave came to the Bullis house. Come to think of it, it might have been Geronimo himself!

Alma told me one time her mother tried to get into an upstairs bedroom, which they call "Room G." It wasn't locked, but try as hard as she could, she couldn't open the door. Finally she went downstairs to get Alma. When the two women got to the room, the door was standing wide open!

There are just lots of little occurrences that take place in the inn, giving weight to the possibility that there are several rather interesting spirit personalities clinging to the historic old mansion.

For a night spent reliving history, call (210) 223-9426 where the owners guarantee you'll find "affordable elegance in the classic Southern style."

# The Gingerbread House: Country Cottage Inn

The Country Cottage Inn, in Fredericksburg, was built in 1850 as a private dwelling. It was the first stone building, and one of the first two-story dwellings, in the small community. German immigrant Friedrich Kiehne built it for his wife, Maria. They came to the new settlement from their home in Everode, Germany. A blacksmith by trade, Kiehne made most of the window hardware used in the construction of the house, which has been carefully restored. It is a charming building, located on Main Street, just cater-cornered across from the old Nimitz Hotel. One of the showplaces of the community in its day, it has matching upstairs and downstairs porches joined by an inside stair and is decorated with beautiful cut-out "gingerbread" work that gives a starched lace character to the front porches.

Barbara Strackbein, a Fredericksburg resident, told me that she believes the house is inhabited by a resident ghost. She ought to know! Employed to clean the house in between bed and breakfast visitors, she has experienced some close encounters with something not quite of this world! Once, when she knocked on a door to be sure the occupants had vacated the room, she said she distinctly heard someone say, "Come on in." When she opened the door and walked into the room, she was shocked to find it empty! And another time, when vacuuming a room where a heavy velvet curtain, or drape, separates one section of the room from the other, a Polaroid picture suddenly just floated down from one of the curtains and landed at Barbara's feet. There was no likeness

Country Cottage Inn

on the strange photograph, only the words "this is haunted" were plainly to be seen on the otherwise blank film. Barbara still has it, and she still doesn't know what to make of it.

There are a number of cold spots in the old house, according to Barbara, and she says another housekeeper told her she often heard mysterious footsteps when she absolutely knew the house was unoccupied. Another girl who once worked there reported she saw a little carved wooden figure fly off the mantel (It didn't just fall, it was propelled!) as she worked at cleaning the room.

Strackbein says the back door which leads into the kitchen area was always kept locked. Once she came to the house about 6 p.m. as it was just getting dark. The door was shut and locked, but just as she arrived, the door opened in front of her, without her inserting the key, and she watched, astonished, as the door swung open into the room. She also told me one of the doors to a certain bedroom swung open alone, and she continually had the feeling that someone was there, watching her, although she knew she was all alone in the house. She has a feeling the resident spirit is Mr. Kiehne. She said sometimes she used to say "Hello, Mr. Kiehne" when she came in, just to acknowledge his presence.

On a recent trip to Fredericksburg I noticed a "For Sale" sign on the inn. I hope someone hurries up and buys the place. Mr. Kiehne may be lonesome.

# The Ghostly Bride:
# The Prince Solms Inn

The Prince Solms Inn, located at 295 East San Antonio Street in New Braunfels, is a charming two-story brick building that was built by German craftsmen in 1898. The soft beige bricks were handmade for the hotel and transported to the building site by horse-drawn wagons. Giant cypress trees were cut from the banks of the Guadalupe River to furnish the wooden parts of the building. It has always been a hotel, located just off the Main Plaza of the little German community founded by Prince Carl of Solms Braunfels in 1845. It is just a block away from the shady banks of the Comal River, which claims the distinction, at 2.5 miles, of being the shortest river in the state of Texas!

The inn sits within a cluster of historic buildings, which include an old feed store where residents bought all sorts of supplies, and the stables which were built around 1845 and which bear the distinction of once quartering Sam Houston's horse when he came for a visit to New Braunfels. The old Joseph Klein house, a tin-roofed, stuccoed structure built in 1852, is also adjacent to the inn.

Lovers of antiques really enjoy visiting the Prince Solms because it is charmingly decorated with Victorian furnishings, lovely artwork, and bric-a-brac. The ten-foot-tall front doors are accented with intricately etched glass panels. It's a lovely place for an overnight visit, or longer.

Amidst all this elegance of the past century, there seems to reside some spirits left over from that era. At least that's what we've been told! The manager, a lovely lady named

The Prince Solms Inn

Carmen Morales, invited us over for a visit, and we brought our psychic friend and advisor Sam Nesmith and his wife, Nancy, along. Sam picked up on several spirits and said they were friendly and just liked being around the inn. One was in the basement level which houses Wolfgang's Keller, a fine restaurant which features Continental cuisine in a quiet, subdued atmosphere. Sam believes this is the spirit of a young woman who may have worked as a waitress or tended bar at one time. When we later went back for another visit, some of the dining room staff told us that around the bar is where they feel the presence of something, and several told me that they, or customers they had waited on, had actually seen the entity of a young woman.

When my husband and I later visited the inn to experience one of their fun-filled murder mystery weekends, we were told by Carmen that the story has been told for many years that the ghost of a young woman, a bride who was jilted on her wedding day, has come back a number of times. The young woman and her family were staying at the inn prior to the wedding. There the wedding party awaited the arrival of the groom, but alas, he never showed up. The family members finally left, but the heartbroken, embarrassed, and puzzled young woman stayed on and on, waiting at the top of the stairs for the lover who never came. The story goes she finally lost her mind with grief and sorrow. They say that her ghost has been seen either on the stairs or standing at the top of the stairs, just waiting . . . waiting . . . waiting. . . .

During our visit when Sam was with us, he told us he believes that there is also an old man spirit that may be someone who lived there when it was used more like a boardinghouse. He picked up that the man had been a Union soldier who came south for his health after the Civil War. He settled in the German community because the Germans were more sympathetic towards the Union than were the other citizens of Texas. Sam believes he may have lived at the inn until he passed away. The Huntsman Room is the one supposed to be haunted, and that is where Sam strongly felt the presence of this man. Well, we slept there during the murder mystery weekend and had no experience except good, pleasant dreams in a comfortable bed!

If you visit the inn, you won't be disappointed. Charming accommodations with names like the Peony Room, the Songbird Room, the Library, the Huntsman, the Rose Room, and the Magnolia Room, all inspired by the wallpapers used in the decor of the various bedchambers, await you. You'll have a restful night's repose, and a delicious Continental breakfast will be ready for you come morning's light. Call Carmen Morales at (210) 625-9169 for information and reservations for either lodgings or the murder mystery weekends.

# New Braunfels' Haunted Hotel: The Faust

The warm September morning when I drove to New Braunfels some thirty-five miles north of San Antonio to interview some of the staff of the old Faust Hotel was somewhat of a nostalgia trip for me. It had been at least twenty years since we used to frequently drive over to the small German community to enjoy Sunday dinner at the hotel, located at 240 South Seguin Street. It was a special favorite dining spot of my parents, the late John and Statira Schultz, and we often brought them for lunch during their periodic visits from North Texas. Especially famous for their fried catfish, the hotel enjoyed a brisk noon trade. Today the hotel no longer serves those great cafeteria-style Sunday dinners.

The hotel has been beautifully restored and is furnished with both Victorian antiques and furniture of the 1920s era, all original to the hotel. The place has a most interesting history, as well as a good bit of mystery attached to it!

In the 1920s some of New Braunfels' leading citizens realized that a modern hotel was needed to attract tourists and "drummers" (traveling salesmen who needed sample rooms in which to show their wares to local merchants) to the area. Also, there were a number of clubs and organizations in the sociable little town that needed meeting rooms and dining facilities for banquets and dinner-dances. But there was no place in the town that met this criteria. Finally, Walter Faust Jr., who was vice-president of the local chamber of commerce and president of the First National Bank, sponsored a committee that raised funds for the construction of such a hotel.

The committee did a great job, and by the time the building was completed, almost all expenses had already been met. It opened as the Travelers Hotel, on October 12, 1929. Over 2,000 excited townspeople came on opening day to see the beautiful new hostelry, which featured a private bathroom in every room!

Faust became the first owner of the hotel. He and his wife lived in a suite there until his death in 1933. The building was constructed on the original site of the Fausts' old homestead, which was moved to the other side of Seguin Street and rebuilt. In 1936, three years after Faust passed away, the hotel was renamed in his honor. From an old, prestigious New Braunfels family, Faust was the son of Joseph Faust who had served as a state senator, mayor of New Braunfels, and a regent of the University of Texas.

The old hotel is really a charmer. The original tile floors intricately patterned with a sort of Moorish design still are an integral part of the elegant lobby. They look to be in mint condition! And the ten fine black wrought iron chandeliers which

The Faust

extend from the black-bladed ceiling fans in the lobby keep
the air circulating, even though the building is now air condi-
tioned. There's a definite look of art-nouveau-Spanish
Renaissance to the decor of the building, which was designed
by architect Harvey P. Smith of San Antonio, who worked on
the restoration projects of the Spanish Governor's Palace and
San Jose Mission.

In its heyday, the Faust, with interesting yellow brickwork and ornamental stonework in the facade, included the
carved faces of Spanish conquistadors. It was considered one
of the finest small hotels of its kind in the entire southern part
of the United States.

For a time, plagued with financial problems and facing the
competition of modern motels growing up in and around New
Braunfels, the Faust barely managed to stay open. For a time
it was owned by the family of Bob Krueger, former congressman and, later, ambassador to Mexico. Finally the hotel was
forced to close in 1975. It was soon purchased, however, and
an extensive restoration project began to update the old landmark. Today, after changing hands several times, it seems to
be in excellent hands, the property of a Houston firm.

Each of the guest rooms is decorated with old 1920s
furnishings. Old armoires, dressers, desks, and beds are combined with modern television and telephones in every room.
And, I was absolutely astounded at the extremely reasonable
room rates I noted for all this comfort and charm!

On the morning of my visit I was warmly greeted by the
attractive young manager, Karen Blakeman. Ms. Blakeman
in turn introduced me to one of the hotel's housekeepers,
Carla Dillard, who seems to be an expert on the status of the
ghostly residents of the hotel. In the two years Dillard has
been employed there, she told me she has had numerous
encounters with them. I gave her my undivided attention and
was soon rewarded with all sorts of information as she mentioned encounter after encounter, both her own personal
experiences and those related to her by other employees.

For starters, when Dillard was cleaning a third floor bathroom she felt something tap her on the back. Turning around, she saw a little girl about four or five years old standing behind her. The child darted into the hallway and went right through the wall! For some reason, Dillard, who professes to be somewhat psychic, said the name "Christine" immediately popped into her head. She also told me the apparition of the child as it appeared to her was somewhat transparent, but the features were easily discernible. Carla believes the child is Christine Faust, an ancestor of the late Walter Faust. The child's picture hangs in the third floor hallway, just outside room 306. It is a charming likeness of a little girl dressed in a checked gingham dress, holding a white cat. Dillard did some research on the Faust family and learned that a Sarah and James Faust had a daughter, Christine, who was born in 1837. She might possibly have lived in the old Faust homestead which once occupied the site where the hotel now stands.

Dillard also told me that other members of the housekeeping staff have both seen and heard the child playing hopscotch in the hallways. Carla has felt a cat brush against her legs, and once she saw the white feline in the hallway on the third floor. However, when a search of the rooms was conducted, no such animal was to be found.

The housekeeper also said she had been cleaning room 411 when the water in the sink started running of its own accord. She also volunteered that once a couple checked out of room 415 in the middle of the night when all of their luggage got up and started moving, handles up, around the room as if it was being carried by the unseen hands of a bellman! She also told me in Walter Faust's old quarters, now an elegant suite, the spirit of the former owner often moves things around. He has also been seen standing at the foot of the brass bed by several occupants of the suite, which is popular with honeymooners.

Dillard volunteered that about a year ago some guests said they saw a bellman running the elevator. They remarked they thought this was "quaint and nice and old-fashioned" to the desk clerk, who promptly told them that there was no bellman or elevator operator! The guests described the accommodating gentleman as being "an older man dressed in a plaid jacket." Some of the hotel staff believe this must have been an appearance by Walter Faust, who seems to do all sorts of things at the hotel. He has also set the fans whirling, locked guests out of their rooms, and has caused the big front doors of the hotel to open and close by themselves in the middle of the night.

While I was chatting with Carla, a gentleman walked into the lobby and Carla called him over. She introduced him as Dave Abram, a painting contractor who does quite a bit of work for the hotel. Abram has also been witness to several ghostly appearances and was glad to sit down and chat awhile.

In 1995, during the infamous O.J. Simpson trials, Abram was repainting all the door frames on the fourth floor. Not wanting to miss the excitement of the trial, he would open the door into a room and turn on the television set so he could follow the proceedings while doing his work. When he was painting the door frame to room 326, a small corner room, he chanced to look up and was totally startled to see the transparent figure of a young woman holding a baby on her hip, as she stood in the narrow space between the television set and an old fashioned chifforobe. The figure seemed to be bathed in a misty, bluish color. A second glance assured the painter he was not imagining things. Knowing Carla was working in a room a few doors down, he called to her. But by the time she got there, the misty figure had totally disappeared. Carla said she went into the room to the spot where Abram had seen the woman, and while she saw nothing, she had a feeling of cold and knew the spirit was still around! Abram said he didn't wait for the elevator to go downstairs. He took the stairs, two at a time, and ran to the lobby to report what he had seen to the front desk clerk. Even as he spoke to me about the sighting, I could tell he was still visibly moved by the experience.

Mr. Abram went on to tell me that he recently restored the elevator doors, covering them with a new coating of gold paint. Shortly afterwards he found a little handprint on one of the doors at just about the height where a small child would have made it. Carla saw it also and verified this. The house-keeper and the painter both believe the handprint was made by little Christine before the pigment dried.

Once when Mr. Abram was working on the fourth floor near the elevator he saw an elderly gentleman going in and out of all the rooms, using no keys to get into them. Abram knew all the rooms were locked. He said a lot of the rooms were even hard to open with a key, yet here was this old man, who first would look up the hall towards where Abram stood, then dart into a room, stay just a minute, and come out into the hall again. Then he would repeat the process as he went into first one room and then the next, all the way down the hallway. He always looked back down the corridor at Abram before he dashed into another room. Now, Abram didn't think "ghost" at first, as the man he saw was completely solid and looked just like anybody else. He did think "crazy" as his behavior was so strange! Abram went down to the front desk and asked who in the world was up on the fourth floor going in and out of all the rooms without a room key. The desk clerk assured him all the rooms were locked and nobody could be going in and out of them without first unlocking them with a key! Carla had come down to the lobby by then and caught some of the conversation. She asked Abram to describe the man he had seen. He told her he was a man who looked to be in his early seventies, well groomed, wearing metal rimmed glasses and clad in a well-tailored gray suit. Carla led Abram to a picture of Walter Faust which hangs in the dining room. Abram said "without a doubt" the man he saw in the fourth floor hallway that day was the former owner of the hotel!

I was also shown an article which appeared in the November 27, 1994 edition of the *Lake Charles American Press*, written by staff writer Jamie Gates, from which I quote:

Rena Whitley was working late one night when the door to the front desk started swinging back and forth. I thought to myself, "Oh my goodness, gracious no, that's not possible," said Whitley, who had worked at the hotel for many years without experiencing anything unusual.

Whitley also recounted a story she'd heard concerning the hotel's bartender. Before locking up at night he would always make sure the full liquor bottles were placed behind the half-empty bottles in the cabinet. After doing so on one occasion, he returned the next morning to find all the bottles switched back.

Gates's article went on to recount what Carla Dillard had told me about seeing the little girl spirit. Then he mentioned the experiences a couple of other employees have had:

On the second floor hangs a picture of a man and woman gazing staunchly at the camera. Joanne Rico claims to have seen the man enter the elevator. "I never thought about it until after a week when I passed by the picture and he looked exactly like that person," Rico said.

Dianna Torres, another housekeeper, recounted the time when all the lights went out during a bad thunderstorm. The night clerk went down to the basement to check the fuse box. He heard someone laughing, became frightened and ran upstairs to the dining room.

A lighted picture of Walter Faust hangs in there and its light happened to be the only light still on in the entire hotel. The outlet was later checked and found to have no electricity running through it.

There are apparently no malevolent or negative spirits around the old hotel. Walter Faust and little Christine are the ones most often sighted or sensed. The child is just playful, and Walter is apparently very protective, keeping a careful watch on the hotel which was his pride and joy.

You are certain to enjoy a trip back in time, when elegance and charm were of utmost importance, and quiet, tranquil surroundings meant more than noisy bars and loud disco music. A stay at the Faust will become a cherished memory, I am sure. Call (512) 625-7791 for reservations. Oh, and do give my regards to Walter.

# The House of Happy Spirits: Karbach Haus Inn

It was on a warm January afternoon that my husband, Roy, and I enjoyed a pleasant visit with Kathy and Ben Jack Kinney, owners of the historic Karbach Haus Inn, located at 487 West San Antonio Street, in the old German community of New Braunfels, about thirty-five miles to the north of San Antonio. Built in 1906, the large two-story beige brick building of over 5,000 square feet has a most interesting background, and like all of the houses in this chapter, it has a history of resident spirits as well!

The land where the spacious house is located was part of a large Spanish land grant given to one Juan Martin de Verimendi. At Verimendi's death, the land was sold by Maria Antonio Verimendi Garza and her husband, Rafael C. Garza, to Prince Carl of Solms Braunfels, who was the trustee for the Association for the Protection of German Emigrants in Texas. Subsequent owners of the tract included numerous pioneer settlers of New Braunfels.

Finally, Catherine and Friedrich Dulm, who had purchased the property in 1869, sold it to a John Muller in 1883. Muller in turn sold it to George and Hulda Eiband around 1890. The wealthy Eibands, who had no children, owned successful dry goods stores in both New Braunfels and Galveston. Around 1906 they decided to build a house on the property. It was considered one of the finer homes in New Braunfels in its day. There was also a large carriage house on the property, built of the same brick. It included space for at least three carriages, two large horse stalls, two tack rooms, and probably had a lodging place for the groom as well. In addition, the building, modern for its day, included a concrete floored room where the horses and wagons could be washed down and the water would drain out of the building. The entire upper level was a loft where hay for the horses was stored. Later on, when horses and buggies were no longer in fashion, the very first electric car in New Braunfels was housed in the old carriage house, which had now been designated the "garage."

The Eibands evidently lived a long and happy life in their fine home. In 1935 George died, and Hulda passed away a year later, at the age of seventy-two. The property was left to three nephews, sons of E.A. Eiband, who was George's brother. None of the heirs wanted to live in the house, all having fine homes of their own, and so it was that the property was put up for sale.

Dr. Hylmar Emil Karbach Sr. and his wife, Katherine Elizabeth Taylor Karbach, purchased the thirty-two-year-old house in 1938. The doctor, who had four children, soon remodeled the house extensively, adding four bedrooms and two bathrooms plus a large playroom in the upstairs portion of the house which the Eibands had previously used as a storage attic. The Karbach family lived there many years, and the lovely house was often the scene of some of New Braunfels' most gala and memorable social functions. Apparently both the Eibands and Karbachs were wonderful hosts, and an invitation to a social function at the San Antonio Street address was greatly coveted by the citizenry of New Braunfels!

Dr. Karbach died in 1959, and his wife Katherine lived on in the house until she died in 1985. The four Karbach children inherited the property. In 1986 the eldest daughter, Kathleen, and her husband, retired Navy Captain Ben Jack Kinney, bought the house from Kathleen's siblings. They have worked tirelessly since that time to restore the house to its original grandeur.

For the past ten years, since 1987, the Kinneys have operated the house as the Karbach Haus Bed and Breakfast

Inn, with four of the six bedrooms in the house available for travelers to the charming little German community.

The rooms are all beautifully and tastefully appointed. No creature comfort has been neglected. The house, with its floors of oak and cypress and original old ceramic tiles, fascinating "secret rooms," and fine antique furnishings, is a wonderful choice for the visitor to New Braunfels who is seeking peace, tranquillity, and comfortable surroundings.

Karbach Haus Inn

Kathleen, or Kathy, as she prefers to be called, is a well educated and interesting woman. She holds a doctor of philosophy degree. The retired educator is a gracious and enthusiastic hostess as well. And she readily admits to believing that her lovely house is occupied by "happy spirits." Often guests who occupy the two second-floor guest rooms have asked the Kinneys about "the children." When assured that there are no Kinney children around, and that the innkeepers don't even let rooms to families with small children, the guests tell them they have heard small children laughing in

the night. The sounds always seem to originate in the direction of the playroom located in the front of the house.

Kathy told us that her mother had twelve grandchildren,
and they often all came at the same time for long summer
visits. The playroom was where they all gathered, often sleeping on blanket pallets spread out on the floor. They loved to
stay up until late at night telling ghost stories. The children
all called the playroom their "magic room," and there was
always lots of laughter and prankstering going on.

Kathy went on to tell us that her youngest child, Roy, died
in a tragic playground accident while the family was residing
in Virginia where Ben Jack was stationed at the Pentagon.
Roy was only twelve years old at the time of his death. Kathy
said he was a happy little boy, always laughing and full of fun.
She firmly believes his spirit comes back to his grandmother's
old house where he spent so many happy childhood summer
vacations with his cousins and siblings, and where his beloved
parents now live.

Kathy says her mother, Katherine Karbach, had a vibrant
personality. She always wanted Kathy and Ben Jack to come
back to New Braunfels to live. Kathy says she and her husband believe much of what they have, or have not, done to the
house has been directed by her mother's spirit. She says they
would not dream of doing anything to the house, or grounds,
that Katherine Karbach would not have approved. Kathy also
said her mother was very frugal with the use of electricity and
always insisted that the lights be turned off when not in use.
Now, when the Kinneys leave a light on in a room or in the
hallways, they often find themselves groping in the dark, as
Katherine's spirit goes about turning them all off. They
always find the switches in the off position, so they know
someone, or something, definitely turned them off. Captain
Kinney says he knows it's his mother-in-law, just keeping an
eye on the budget! Kathy also believes that Mrs. Eiband may
come around as well. After all, she was the first mistress of
the household!

On the broad wrap-around porch, there's a rocking chair that often rocks by itself. It was Katherine Karbach's custom to sit on the porch on nice afternoons to watch the San Antonio Street traffic pass by. The chair was her favorite. Kathy says the chair will rock when there is absolutely no wind blowing, and they know it's just Katherine's way of making her presence known.

Kathy also often senses the presence of her younger sister, Martha Jo, who was just a year younger than Kathy. The girls were very close, almost like twins. Their bedrooms shared a bathroom, and the girls often spent the nights in one another's rooms as they were little girls growing up. Kathy misses her sister, and she believes her spirit is often in her old room.

The Karbach house has a huge backyard, which boasts a spa and a big swimming pool located beneath the sheltering limbs of magnificent magnolia and cypress trees.

At present there are four guest rooms available to the public, but the Kinneys are now remodeling the old carriage house. In the early spring of 1997 two more rooms will be made available, where the old hayloft was once located, while the lower carriage area will be converted into a large party room available for all sorts of catered affairs. The property is really a great place for a party, and I would rather imagine that suits the spirits of Katherine Karbach and Hulda Eiband just fine!

To reserve your own lovely room in a unique and elegant old house where you'll enjoy a full gourmet German breakfast and the company of interesting and genial hosts, just call Kathy and Ben Jack Kinney at (210) 625-2131.

# The Weinert House Inn: Showplace of Seguin

Five years ago, Tom and Lynna Thomas opened the first bed and breakfast inn in the historic community of Seguin, some twenty-five miles east of San Antonio. The spacious two-story rose-pink Victorian house at 1207 North Austin Street was built in 1895 by a prominent local citizen, F.C. Weinert, for his wife, Clara Maria Bading Weinert, and their seven children (four boys and three girls). Weinert served in the Texas State Senate in the 1800s, and he also served as Secretary of State. He was generally referred to as "the Senator."

The present owners purchased the house and beautifully landscaped grounds from a granddaughter of Senator Weinert, Johnnye Jean Weinert Lovett, who had inherited it from the estate of her aunts, the old senator's three daughters. Johnnye's father, Rudolph, one of the Weinert boys, had followed closely in his father's footsteps, having been elected to the Texas State Senate in 1936, where he served for twenty-six years. Rudolph was often referred to as the Dean of the State Senate. Lynna also told me that Rudolph and Congressman Henry B. Gonzalez had served in the state house in Austin at the same time and had always been good friends.

Lynna told me the house remained in the Weinert family for ninety-seven years until she and her husband purchased and restored it. They added a few extra bathrooms for the comfort of their guests, but basically the integrity of the house has been maintained. The woodwork, including fine fan-shaped fretwork cornices framing the arched entrances to the front parlor and the staircase have been beautifully restored and are in pristine condition. The whole house looks like it should be a featured spread in *Victoria Magazine*. It is furnished with many of the original Weinert family heirloom pieces, and as Lynna says, "It really is the Weinert house. We've just become its caretakers for a while."

The Weinert House Inn

All of the guestrooms bear the names of Weinert family members. The Senator's Suite includes a beautiful glassed-in porch with inviting wicker furniture, and a small sleeping nook for a child or third party who might want to share the suite. The Senator's portrait hangs on the wall in "his" bedroom. Ella's Chambers, another lovely bedroom, bears a photograph of the stern-faced Ella Weinert, the daughter who never married, on the dressing table.

A feminine bedroom with a lovely canopied bed is named Tanta Clara's Room. When I asked Lynna what that meant, she said *tanta* is the German word for aunt. The room is named in honor of the beautiful Clara Hedwig Weinert Brustedt, whose photograph occupies a prominent place on the wall of her namesake bedroom. The comely brunette is pictured wearing a long white Victorian gown. The fourth bedroom is called Kathinka's Quarters in honor of the third Weinert daughter, Kathinka Weinert Eilers.

According to the Thomases, when Clara and Kathinka were widowed, they returned to live in the old family home. Ella, the spinster sister, had always lived in the house with the Senator and his wife. As far as she knows, Lynna said, all the daughters plus the Senator and his wife passed away in their beloved home.

The Saturday in early January when I visited the Weinert House was fortunate for me, because Lynna had not yet removed the exquisite Christmas decorations, including gilded magnolia leaves arranged with candles on a lovely lace cloth in the dining room, a collection of charming antique and contemporary Santa Claus figures displayed on the greenery bedecked shelves of a Victorian secretary, and two magnificent, heavily ornamented live Christmas trees, one in the front parlor, and the other in the music room. Lynna Thomas has excellent taste, and her decorations showed that much time and skill had gone into their execution.

The innkeeper is convinced that the Weinert family members still occupy the rooms of their old home. The spirits are all friendly and benevolent, and Lynna is not at all frightened by them. But the evidence certainly points to a house still occupied by at least three of the former residents: the Senator, the lovely Clara, and the spinster sister, Miss Ella.

The spirits seem to make their presence known when a member of the staff or Lynna are in the house working alone, or when just one guest, or guest couple, is staying there, or conversely, when the house is absolutely full of guests, but, then, only when the guests are of all one family group, such as a big family reunion, a wedding or anniversary or birthday celebration, or something of that nature. Sometimes then the sounds of music are heard, and even the piano has been heard to play, even though it is not a player piano!

One night a woman guest saw the figure of a beautiful young woman dressed in a white gown as she brought what appeared to be a fully laden breakfast tray into the room. The startled guest nudged her husband to wake him so he could see the apparition. But when she did this, the figure disappeared. When the lady spoke to Lynna and described the young woman she had seen, Lynna showed her the photograph of the beauteous Clara, and she positively identified her as her nocturnal visitor!

A gentleman guest also saw Clara standing at the top of the staircase one evening.

Once, a startled guest couple who occupied the Tanta Clara's Room witnessed a blackout shade as it flew up and then just kept going around and around on its roller. Since Clara probably didn't have blackout shades to darken her room, maybe she just doesn't like for them to be a part of her room now.

Other guests have reported they've had the sensation of being gently tucked into bed at night.

According to Lynna, Miss Ella likes to move things around. One housekeeper constantly complained that things like small accessories, clocks, vases and various art objects were always being relocated. The Thomases just think Ella's spirit likes to redecorate.

One guest, a travel writer, reported being awakened by the sounds of timpani during her visit to the inn. There's not a clue as to who the kettle drummer might be.

Lights are often turned on and off, according to the whims of the spirits, and doors gently open and close of their own volition. No slamming, of course! Victorian ladies would never have had the ill manners to slam doors!

The senatorial spirit has a different personality. A strong personality in life no doubt, he likes to remain "in charge" even in the spirit world. Sometimes Lynna feels he is there with her as she goes about her chores. And sometimes she senses he wants her to leave, so then she usually just locks up and goes home! Lynna and Tom don't reside at the inn, although Lynna joked that she really lives at the inn and just sleeps somewhere else! I explained to the attractive inn-keeper that the Senator was no doubt used to getting his way. A persuasive senator and politician would have been of that turn of mind. And in his day and culture, German patriarchs really ruled the roost in their households. So there he is, very possessive of the old home which he built for his wife and children. It may be a little hard for his spirit to fathom that someone else owns his property now.

None of the spirits are at all threatening or frightening to Lynna. They just sort of come and go, adding a special personal touch to their beloved old home.

The showplace of Seguin in the 1890s is still a real showplace today. Besides providing a charming place for her guests to find peace and rest, Lynna serves a fabulous full gourmet breakfast. She caters luncheons and parties of all kinds on the spacious sun porch, and stages elegant weddings and receptions in the house and on the grounds as well. A special Victorian high tea is served on the second and fourth Thursdays from 2:30 to 4:00 p.m. at the inn. I once attended one of these, and they are really splendid, with fine china, linens, and silver being put to good use.

Tom and Lynna Thomas state on their attractive brochure that their mission is to create a peaceful, serene experience for those who pay a visit to the Weinert House, so that heart, body, and soul may be refreshed. For information and reservations for your own memorable stay at the Weinert House Inn, or for a special catered event, call Lynna or Tom Thomas, the gracious hosts, at (210) 372-0422.

# CHAPTER 2

# FOOD, SERVICE, AND SPIRITS: HAUNTED EATING ESTABLISHMENTS

*Millions of spiritual creatures walk the earth
unseen, both when we wake and when we sleep.
Spirits when they please can either sex assume,
or both, so soft and uncompounded is their
essence pure, not tied or manacled with joint or
limb, nor founded on the brittle strength of
bones.*

John Milton

# A Host of Ghosts:
# Victoria's Black Swan Inn

The elegant white house that looks very much like a plantation home in the Deep South, sits atop a natural knoll overlooking Salado Creek. The address is 1006 Holbrook Road, and it's called Victoria's Black Swan Inn.

I devoted a dozen or so pages to the inn in *Spirits of San Antonio and South Texas.* The place is still haunted, according to the owner, Jo Ann Rivera. When I interviewed Jo Ann back in 1992, she was Jo Ann Andrews. She married Robert Rivera soon afterwards. Today they jointly run the inn, which is a party house and fine restaurant, not an overnight stopping place. They've also added little Victoria, who is now three years old, to the family.

A recent addition to the activities at the Black Swan is the staging of elaborate Victorian high tea parties for ladies who belong to the "Queen's Court," a social club that was instituted by Jo Ann and her friend Mary Kathryn Knowlton, who owns a charming boutique on the grounds called Exclusively Victorian. These affairs, complete with fine linen, silver, and china, and tasty little teatime tidbits offer morsels to tempt even the most jaded palates. The ladies who attend listen to lecturers, share book reviews, and enjoy fashion shows of vintage clothing. I was pleased to be invited to speak at the July soiree, and I met a lovely group of ladies who arrived to "take tea." Period hats were offered to each arrival, and soon all the ladies were wearing a suitable chapeau to top off their afternoon ensembles.

Victoria's Black Swan Inn

I was reminded of some pleasant high teas I enjoyed during the three and a half years I lived in England back in the 1950s.

After the tea party, I was able to remain and chat with Jo Ann and Mary Kathryn, and a friend of Jo Ann's, Sam Davidson Faires. I needed an update about the ghostly residents of the inn which I had previously written about. Although they've settled down quite a bit since I last was there, there are still the sounds of tinkling music boxes which follow employees around the house. Piano music is often heard, even though there are no signs of a pianist seated at the console. Jo Ann and Robert and their employees seem to just take the presence of other-worldly entities for granted!

Sam Davidson Faires, a most attractive woman who was wearing ecru lace on the day of the tea, told me of a recent experience she had there. She was in a room in the south wing which they call the Bride's Room, giving Jo Ann's mother, Fay Marks, a manicure. She glanced up and saw a man walk in and stand behind Mrs. Marks. She looked at him to see what he wanted and he totally disappeared! In about thirty minutes another man walked into the room, and again, poof! the same vanishing act! No one in the house has a clue who these figures might be.

I also visited with Libby Bishop, who, with her son, gifted designer Justin Stutz, runs Possum Flats Haberdashers on the estate. They headquarter in a building behind the Black Swan, built on the site of an earlier garage and storage building which was badly damaged in a windstorm and had to be torn down. Possum Flats and Exclusively Victorian share the same building, and both are well worth visiting.

Libby and Justin have a unique business, creating custom-made authentically constructed clothing of the Victorian and Edwardian eras. The Stutz family (Libby was a Stutz) has long been occupied with tailoring. Justin's great-grandfather, Paul Stutz, owned a fine tailor shop back in 1883. When the St. Anthony Hotel opened in 1909 he moved his successful business there, where he created custom designed clothing for many of San Antonio's most prominent citizens. Justin is so proud of his Stutz family heritage he had his surname legally changed from Bishop to Stutz.

Soon after Justin and his mother settled into their new shop location, they noticed "things" happening. Pictures fell off the walls and broke. Small objects flew off console tables and shattered. Various articles disappeared and then, just as fast, they reappeared. Justin told me there were a lot of times when he needed to complete a costume, he would have the buttons, buckles, and other trim all laid out ready to go on the finished garment. Then he would turn around and the items would be gone! A thorough search all over the premises would turn up nothing, and often he had to dash downtown to buy a substitute for what he had laid out so carefully. Later on the missing item, or items, would turn up, just exactly where they had been laid out in the first place! This has become a frequent, irritating situation at the shop. Justin thinks his great-grandfather is there with him, and maybe it is he who does some of these things. San Antonio psychic Kathleen Bittner visited the shop soon after Justin opened, and she sensed the presence of a "little short German man, very serious, almost harsh, standing with his arms crossed across his chest." He seemed to be keeping an eye on things in the shop. Libby, who knew her grandfather, Paul Stutz, says the description fits the old tailor perfectly. Since he was a skilled craftsman, and now, in his own fashion, his great-grandson is also following that line of endeavor, maybe Paul Stutz' spirit has moved in to oversee the family business!

Libby and Justin agree there's also a mischievous child spirit in the place as well. "A spoiled little girl spirit," is how Justin describes it. Whenever children come into the shop, something immediately seems to happen as they leave. Pictures, securely attached to the walls, mysteriously fall and break. Things a child might like are moved about the room. It's like a childish temper tantrum is being acted out. Recently Libby and Justin did a costuming contract for a local private school. Numerous children had to come in for fittings. After all the children left, things started falling and breaking, and it was some time before order was restored to the shop. One might think this child spirit just doesn't like sharing her limelight with mere mortal children, and so she chooses this way to make her presence known!

Some months after the summer tea party I had another chat with Jo Ann Rivera and she told me that for some time now the staff at the inn has seen a white-gowned, dark-haired young woman spirit come out of the front door and walk down the front steps onto the grassy knoll upon which the Black Swan Inn sits. The wraith always strolls to the gazebo at the foot of the hill, and then she disappears from view. This has become such a frequent occurrence that the Riveras and their employees pay little attention to her comings and goings.

A reporter and camera crew from Sci-Fi Channel's show *Sightings* visited the inn in December of 1996. They brought Peter James, their psychic consultant, and he agreed the place is literally overrun with spirits. He found a woman on the stairs, another in the main reception room, two spirits in the south wing, and another in a hallway. He also saw a man looking into a window. James says the little girl spirit who pulls the pranks at Justin's shop is named Sarah, but she was always called "Suzie." The renowned psychic also told Jo Ann that Park Street, a former resident, is trying to contact her, and he wants her to find something he left hidden in the house.

The findings of the renowed psychic only solidifies my own opinion that Victoria's Black Swan Inn on Holbrook Road is one of the most fascinating and most spirit-filled places I have ever visited or written about!

# A Gathering Place for Ghosts: The Alamo Street Restaurant

The Alamo Street Restaurant was mentioned in *Spirits of San Antonio, and South Texas* which I coauthored with Reneta Byrne in 1992. Located at 1150 South Alamo Street (at the corner of Wicke Street), it is home to at least four other-worldly entities. The old church building was erected in 1913 and was sold by the Methodist Church in 1976 to Marcia (Marcie) Larsen and her late husband, Bill. They did a great deal of work to restore the old building, which had been deserted and vandalized for a number of years, and converted it into a dinner theatre in 1976. The building is on the *National Register of Historic Places.*

Today, the basement's old Sunday school rooms serve as the restaurant and kitchen, and the upper floor, the former sanctuary, has been converted to an intimate and cozy little theatre.

I've been taking groups of people there, for dinner and a visit with the jovial owners, for a number of years. Finally, I prevailed upon several psychics, including Sam Nesmith, Robert Thiege and his wife, Joie, and Liz Null, to come visit the place on an evening when no productions were scheduled. All gifted, these people came up with some rather astounding information! Marcie and Bill had always thought they had "a" ghost, but the psychics said there are at least four resident spirits, and they apparently are so happy there, they probably will just stick around!

While the best known spirit seems to be a woman in a white Victorian dress who has frequently been glimpsed in

The Alamo Street Restaurant and Theatre

the former choir loft, or even out in the audience during productions, there are three other interesting personalities in the
old former house of worship. Two are major and two are minor
entities in the ghostly scheme of things.

The woman in white told the psychics her name is
Margaret, and it is believed she might be the spirit of
Margaret Gething, who once lived on Guenther Street, just a
block away from the old church. She died in 1975. The woman
in the white Victorian dress started appearing in 1976 soon
after the Larsens bought the building. Now, there are several
reasons why this might be the spirit of Miss Gething. First,
the ghost seems to want to stay upstairs where the plays are
produced. She usually is seen only during the rehearsal or
actual performance of a play. Margaret Gething was an
actress on the old legitimate stage. She often played in New
York and also in Europe. She even starred once on Broadway,
with the late Clark Gable! She was attractive and she always
wore white dresses cut and styled in a Victorian manner.
There is a good likeness of Miss Gething in her former home,
which is open every April, during Fiesta Week, for special
tours. The photograph looks just like the woman who has

frequently been seen by a number of actors at the Alamo Street Theatre! And the clincher, the psychics say the spirit they actually saw told them her name was Margaret!

The second ghost, and the one who is the most fun, is Little Eddie. He seems to have arrived at the theatre when they brought an old Victorian wicker wheelchair in as a prop for one of the plays. It seems Eddie, a youngster of ten or so, was confined to a wheelchair in life. Not so now! He enjoys playing pranks and is making up for lost time as he enjoys being an active little boy again. The old wheelchair is still upstairs, in a prop room. The psychics said they could see him there, and he told them his name was Edward, but he preferred to be called Eddie. He is active and mischievous as one might expect a youngster of that age to be. He is especially fond of teasing Victoria Sotello, the cook.

When Victoria arrives in the mornings, the first thing she does is light the oven to bake the muffins and breads she will need to have ready for the noon meal. But Eddie often turns it off just as soon as Victoria's back is turned! Finally, in exasperation, she'll say, "All right, Eddie. Let's cut that out!" Usually he gets the message and the oven stays on. Sometimes when Victoria leans into the big refrigerator to retrieve something, she feels a push from behind as Eddie tries to shove her into the 'fridge. She has even heard him call to her... "Victoria... oh, Victoria!" A few times he has gotten so carried away with his pranks, he has pulled shelves out of the refrigerator or microwave.

Several times, when the noon crowd is at the restaurant, Marcie says a big serving spoon has risen up off the steam table, levitated across the room, and landed on the carpeted floor among the dining tables. Numerous customers as well as staff members have seen this happen. Recently when Marcie offered to help an elderly lady carry her plate from the buffet something snatched the plate out of her hands and hurled it to the floor, spilling the food and breaking the crockery. Marcie swears she did not drop the plate. It was snatched from her grasp!

The psychics, Sam, Robert, Joie, and Liz, also say there is an elderly lady there named Henrietta. She was once a seamstress. She doesn't do much of anything but sit up in the tower and watch the Alamo Street traffic go by. Sometimes she is joined by another ghost, an elderly man, whom the psychics say is a bland character who is just "there." They couldn't seem to pick up much on him. He is probably the figure that Deborah Latham, the director and playwright of many of the productions at the dinner theatre, once saw. Latham stayed late one night to work on some sound tapes for an upcoming production. She made sure all the doors to the building were locked since she planned to stay alone, and very late, in the place. After a couple of hours, she got up and walked through the dining room to the ladies' room. When she came out and started back across the dining room headed for her workroom, she was startled to see an elderly gray-haired man sitting at one of the tables. Her first thought was "oh, my... I'm a goner!" She didn't know what to think about the visitor, but decided to get up the courage to say, "Good evening, sir. Is there something I can do for you?" The old gentleman just looked at her and poof! disappeared! Deborah promptly decided she'd worked enough that night, locked up, and headed home!

A couple of years ago there was an Elvis Presley collection of memorabilia on loan in the restaurant for a few months. One of the items was a life-sized full figure photo of Elvis, which hung on the wall. One day when a group of the actors were in the dining room discussing an upcoming play, the figure suddenly came off the wall and traveled across the room, landing on a table. It did not fall. Deborah said, "Little Eddie! Put that back!" and would you believe, the cut-out figure arose from the table and backed across the space to the wall where it reattached itself to the hanger! Oh, my!

New Year's Eve 1995 was a gala time of celebration at the restaurant. The party was just about over, 1996 had been ushered in. The band was packing up to leave, just one couple remained at a table, and Marcie and some of her staff were about to close up and go home to leave the shambles of paper hats, confetti, noisemakers, and dirty dishes for the morning clean-up crew to tackle. All of a sudden Marcie saw a champagne flute arise from an empty table and hover in the air a moment. Then the stem snapped in two and the flute fell back on the table. Marcie is still talking about that strange occurrence!

The ghostly manifestations are so frequent that nearly every time I drop by the restaurant, Marcie or Deborah have a new adventure to relate. In fact, the ghosts are so well known there is a printed give-away sheet about them on the cashier's stand for diners to take and read. Marcie Larsen, her restaurant staff, and Deborah Latham and her thespians just take the quartet of ghostly residents for granted. In fact, when someone suggested an exorcism be held to get rid of them they were all horrified! They say the ghosts bring good luck to the place and it would really be boring if they were to leave.

# A Magical, Mystical Place:
# The Grey Moss Inn

As many times as I've passed through Helotes en route to the "Cowboy Capital of the World," Bandera, for some reason I've always just zoomed right past the cut-off marked "Scenic Loop Road." My goodness, what I've been missing!

Recently, my husband, Roy, and I had occasion to drive out to visit in the small community of Grey Forest, where we understood we'd find a good ghost story or two. We were not disappointed.

The two-lane Scenic Loop Road traverses a valley through which flow Helotes Creek and various other small spring-fed streams. The whole area is lush and green with plants and trees in contrast to the hill country's arid rocky slopes just to the north.

Wildflowers, mostly little yellow ones, were blooming in profusion on the day of our visit, and most of the yards in the small community of Grey Forest were overgrown with tall grass, the result of a recent downpour. There was a magical, mystical aura about the whole place. I would not have been at all surprised if a band of little leprechauns had materialized to escort us as we turned into the driveway leading to our destination, the historic Grey Moss Inn.

Because I had heard from various sources, including an interesting article by the *Express News* writer Paula Allen, a few ghost stories connected to the inn, I called the present owner, Nell Baeten, and made an appointment to drive out and see her. While my husband and I waited for Nell to appear, her bookkeeper-secretary Linda Young proved an able guide as she showed us around the lovely dining rooms and spacious patio with tables shaded by colorful umbrellas. The four dining rooms were all appointed with various antiques, lots of green plants, hand-painted china plates, and lovely portraits and still-life paintings. The place has the look of what it is; an old-fashioned country inn. I could well see why it is a favored spot for anniversary celebrations and romantic rendezvous. There are huge candles formed from many small tapers of various colors which have dripped and built up the colored waxes over the years. These illuminate the tables at night. The mantle in the main dining room boasts a pair of candles over three feet tall! They have doubtless been around a good many years.

It was not long before Nell Baeten, the attractive proprietor, appeared, and a fascinating visit ensued. First, she filled us in on the background of the inn which she and her husband, orthodontist Dr. Lou Baeten, have owned since 1987.

Grey Moss Inn Owner Nell Beaten

A woman named Mary Howell, a part-Cherokee Indian, who was brought up in Oklahoma, arrived in the valley with her husband, Arthur, back in 1929. They had come here from Waco, where previously they had made their home. Arthur was a fireman with the Katy Railroad. When they drove through Grey Forest, Mary fell in love with the area. She noticed a big rock building, which had once served as the headquarters for the old Requa Realty Company, was up for sale. It looked like just the place where she could make her longtime dream of owning her own "tearoom" come true! She had already had experience with the restaurant business, since she had managed a tearoom in Waco for the Business and Professional Women's Club.

After Mary and Arthur purchased the building a big kitchen was added and the open front porch was eventually closed in. Mary named the place the Grey Moss Inn because it is circled with giant live oak trees from which long fronds of silvery Spanish moss slowly wave back and forth in the breeze. The Grey Forest Playground, which was close to the inn, was a popular weekend attraction for wealthy San Antonio families. Many of them built cottages and cabins of limestone and wood close by the playground area which featured a beautiful natural limestone swimming pool fed by springs. The pool is still there. The walls of the little changing houses are there as well, on the high banks overlooking the pool. The old metal stand for the diving board is still firmly anchored in the limestone escarpment. What a beautiful place it must have been in its "heyday." Nell took us to see it and said the pool, which was empty, still fills up after a rain. Lush green ferns and watercress grow along the banks of the creek and the dam which was built to hold the water in the swimming area. In the 1930s and '40s artists and various celebrities flocked to the playground to enjoy the scenic landscape and the pleasant climate. Mary Howell often cooked for such well-known "neighbors" as John Floore, artist Robert Wood, and movie star Sonny Tufts. She sold homemade candy, too, made in the kitchen at the inn.

It didn't take long for Mary's tearoom to catch on. Nell told us that many families who were regular customers came every Sunday and always insisted on sitting at the same table. Mary was a fabulous cook, and the recipes used today are still from her files of tried and true favorites. The recipes and techniques have not changed in over sixty years. Four meats are served: steak, chicken, lamb, and seafood. Only choice, heavy-aged beef is used, lightly basted with what Nell calls "witch's brew," an original inn recipe. The water used at the inn is drawn from fresh spring wells, and all the desserts they serve are made "from scratch."

Across the driveway leading to the inn there is a little cottage which was where Mary and Arthur Howell lived. It is built of old limestone, and its quaintness calls to mind the dwarfs' house in *Snow White and the Seven Dwarfs*. Consisting of just one big room that was a combination bed-sitting-dining room, with a kitchen and a little bathroom, which was obviously a later add-on, it today makes a charming small party house. At one time, Nell told us, it was a part of Requa Realty's properties. The building converted to the inn was the company headquarters and the small building housed the Realtors who lived there and ran the business. The Howell's twin boys, Arthur Junior and Tynus, lived in another small stone cottage situated just behind their parents' small house.

When Mary opened her tearoom she decorated it with some favorite plates and antique bric-a-brac. Arthur was busy with his railroad job and left the operation of the restaurant to Mary. From what the current owner told us, the place hasn't really changed all that much in its over sixty-five years of operation, except for a few additions which have added to the capacity of the restaurant.

The Baetens purchased the inn from Mary and Jerry Martin who owned it for several years. The Martins had purchased it from Mary Howell's son, Arthur Junior, who managed the property for a number of years after the death of his mother.

Nell Baeten was a most gracious hostess to my husband and me during our visit. She not only took us on quite a tour of the inn and to the little house that had belonged to Mary and Arthur, but we visited her small office which is housed in the tiny building where the Howell boys lived. Nell is not only a restaurateur, she is also a licensed family counselor and a reflexologist as well, and she uses the office for her work in those professions.

Just visiting the inn wasn't enough. Nell insisted on taking us on a long drive over the green hills and valleys of Grey Forest. We saw many of the old original playground houses, many doubtless purchased from Requa Realty! We learned much of the colorful local history from Nell, who is a former city councilwoman of the small community of some 400 inhabitants. She knows every rock and rill in the area! While we came away thinking the inn is certainly a special place, I would have to say that Nell Baeten is the real treasure of Grey Forest!

We finally, of course, got around to talking about the spirits who are said to inhabit the area. Nell told us numerous incidents have occurred during their ownership to convince the Baetens that the inn is frequented by several spirits. Mary Howell's spirit seems to be the most dominant. It is evident she likes to know what is going on at the restaurant. Why not? The inn was the culmination of her dream to own her own place. She was very happy there, made many friends, and was undoubtedly proud of her accomplishments. Why wouldn't she want to return to see that things were kept up to her standards?

Nell says if Mary is at all displeased, she usually manages to make it known. Sometimes Nell gets a strong whiff of the rose cologne she has been told was Mary's favorite fragrance. It is most often evident in the main dining room, where Mary's presence is often sensed near "her" table, which is located close to the kitchen door.

Linda, Nell's bookkeeper, told us she had an experience where she heard a big coffee maker fly apart in the kitchen when no one was around. She has often witnessed the alarm system going off for no reason at all, too.

Nell said when Mary is not pleased with the operations at the inn she causes the tray jacks to fall over, ice buckets full of water and ice to fall, and dishes to break. Once, when a couple was there to celebrate a wedding anniversary, they were given what Nell says was a warning from Mary. The wine bucket next to the table fell over, although there was no plausible reason how it could have done this. In six months the happy celebrants had parted, headed for the divorce court!

One employee of Nell's has reported the adding machine sometimes starts to add figures all by itself. The same woman also reported that once, when she had her arms full of things, the gates suddenly opened up right in front of her. She thanked Mary for helping her! Linda seems to have a lot of trouble with the computer. When the new system was installed a few years ago it looked as if Mary was reluctant to accept the new technology. The technician, who was a computer science instructor, was baffled when the programs failed, hardware stalled, and discs died. The day we were there, Linda had a lot of trouble getting the computer to work for her, and she's apparently a skilled computer operator! Mary just doesn't seem to like any kind of change!

Nell has placed Pennsylvania Dutch hex signs in all the dining rooms, and in Mary's little house that is now the party house. Mary Howell's upside-down horseshoe (holding the good luck in, you know!) still hangs over the front entrance, which is now the entrance to the main dining room as one comes off the former porch.

Nell said whenever she plans to leave on a trip she always goes into the main dining room, which seems to be Mary's favorite bailiwick, and she talks to her, "like she was still a live, human being." She tells her that she is going away for a few days, but capable people will be running the inn in her absence and everything is going to be just fine. She started doing this after a number of manifestations occurred during her absences. This past New Year, however, Nell forgot to tell

Mary she was leaving. Right after Nell left, the alarm system went completely haywire, going off every fifteen or twenty minutes for no reason at all. This went on all night long. Dr. Baeten, who did not go out of town with his wife, had the alarm people out the next day to check out the system. They cleaned and checked the system and said that absolutely nothing was wrong, and there was no earthly (what about unearthly?) reason the alarm should have acted up like that.

One room at the inn, the Garden Room, seems to have another spirit attached to it. Unlike the benevolent spirit of the former owner, this spirit seems to be rather hostile. One strange event took place there about five years ago. That night Nell had personally checked to see all the candles had been extinguished before she locked up the inn. A last glance revealed not a glimmer of light from any of the candles. Satisfied, Nell went home. The next morning they were startled to find that there had been a fire in the Garden Room! It was just at one table, underneath a giant hex sign on the wall that stands for "Justice." The placemats, which had been placed over the tablecloth, had totally burned up. But the stitching, a series of round concentric circles, was still there on top of the charred tablecloth, which had been reduced to just a black tissue-thin bit of ash, except for the area just beneath the hex sign, where the cloth was intact and had not burned at all. There was also a basket of sugar packets there on the table. Neither the little basket nor its contents had burned at all. The napkins on the table for two had burned up completely except for the portions under the forks. The candle on the table had completely burned down and the wax had formed a big puddle on the floor beneath the table. The plate that had been beneath the candle had cracked in two. The fire alarm had never gone off and there was absolutely no smoke smell in the building!

Furthermore, the table top, which was formica, was unharmed, but the woven straw back of one of the chairs pulled up to the table had completely burned away.

A visiting psychic recently told the management that there was an unfriendly or malevolent spirit that hangs out in the Garden Room. They believe it must be a male entity, but no one has a clue as to who he might be.

Once, after work, a few of the cooks were just "hanging out" and visiting while drinking a cold beer after work. They were out by the little stone building Nell uses as an office. Nell had left a light on in the building. The men suddenly saw a large shadow go by the window. At first they thought Dr. Baeten might be inside. Then, whatever it was (they just call it the "spirit") materialized into a big black form that literally walked through the wall and went out to the bird bath. It didn't take long for those cooks to all take leave!

Nell claims an Indian woman spirit has been seen walking from the herb garden to the area where a big fallen tree now lies in the meadow. She said there is a vortex of waters under the tree, and the woman, according to Nell, may be headed towards that water source. There are underground springs all over the area, according to Baeten. Sometimes water literally oozes up in the patio area of the restaurant.

It wouldn't be at all strange to surmise there are Indian spirits around. There were Indian trails all over the area, and the heavily forested area was a favored hunting ground for Indian tribes for hundreds of years. The first white family to arrive was a man named Juan Menchaca, who obtained a land grant and brought his Aztec Indian wife to settle down there. Later on, the little road that ran through the valley became a stage route and often the stagecoaches were raided by either Indians or bandits. There are a lot of caves in the area which provided both cover for the stage robbers and a handy hiding place for their loot. Pioneer Texas Ranger Captain Jack Hays pursued many a bandit through the area, and for a time the famous lawman was the main source of law and order in the little valley.

Nell also cited an experience some of the help had fairly recently. They were in the employees' parking lot across from the inn, chatting and have a cold drink after work. Suddenly they heard the tremendous clashing of cymbals coming from the inn! They hurried over to see what was wrong. The sounds had set off the alarm system, and soon the police arrived. Nothing could be found out of order, however. Later on, that same night, the Baetens, who live in a house adjacent to the inn, had just retired for the night, when the same cymbal clash routed them from their bed. Again, nothing was out of place and there was no explanation for the racket. This same thing happened one more time that night. Nell still doesn't know what set off the sound of cymbals.

According to Nell, various nomadic Indian tribes battled one another over the years, fighting over land rights and such. There is a majestic old oak, located in the meadow adjacent to the Grey Moss Inn, which is said to have been used by the various Indian tribes as a place to meet and settle their differences. It is said to possess a "peaceful energy" and was used by the Indians because they believed it grew on spiritually healing ground. Here treaties and alliances were negotiated. It, like many of the trees around the inn, is festooned with draperies of grey Spanish moss.

Nell firmly believes there are several "old souls," as she prefers to call them, living both in the inn and in her home. She takes them for granted. Mary Howell's is the presence that Nell most often senses. Because she is such a loving spirit, Nell feels comfortable having her there. Strong as her presence is, Nell says as far as she knows, no one has ever actually seen her apparition.

If you would like to experience an evening spent dining on delicious food served in an atmosphere of country charm and romantic seclusion, you might look no further than the Grey Moss Inn, which is the oldest continually operating restaurant in South Texas. It's long been popular with generations of South Texas diners, so we suggest you call (210) 695-8301 for reservations. You're sure to enjoy a memorable, magical evening in this special place.

# Genteel Spirits: The Bright Shawl Tearoom

Several times in the course of dining at the Junior League's Bright Shawl Tearoom, of which I've long been a member, I have heard little whisperings that there just might be a ghost story or two connected to the popular gathering place. Finally, I spoke with Barbara Perkins, a former manager of the property.

The Bright Shawl was named after a popular novel of the 1920s by author Joseph Hergerheimer. The older section of the semiprivate club was once a limestone house built at the corner of Brooklyn and Augusta Streets by Dr. C.E.R. King for his wife and family of nine children. The residence was designed by popular architect Alfred Giles sometime in the 1890s. Giles is the same architect who designed many of the fine homes in the King William Historic District and the beautiful stone officers' quarters along Staff Post Road at Fort Sam Houston.

The Junior League established a tearoom as a source of income for altruistic endeavors of the organization back in 1925. It was moved to the present location in 1929. Since that date, there have been major additions to the property; one in 1975 and another in 1990, so today the place extends from Brooklyn over to McCullough, but still fronts on Augusta Street.

Barbara Perkins told me she recalled, during her tenure at the club, that once a portrait of Mrs. John Bennett, the first Junior League president, was moved from the living room to the boardroom, in the old section which was formerly the King

The Bright Shawl Tearoom

house. Every day when the staff arrived to open up, they would find the portrait off the wall and on the floor. Finally, they moved the painting back to its original place, where as far as I know, it still remains.

Ms. Perkins recalled one time when one of the accountants was working late in the evening. The young lady went to the restroom, and when she passed the boardroom, the large room to the right of the front door in the old house section, she noticed the light was on. She turned it off and then went on into the powder room. As she came out, she was astonished to see the light was again turned on in the boardroom. The lights continued to go on and off, with no visible explanation, several times during that evening. Finally, as the bookkeeper left for the evening, she turned the lights off in the boardroom again just before setting the alarm and going out the door. She got into her car, and as she started to drive out the Brooklyn Street exit, she looked back at the building through her rearview mirror, just in time to see the lights in the boardroom flash on again!

There are monthly art shows featuring local artists in the gallery section of the Bright Shawl. These are popular events and afford exposure for the artists and opportunities for the members to purchase some fine works. Once an artist who painted in a modern, contemporary manner, was featured. Perkins recalled that at least three of the works were of purple cows! Evidently the spirit that seems to watch over the Bright Shawl didn't like purple cows. Barbara said for three nights in a row she was called at home around 3 a.m. to come to the Bright Shawl because the burglar alarm was going off. Each time she came the three renderings of the purple cows were lying, facedown, on the floor! The wall hangers were still in place and the wires across the backs of the pictures were undamaged. Someone, or something, that didn't want the pictures to remain on the walls had purposely lifted them off their hangers and placed them on the floor, causing the motion detector to set off the alarm system. Finally, for the duration of that particular artist's showing, the staff removed the purple cow paintings every night prior to departing the building, and placed them on the floor. Barbara had no more disturbing middle-of-the-night calls after that.

Haunted or not, the Bright Shawl is still a popular gathering place, and the orange sticky-buns and the almond crunch cake are among the best taste treats in town!

# The Ghost Wears White at the Cadillac Bar

My friend Franklin Rowe was at the Cadillac Bar at 212 South Flores one morning in April 1996. He had loaned the restaurant some saddles, harnesses, chains, and other tack to add atmosphere to a Western party that was held the night before in the upstairs party room. Now, he'd come for his paraphernalia and was in the midst of half dragging, half carrying the heavy items down the sweeping staircase that leads to the upstairs party room. Jesse Medina, the general manager of the Cadillac, remarked, "Good grief, Frank, that sounds just like some of our night noises around here." When Frank asked Medina just what he meant, Jesse told him that they often heard strange noises late at night after the customers had all left, noises like chains rattling and heavy saddles and bridles and such being dragged down the stairs. He also said that childish screams and laughter of children at play were heard around the place at various times. They've also frequently heard the sounds of glass shattering as if a car might have driven right through one of the plate glass windows there on South Flores Street, but thorough checks always reveal nothing is broken or out of order. Frank asked Jesse, "Are you trying to tell me the place might be haunted?" When Jesse told him yes, that was indeed what he and his employees thought, Frank told him he knew just the person he should talk to about the situation . . . me!

Frank called me the next morning to tell me of his ghost discovery. He asked if I might be free for lunch that day and asked if I would meet him and his business associate, June

The Cadillac Bar

Bratcher, who was also interested in the whole thing. I had no
pressing plans, and I always enjoy learning of another "new"
ghost, so I accepted his invitation. I hurried on downtown to
meet Frank and June and one of their employees, Chris
McKinney, who also wanted to learn about the ghosts at the
Cadillac. We had a delicious Mexican lunch and a good visit
with Medina, who told us he'd been there for about twelve
years and had heard all sorts of weird night noises over that
time. He also said the alarm often turns on and off by itself,
usually very late, just before closing time. Sometimes large
utensils, such as serving bowls and chafing dishes, fly off the
shelves in the kitchen. He recalled one day when the water
faucet turned on and off all day long. It did this at least six or
seven times. They actually saw the faucet slowly turn as if
unseen hands had hold of it, and then the water began to flow!
Finally, not understanding what on earth was going on, they
called a plumber. He checked the faucet and said there was
absolutely nothing wrong with the spigot, and there was no
possible way it could turn on by itself. The only thing . . . it did!

When Jesse first came to work at the Cadillac and he'd hear a strange noise late at night when he was there alone in the building, he would just lock up fast and go home! It happens so frequently now, he is used to all the strange noises and takes them all pretty much for granted. He says he expects something to happen nearly every night after midnight.

I felt I needed to know some of the background of the building, which is actually two old buildings which have been joined. One is a large stone-walled room, where the main restaurant operation is located, and this is then joined to an older two-story structure, which has two large party rooms, one on each floor. Jesse gave me a menu, which has some of the history of the place on it. I would like to share some of this information with you:

The nation of Texas was young. Just two years earlier in 1845, the Alamo had fallen and rebel Texicans had won independence from Mexico. Herman Dietrich Stumberg, a young German immigrant, left Missouri for San Antonio. Time passed. Texas became the 28th state and Herman and his son George became successful in the general mercantile business. In 1870, they built a fine new limestone building on land Herman had purchased in 1863. Their business flourished. Farmers and ranchers from across South Texas drove wagons to the campyard behind the store, checked their guns with the storekeeper, bought supplies and headed for the saloons to the north or maybe the red light district to the west.

The nineteen twenties brought wild times along with Prohibition. Mayo Besan, the owner of the Cadillac Bar in New Orleans' Roosevelt Hotel, was not satisfied to sit out this country's moral evolution, so he packed up and headed for Nuevo Laredo, Mexico. Although he found the liquor laws more permissive, he also found that Nuevo Laredo already had a Cadillac Bar. Besan opened as the White Horse Bar and a year later, when the competition closed, changed back to his beloved Cadillac Bar.

The Depression changed the face of the country and part of that change was the demise of the Stumberg General Store in 1932. After its closing the building was used for many purposes. John Wayne had a saddle made for Queen Elizabeth by one of the tenants. The Cadillac flourished.

Time passed. Mayo Besan was succeeded by his son-in-law, Porter Garner, who retired in 1980 and left the Cadillac to its employees. Shortly thereafter, they sold to "Chito" Longoria and Ramon Salido.

The 1980s also brought change to the old Stumberg General Store. The buildings were restored and renovated in a redevelopment known as Stumberg Square. The project won the 1985 San Antonio Conservation Society Award for Excellence. The Cadillac Bar became the project's flagship tenant in 1984 when the operation returned to the United States for the first time since Prohibition.

In December 1991, the latest chapter in these two histories was written when the partnership in Nuevo Laredo split. This event saw George Stumberg, the great great grandson of the German immigrant, become the operating stockholder of the Cadillac Bar in San Antonio.

After I had read over this information, I was even more fascinated by this unusual old building. When I questioned the present owner, George Stumberg III, about the saddle shop, he said a family named Carvajal had run this shop and it had been popular and successful. Sounds of chains and the sort of equipment associated with a saddle shop come from the area of the building where the saddle shop was located.

In addition to strange noises, numerous employees have actually seen the ghostly figures of some former occupants of the building. No one seems to have a clue as to who they might be. One of the kitchen helpers told my husband that he had seen an older man on the back steps leading from the kitchen to an upper storage room. The man had a white handlebar mustache and was tall and thin. George Stumberg said he has a photo of his ancestor Herman, and he was clean shaven. George, Herman's son, once had a full beard. Neither man wore a handlebar mustache as far as George could determine.

However, Stumberg volunteered that there had been an "Uncle Herman." He wasn't sure what he had looked like, but he might have had a handlebar mustache. He was sort of a family "black sheep." While he did hang around the mercantile business quite a bit, he was a habitue of the old Silver Dollar Saloon, which was located at the corner of Main and Commerce, where now stands the old Frost Bank Building, now used for city council meetings. In fact, he was such a frequent visitor to the saloon, the management gave him one of the old gaming tables when they closed up! Uncle Herman just may be the man that the cook saw on the back stairs that night.

After my initial visit to the Cadillac with Frank, June, and Chris, I discussed the place at length with my psychic friend Sam Nesmith. Sam concentrated hard on the building, and he called me to say he believed that there were two spirits hanging around the building. One, a man, was tall, thin, and had a handlebar mustache, and he believed his name was either Herman or Henry! He told me this before my husband had visited with the cook or before I talked to Mr. Stumberg!

Nesmith also said there was a young woman, a rather sad spirit, hanging around. He couldn't determine just why she was there. The place stood on the outer fringes of the notorious red light district, and she might have been one of those nighttime ladies. I mentioned this to Mr. Stumberg, and he said he was positive the building had never been a brothel or anything like that. The upstairs portion was used for a long time as a storage place for goods and supplies needed for restocking the mercantile business. It once was served by a hand-operated elevator. However, the amazing thing here, Sam told me the girl might have been named Beatrice. This was the name he kept picking up on, and he said she was not particularly attractive. She knew she was homely, and this made her sad. She was very thin, had stringy dishwater blonde hair and protruding teeth. For some reason she has more or less taken up residence in the upper floor party room of the building.

Several of the employees of the Cadillac Bar have actually seen a woman matching the exact description Sam gave me. She has always been seen upstairs as the viewers glance up towards the glass windows of the room. Two waitresses at the establishment, twin sisters Deborah Fresco and Linda Frazier, truly believe there is someone there. Linda, a vivacious blonde, says she saw a girl spirit late one night as she was cleaning up a bar she had been working at on the lower level next to the stairs. She chanced to glance upstairs and saw a slender young woman in a white dress standing behind the glassed-in portion of the party room, just looking down at her. She said the woman bore an angry expression on her face. It wasn't a "nice ghost," she said. She went on to say the wraith had stringy, brownish-blonde hair, a thin face, and could not be considered at all pretty. This was much as Sam had described the live-in ghost. We later spoke to Brenda Cordoway, a comely brunette bartender. She has also felt a presence and says whenever she walks up the stairs at night she feels somebody is there, staring at her.

Lorenzo Banda Junior, a security guard who works on Friday nights, said he often feels a presence up on the second floor, and it gives him chills because he feels like he isn't alone, although he knows he is.

June and Frank and my husband and I went to the bar one Friday night, right at closing time. However, we didn't sense anything out of the ordinary on that one evening. I think there was too much noise from the serving staff as they cleaned up the place, and when they heard that "ghost hunters" were there, they all wanted to come up to the party room where we were to tell us of their own particular experiences. It just wasn't the right time for one of the spirits to appear.

However, just a few days after our fruitless midnight visit to the Cadillac, we got a call from Linda Frazier. She and several others had again seen the female wraith. They were all out on the patio in the rear of the building which is lighted by some wonderful old lamps. In fact, they were the first electric street lights in Texas. As they went about their work of cleaning up after a patio party, they chanced to glance up to the second floor windows. There she was! The ghostly young woman was just standing there, looking down at them. She walked away, then turned and walked back to the window. Then she sort of knelt down and peeped out of the window from a lower position. The group of Cadillac employees were all just fascinated by what they saw!

When I reported this latest sighting to Sam Nesmith he said he thinks this type of haunting is a replay of something that took place in the past and is a registered emotion, rather like a photograph. It can continually reoccur. He thinks the young woman either lived or worked in the vicinity and for some reason has become so attached to the old building she doesn't want to leave it.

All of the people we spoke to at the Cadillac Bar are convinced the place is haunted. No one knows who the spirits might have been in life or why they've decided they want to hang out at the Cadillac. But they are there, and they don't appear to be in any hurry to move on.

There's one thing I can tell you. The Mexican food is great, and the icy margaritas are memorable! I can't guarantee you'll see or hear a ghost, but come on down to the Cadillac anyway. I'll guarantee you'll have a good time!

# Ghost Adds Spice to Menu at Cafe Camille

Tracy Becker says she's very sensitive to presences. And she definitely has sensed unexplainable feelings in the front portion of her husband's Cafe Camille, located at 517 East Woodlawn.

Tracy met Scott Becker about six years ago. She had long been fascinated with the old Monte Vista section of San Antonio and hoped to eventually make her home in that area. While out driving around one day she chanced to stop at a newly opened restaurant which occupies one of the old houses on East Woodlawn Street. She became acquainted with the owner, and since she had also had considerable experience in the restaurant business, the two young people soon found they had much in common. One thing led to another, and they soon were married!

The restaurant, which Tracy says is really more of a bistro, has a loyal clientele of neighborhood patrons. Both lunches and dinners are served, featuring a varied Continental cuisine in the establishment which Scott named for his mother and grandmother, both of whom were named Camille.

Tracy told me the place was once the property of an elderly gentleman who is now over a hundred years old. After Tracy and I discussed what has happened from time to time in the cafe, we decided the spirit might possibly be the deceased wife of the former owner. Much of the activity took place while a great deal of renovation and remodeling was taking place, as the house was being converted into a restaurant. This did not surprise me as spirits are generally upset by remodeling in places where they once lived. There are still the occasional incidents of doors opening and closing unassisted by human hands, and Tracy often gets the overwhelming feeling that there is someone, a sort of presence, in the room with her. This is most noticeable in the front section of the establishment.

Tracy told me that once a mirror, which was firmly attached to the wall, fell and was shattered when it hit the floor. A hanging cupboard once fell on a glass topped counter, breaking the glass. Tracy said that had the cupboard fallen "normally" in the direction from where it was hanging, it would not have landed on the counter at all. It had to have been picked up and moved over before being dropped on the counter!

Tracy has begun to work regularly at the cafe with Scott. She has promised to keep me informed of any other ghostly activity there.

For a pleasurable dining experience in a friendly atmosphere, with really good food, the Cafe Camille is a place you are sure to enjoy. Call 735-2307 for reservations and information about hours of operation.

Cafe Camille

# CHAPTER 3

# PHANTOMS IN PUBLIC PLACES

*It is all very well for you who have never seen a
ghost to talk as you do, but had you seen what I
have witnessed, you would have a different
opinion.*

**William Makepeace Thackeray**

# Phantoms in Public Places

In researching the resident spirits of San Antonio, it's been interesting to discover that they don't cling to any one sort of locale. All these confused, mixed-up, lost souls wander around the places they once knew and had some attachment to in life, as they try to settle a debt, disclose some hidden secret (oftentimes the hiding places of money or valuables), or finalize some unfinished business. Many of our well-known San Antonio landmarks are haunted by former residents who once occupied some location as either a place of business residence or oft-visited site.

In *Spirits of San Antonio and South Texas* many of our better known historic landmarks were covered. Because there has been little change in the "ghostly status quo" of these places, I will only briefly mention them here.

The Alamo, the Spanish Governor's Palace, the Yturria Edmunds House, and the Jose Antonio Navarro House are all haunted, or at least have been. So is the Institute of Texan Cultures, the Wolfson Manor on Broadway, and the John Wood Courthouse. Many old buildings in La Villita were also previously mentioned, but at least one new story has turned up, which I mention in the chapter on haunted houses.

In addition, you'll find interesting accounts of such local landmarks as the Alamodome, the Hertzberg Circus Museum, and the Witte Museum. The list goes on and on. You'll also read about businesses, such as the Reed Candle Factory and the former Menger Soap Factory, and their hauntings.

I dare say, if I were to contact every business establishment and public building in San Antonio, and were the responsible parties at each place to really unload their noteworthy experiences, I'd have enough material to fill a good-sized library! I truly believe there are that many hauntings in this historic city!

# The Alamodome:
# Is It Haunted?

They say it's haunted. But how can that be? The 65,000 seat stadium on Highway 37-281 in downtown San Antonio known as the Alamodome was only built a few years ago, in 1993. It's a modern structure, admired by some and intensely disliked by others. Everyone agrees it's HUGE and it was costly to build, and the hoped-for purpose of attracting a National Football League team never materialized. It was a project instigated by former mayor Henry Cisneros, and like it or not, most of San Antonio's citizens have to agree that it didn't become what Henry said it would be: a big convention center and the playing field for an NFL team. Today it's the home base for the San Antonio Spurs, our NBA basketball team, who are not too happy with the layout, a sometimes locale for ice capades and hockey games, big concerts, and mammoth convention gatherings. It is definitely NOT in use all the time and is therefore not a steady producer of income for the city coffers.

And somewhere in all this there comes the idea that the huge stadium just may be the choice of residence for some interesting spirits from other-worldly realms. Although I questioned numerous Alamodome staff members, security guards, and custodians, not one would own up to having seen, heard, or felt any presences in the cavernous spaces of the Dome. It's been plagued with enough problems already: a leaky roof, several deaths among workers, and the death of a stock car race driver at one of its first big events. There has been a lot of criticism from people who either don't like its

The Alamodome

appearance or didn't want it built in the first place. It certainly doesn't need the added complications of a ghost to add to its other challenges!

Be that as it may, I would be remiss if I didn't at least touch on what has been rumored, and although I have never been told, firsthand, about any manifestations, I have read numerous articles by other writers and would like to at least mention a couple of them, just for the record.

Writer Charles Booker wrote a feature article for *Current Magazine* (February 17, 1994) in which he told about taking a couple of psychics to visit the Alamodome. Both ladies, Marie Simpson and Mary Nichols, zoomed in on the spirit of an Indian woman who hangs out in the upper level in the northeast corner of the building. They perceived her to be a sad little spirit. She seemed to be in a dwelling, just a hut really, and she appeared to either be doing laundry or stirring something over an open fire. Both psychics said they believed she had died tragically and painfully, either being murdered or so badly beaten she succumbed from her injuries. The best time frame these ladies could place the Indian woman in was the mid to late 1700s. Strangely enough, several Dome employees had mentioned they'd heard the mournful sounds of a woman sobbing, coming from that portion of the building. However, I must say, it's a big building, and perhaps a sudden draft could cause some pretty unusual noises. It could be a pretty frightening place to be in, alone, at night, and I expect it would be easy for one's imagination to work overtime!

Kevin Duvall, who was a member of the Dome staff at the time Booker wrote his article, was quoted by Booker as saying "There have been some strange things happening in the northeast portion of the Dome. I know the alarms go off with no apparent reason, and the doors which are supposed to be closed, suddenly open. I have heard some of our people say they've heard voices when no one is there."

Another article appeared in 1994. This one, dated November 20, was written by *Express News* staff writer Becky Whetstone Schmidt. She also mentioned the possibility of the Dome being haunted. Schmidt quoted several employees, including Janet Vasquez, then the public information director for the facility; Rachel Castillo, an usher; Gisela Radloff, a tour guide; and Yolanda O'Bar, the event service manager. At the time of her visit, Schmidt asked psychic Irma Latham to accompany her.

Again, as with the psychics that were quoted in the *Current Magazine* article, Latham agreed the fifth floor level of the northeast corner of the building seems to be the most haunted area. Schmidt was told that employees have heard strange noises there, and one maintenance worker claimed he had seen ladders go, unassisted, from one side of the Dome to the other.

Castillo claimed she and several fellow employees had seen curtains on the top floor flapping in the wind, only there was no wind, and the air conditioning was not even turned on! She stated "There was no breeze and the curtain was moving and waving, and there was just no possible way for it to move by itself."

Strange things seem to happen on the elevator located on the east side of the Dome. The numbers register where the passengers are going, yet the elevator doesn't stop there. Numbers also display nonexistent floors, and the elevator stubbornly refuses to take people down to the first floor without making another trip up to the top level first!

Unlike Simpson and Nichols, psychic Latham made no mention of an Indian woman. She said she felt the presence of several prankster ghosts who are harmless, more or less just playful. She says the fifth floor ghosts like to make people uncomfortable, making chill bumps rise on their arms. The northeast corner of that floor is one of their favorite playgrounds. They don't want to leave and don't particularly like the intrusion of mortals on their turf.

My friend Johnny Keith, a longtime driver with Kerrville Bus Company, recently called to tell me he had an unusual experience connected with the Alamodome on Friday the thirteenth of December 1996. Johnny drew the charter to drive the Dallas Mavericks basketball team to the Dome for an evening practice session prior to the game they were to play with the Spurs on the following day.

The motorcoach was in excellent operating condition. Johnny off-loaded the team members and then went and parked his vehicle in the southeast parking lot. After shutting off the engine, he strolled into the Dome to watch the practice session and visit awhile with one of the security guards. As he came into the playing area, he had a strange experience. He said he was "buzzed" by two little brown bats and thought at the time, how appropriate that was for a Friday the thirteenth! Johnny had never seen a bat in the Alamodome before that night.

Later on, he strolled back outside and started the coach up and drove it down onto the ramp which leads right into the Alamodome. This was so he could load the players and their equipment when the practice session was over. He said the bus started up just fine in the parking lot. He turned off his engine, got out, and just stood around waiting for the players to start arriving. About 8 p.m. they started walking to the motorcoach, and they loaded up their equipment. Johnny got into the bus, and when he tried to start it he had no power at all. The engine simply would not start. Most of the players got off the coach, deciding to walk back to their hotel, which was only about four or five blocks from the Dome. Johnny called the Kerrville Bus Company, and they sent their head mechanic over in another bus. He checked Johnny's coach and couldn't find a thing wrong with it, other than it just didn't want to start! There was nothing wrong with the battery. Finally the mechanic put the jumper cable to the engine directly and they got the vehicle to start. Then Johnny drove the bus the short distance back to the shop, where several mechanics on duty checked it out. It was in great shape and made an incident-free trip to Dallas the next morning! The coach only had a problem while it was actually within the confines of the Alamodome!

Keith said he also chatted at some length that same evening with a security guard at the Dome, and he told him he had heard, from various maintenace personnel, of strange occurrences centering around one of the elevators. The guard told Johnny the elevator had the habit of suddenly stopping, for no reason, and the intercom button in the elevator, which has to be manually pushed to activate, has activated several times all by itself. When checked, no one is in or around the elevator. The guard, whom I later contacted, told me this was true but asked me not to use his name. He recommended that I speak to the public relations department. I did not tell him that I had already met with an impasse there! In my opinion, I believe that the Alamodome management has enough problems without the added publicity of ghosts lurking among the rafters! This is too much for them to cope with just now, and so they like to side-step the probability that the place is harboring some other-worldly tenants!

Frankly, after giving it careful thought, if there really are ghosts at the Alamodome, I think they are pretty smart entities. After all, they have choice seats for all the Spur's home games!

# Is the Hertzberg Haunted?

The San Antonio public library's Hertzberg Circus collection is housed in the old white stone former public library building at 210 West Market Street, just one block west of Alamo Street.

Back in 1993 I was invited by Barbara Celitans, curator at the museum, to come and tell ghost stories to a gathering of youngsters. It was around Halloween, when my storytelling seems to become most popular. After my program, several of the museum staff made it a point to chastise me for not including the Hertzberg in my book about San Antonio's ghosts. I promised them if I were to ever do another book I would certainly include their story.

When Dr. Robert O'Connor, the museum administrator, sent me a copy of an article by Bruce Milligan that ran in the October 30, 1983 edition of the *San Antonio Express News*, I realized the museum did indeed have a fascinating story that deserved to be researched further. The article was titled "Murder Victim Haunts Hertzberg." It's a most intriguing story that takes us way back to the early days of Texas settlement.

John McMullen and James McGloin were two early Texas impresarios. In 1829 they founded the largely Irish McMullen-McGloin colony. It soon became known as the San Patricio Colony, and there is still a small town near Corpus Christi known by that name. McGloin stayed in San Patricio, but his friend McMullen, seeking a more affluent lifestyle, moved to San Antonio in 1837, just after the tragic Battle of the Alamo. He became a successful merchant and influential citizen. The wealthy, highly respected McMullen built a fine house which

was located at the spot where the Hertzberg Museum is today.
There he presided at many fine entertainments and lived the
life of a prosperous businessman until 1853. It all came to an
abrupt end on a cold January night when a thief slipped into
the house, bound and gagged McMullen, rifled his posses-
sions, and slit his throat, leaving him to bleed to death. The
murderer was never brought to justice, and it still remains an
unsolved crime.

Hertzberg Museum

The strangest twist to this story of heinous crime concerns
James McGloin, McMullen's former partner and close friend.
He had just arrived home from a trip to Matamoros, down in
Mexico. He had experienced a severe case of depression, and
a sense of foreboding had haunted him as he rode the last few
hours towards his home. When McGloin got home, he unsad-
dled the beautiful Arabian horse he had been riding and went
into his home on Constitution Square.

After supper McGloin settled into his favorite chair in
front of the fire while his wife, Mary, went out behind the

house to bring in her washing. Just then, McGloin heard the sound of wings beating frantically on the front door, and he was filled with a sense of terrible dread. Turning towards the door, which was barred against intruders, he saw a white mist float in and suddenly take on the shape of a human being. From out of the mist stepped the image of John McMullen. He was wearing a white nightshirt and blood was spurting, geyser-like, from a wound in his neck. Although his lips were moving, McGloin could not make out what his friend was saying, and the apparition soon vanished into the mist from which it had come, leaving McGloin extremely shaken.

Terrified, yet feeling compelled to find out why McMullen had appeared to him, he hastened to tell his wife he had to ride to San Antonio to take care of some pressing business. He went to the larder and packed up a few morsels of food, took his hat and coat, and resaddled his horse.

It is a long ride to San Antonio from San Patricio. The horse, already exhausted from its trip from Matamoros, still did the best it could to keep up the pace that McGloin demanded of him. Just outside San Antonio, near San Jose Mission, McGloin was encountered by a Texas Ranger who asked him if he had seen a green-eyed Mexican boy on the road. He told the ranger he had not, and he and the horse, which was beginning to stagger, continued on their journey.

McGloin got to San Antonio just in time to hear the Angelus tolling from the bells at San Fernando Cathedral. He saw candles glowing from the lower windows of McMullen's house, and there were a number of men gathered on the front porch. As he dismounted, McGloin's faithful horse shivered, gave a loud snort, and dropped dead on the ground. He had served his master well.

One of the men assumed this was McGloin and asked him how he had heard. He answered that he had heard nothing, but he just felt somehow that he needed to hasten to San Antonio. The men led him into the front parlor where McMullen had just been laid out in a coffin. His throat had been cut!

Later, McGloin was told that McMullen had adopted a Mexican boy, and they all believed it was he who had murdered his wealthy benefactor. It was never proved, however.

The story of McMullen's death was told in Rachel Bluntzer Hebert's book *The Forgotten Colony*, according to the *San Antonio Express News* article. Hebert had the story from her mother, who had been told about the murder by Patrick McGloin, a nephew of James McGloin.

According to Dr. John Flannery's book *The Irish Texans*, a current story states that John McMullen's ghost walks the hallways of the library building that was built on the site of his old home, the home in which he was murdered, and his specter will continue to appear until such time as someone is able to bring to light who the perpetrator of the crime was. Since it was all so long ago and the players in the tragedy are all dead, it might seem the spirit will always remain there, within the confines of the library building.

As with most of my stories, I wasn't just content to read about the murder and subsequent haunting in the works that had already been written. I decided to question some of the current staff at the library building. I came to the conclusion that there is little doubt that some spirits of the past do indeed cling to the museum. Whether it's the spirit of John McMullen coming back to the site of his old home, or whether it's the spirit, or spirits, of some long-dead circus great whose personal effects are displayed in the museum, it's hard to say. Maybe even Mr. Harry Hertzberg, who so lovingly compiled the collection, comes back to see all is going well. Whoever or whatever it is, strange things continue to take place from time to time in the library building that today houses the circus collection.

A visit with Mario Lara, who has served as custodian there for a little over four years, brought forth some interesting information. Often Lara has felt cold spots in the building, especially in the basement near the bookstore where he often feels a sudden unexplainable chill as he comes to the stairs leading up to the ground level. He says the hair on the back of his arms stands up, he has goosebumps, and his skin crawls. He doesn't dare look behind him as he goes up the stairs! Often Lara has seen a dark, shadowy form moving about, out of the corner of his eye, as he goes about his work. He said recently an electrician doing some rewiring in the building asked him, point-blank, "Is this place haunted?" The workman went on to say he had seen a strange dark, shadowy form pass by his peripheral vision and was quite sure it was a ghost.

Often, Mario told me, up in the rare books collection on the upper floors, the noise of keys jangling has been heard. He said Jill Blake and Thomas Smith, both former staff members, had heard this sound on numerous occasions but could never locate the source. I decided to talk to Smith, who was on the museum staff from October 1993 to April of 1996. He said he often heard keys rattling, and he also heard footsteps in the third floor hallway. He would look out and see no one. He finally heard the sounds so often he just ignored them. He said he was never frightened, as much as he was just curious as to what caused the sounds. He said he did most of his work on the third floor, in the Hemisfair Room, which faces the Hemisfair grounds and Convention Center, although the Hilton Hotel now blocks the view. Smith also said he often had the distinct feeling he was not alone, even when he knew he was.

One strange incident involved both men, Smith and Lara. One evening both of them were working rather late up on the fifth floor, unloading some papier-mache animals from the elevator, taking them into a storage area. The elevator only ran to the fifth floor, but Smith distinctly heard loud banging noises on the elevator door coming from the sixth floor. He looked up the elevator shaft (there was no ceiling on the open lift) and saw the door on the level above him shaking under the onslaught of someone banging hard on the door. He called to Mario to see if he'd gone up the stairs to the sixth floor, and if so, was he banging on the door? But no, Mario was there on the fifth floor, and he also had heard the commotion. Neither man could satisfactorily explain the noises, since they knew no one else was in the building that evening.

Lara told me that about the second year he was there, he was up on the third floor where a kitchen is located. Two female employees were there with him. He clearly heard someone softly say, "Mario." He turned to see who had spoken to him and was surprised to see the ladies had left the kitchen and he was just there alone.

One time when he was up on the fifth floor at work, Lara heard a lot of books drop. He ran down the stairs to the fourth floor and found a number of books on the floor but could find no reason for them to have fallen and could find no one who had heard or seen them fall off the shelves. Smith said on the fifth floor there were some bookshelves right in front of the elevator. He got to noticing that new books kept appearing on the shelves, and the books were rearranged nearly every day. Since the general public didn't go up there, he couldn't explain it. In fact, he said, there were just a lot of things that happened there he couldn't explain!

Lara also told me that he once saw a bright shimmering light that sort of moved around and floated between the book stacks, down the long aisle between them, going towards the wall. This was on the second floor. It happened during daylight hours, but because the room was rather dark between the tall book stacks, the light really stood out.

To this day, Lara says he often feels a presence as he works and knows he is not alone. Curator John Slate, who has not been on the staff long and to whom I spoke briefly, said he sometimes feels he is not alone when he knows he really is, up in his third floor office.

And so it goes. Is so much energy around, due to the collection of circus memorabilia stored within those white stone walls, that it must manifest itself to those who labor there? Or is the restless spirit of old John McMullen still seeking his killer after over a hundred and fifty years? Your guess is as good as mine.

# The Mission Walls Still Shelter Spirits

Mission San Jose de San Miguel de Aguayo was founded in 1720. Situated on Roosevelt Street at Mission Road, it is the best restoration of all the missions. A visit within its walls is like taking a trip back in a time capsule to the early Spanish colonial days.

The National Parks Department has recently added a fine new visitor's center to the San Jose Mission complex. A beautiful twenty-five-minute film outlining the history of San Antonio's five missions is shown every half hour. The photography is exquisite. While mystical sounding music plays in the background, the narrator takes the viewer through a series of vignettes of mission life peopled by the spirits of long-dead mission Indians whose names and faces have been lost in time. The film leaves a definite impression on those who see it. I believe, as the screenwriters obviously did, that the missions are still peopled by the spirits of those who lived, toiled, and finally died within the confines of those thick, gray stone walls.

Marjorie Mungia, a Parks Department volunteer, enjoys meeting people who come to the new visitor's center at San Jose Mission. She was born just a few blocks from the old mission and has been a lifelong member of the parish of San Jose, which was known as the "Queen of the Missions."

The little houses where Marjorie's parents, Claude and Alvina Guerrero, and her aunt, Della Flores, lived, were torn down to make way for the construction of the visitor's center.

Mission San Jose de San Miguel de Aguayo—The Church

Mission San Jose de San Miguel de Aguayo—The Convento

Marjorie recalls hearing lots of ghost stories about the mission when she was a little girl growing up just outside its walls. There were numerous stories about a Franciscan monk clad in a dark robe. (The earlier priests wore dark indigo blue habits instead of the brown ones worn by Franciscans today.) This figure was seen walking in the convent courtyard on moonlit nights. Sometimes he appeared to be headless! The courtyard must look eerie at night anyway, with the moonlight shining through the Gothic arches that once were the windows and doorways in the ruined portion of the mission. Add a headless friar, and it could really get your attention!

Once, in the mid-1940s, when Marjorie was a small child, she recalls the family talking about seeing a tall figure of a priest clad in a dark robe as he came out of the gate where tourists enter today. The gate was tightly closed off then, and the monk actually came right through the wooden gates. Marjorie remembers that her parents said he was "very, very tall," and they were extremely frightened!

Once, Marjorie believes it was around 1969, her mother and father saw a group of young boys come running down a path that used to run along the side of the mission and on across to Mission County Park. It was obvious the kids were terrified. They'd seen a figure of a dark-robed, headless priest walking near the stone rectory which is just outside the mission gate.

After Marjorie's mother died, her father remarried. Marjorie said her stepmother was active in the parish. Once she recalled entering the church through the sacristy when she saw a priest standing with his back to her, near the little altar. She turned around for just a moment and looked out the back door. When she turned back around the priest was gone. He couldn't possibly have gotten out of the chapel that quickly. She walked on through the church and was astonished to see the parish priest, whom she thought she had seen in the sacristy, out in front of the church, chatting with some of his parishioners. When he was questioned, it turned out he'd been there for some time. She is convinced the priestly figure she saw in the sacristy was a ghost!

Not just the clergy haunt San Jose. One of the ushers at San Jose church told Claude Guerrero, Marjorie's father, that recently an old lady had come up to him and asked him the hours of the masses. He told her to wait there just a moment and he would go and get a church bulletin for her that listed the times of the various services. When he returned, the old lady, who had told him her name was Mrs. Huizar, had disappeared. He mentioned this to Mr. Guerrero, and he told the usher that he had known that lady, and she couldn't have been there asking for information. He said she had been dead for over fifty years!

According to Marjorie, there were also stories of a big black dog seen in the vicinity of the mission. It was a phantom animal that would suddenly appear, grow to an enormous size, and then disappear. Marjorie recalled that two boys were riding by the mission one afternoon late. They saw a little black dog behind a tree they passed, and it just looked at them. They kept on riding their bikes. Suddenly they heard a real loud bark and looked back. A HUGE black dog as tall as their bicycles was chasing them and rapidly gaining on them. And the animal continued to get bigger. The boys were so terrified they fell off their bikes. Luckily for them, the huge animal then disappeared. However, they said a lingering smell of sulfur permeated the air!

Marjorie's grandmother also saw a similar huge dog as she walked home from a midnight mass one time. It crossed Mission Road and she said, "It was so big it seemed to stretch clear across the road." Now the National Park Service is taking such good care of the things at the mission property, it seems like sightings of headless priests and phantom big black dogs have become a thing of the past.

Just a few miles down Mission Road from San Jose is the quiet little compound of Mission San Francisco de la Espada, built around 1731. I have been told that something strange exists, or at least used to exist, around the old church. A friend

Mission San Francisco de la Espada

of mine told me that a priest, now deceased, who used to live on the property, told her he had once seen a large, dark, hairy animal, that looked like a wolf or a big, black dog, with a broken chain dangling from around its neck. He had seen it from the window of his quarters at the mission late one evening. It was clearly visible in the moonlight as it darted across the courtyard and disappeared in the vicinity of the well outside the chapel. A search outside for the animal revealed nothing. Then, when two young priests were visiting the elderly padre in his study on another evening, he reported that all three of the men had seen the same thing. Another search outside revealed no trace of any animal in the vicinity.

A recent conversation with a woman who lived in the neighborhood of the old mission during her childhood verified that she also had heard of such a creature, and her mother had always warned her to stay away from the mission grounds at night.

A young woman acquaintance of ours told us that her mother, while visiting the chapel as a young girl, had clearly seen the figure of an Indian man standing near the altar. The apparition, clad in ceremonial regalia, suddenly appeared, and then just as suddenly it disappeared.

Mission San Juan de Capistrano, which was founded in March of 1731, located in far south San Antonio near the river, has a lovely little jewel-box of a chapel, which was actually built as a temporary place of worship. A larger church was begun in 1760, but for some reason it was never completed. The little chapel is small, probably seating no more than a hundred people. The retablo is of polychromed wood, beautifully carved. Featuring several carved images, it is centered with a fine likeness of San Juan de Capistrano, the namesake of the mission. It is still a parish church, and many of its parishioners are descendants of the original mission Indians.

Mission San Juan de Capistrano

It was to this lovely little house of worship a young tourist couple wandered in the late afternoon hours of a summer day in 1994. Most of the other tourists had already departed, and the park ranger was about ready to close his little visitor's center and call it a day. Suddenly, the young couple burst into the center and excitedly told what they had just witnessed. As they sat in one of the little pews, absorbing the beauty of the chapel and the quiet tranquillity of the afternoon, there appeared to them the figure of an Indian man, standing beside the altar. Then, just as suddenly as the apparition had appeared, it vanished, absolutely disappearing before their very eyes. It was readily apparent to the park ranger that this couple was not making up ghost stories. They were fully convinced that the spirit of a long-departed mission Indian had come back from out of the distant past, perhaps to welcome them, to the place where he had found the Christian faith so long ago.

# Phantom at the Fire Station

Fire Station Number 12, located at the corner of South Flores and Alamo Streets is an old-timer. It was built in 1925 on the site of a still older facility, which was destroyed by fire.

Roland Trevino, one of the firefighters assigned to Number 12, is a friend of mine. He told me there was a ghost story connected to the station and suggested that I call Tana Jaroski, a firefighter who had actually seen the "phantom of the fire station."

Tana told me she actually saw a man downstairs one evening when all the other firefighters were on the upper level. She asked him what he was doing there, and he told her he was just checking up on things. She ran upstairs and asked some of the men the identity of the man roaming around downstairs. When they all went down to look, the man had left. She later identified the figure she had seen as being a former captain whose photo is mounted on the wall at the station. He was Captain Ike Bowman, who died at the age of sixty-one. One of the current firemen, Chris Silva, told me he had heard the captain died in the line of duty, but he didn't know if this was true or only a rumor.

Silva also told me he had heard ghost rumors, and he did know that footsteps have been heard upstairs when no one is there, and the commode flushes by itself on occasion!

Tana said that she was upstairs talking on the phone to a friend when she suddenly heard footsteps coming up the stairs. She told her friend to hang on a minute, and she went to the doorway where she could look out at the landing to see who it was. She glimpsed a figure there: a dark figure with glowing eyes, sort of rose colored, "like an animal's eyes that glow in the dark." It frightened her. Often, she said, when she is upstairs she feels strange, like there is an unseen but keenly felt presence there beside her.

At the present time Jaroski is the only female firefighter assigned to Station Number 12. She wonders if the former Captain Bowman, being of the old school, might possibly disapprove of a woman being in a profession formerly associated with men. Maybe he's trying to frighten her into leaving. She said there have been several other female firefighters there, but they've all left, for what reasons she doesn't know. Maybe Captain Bowman knows.

# Another "Extra" at the Express News

I wrote briefly about the ghost at the *San Antonio Express News* in *Spirits of San Antonio and South Texas*. Helen Lampkin, a sales representative, had told me about her only encounter with the ghost at the newspaper which occurred in 1990. During a smoking break, as she stood in the hallway near the freight elevators, she glimpsed a gentleman in an old-fashioned black wool suit standing just behind her. He was there one minute, and had totally disappeared the next! The encounter was so upsetting to Lampkin she still will not go near the spot where she saw the man.

The apparition of the gentleman dressed all in black, in clothing reminiscent of the last century, has also appeared on a fairly regular basis to occupants of the pressroom at the *San Antonio Express News*. Sometimes he appears quite often, and it's usually in the late afternoon. It has gotten to where he sometimes acknowledges the people there; and at other times he totally ignores them, walking straight at, or even through, the startled employees! A friend of mine who is employed at the newspaper, telemarketer Jerry Salazar, told me about the strange visitor to the newspaper offices. He says they've gotten so used to him they more or less just ignore him now!

Salazar first noticed the ghost on the fourth floor of the main building. He has also felt it from time to time on the third floor. Although he has only seen the apparition twice, he has experienced the presence of the spirit in other ways.

Jerry, who is quite sensitive, says "It passes through you, and gives you a chill."

In the basement of the building, where the old presses are located, there was a period of several years when the ghost was quite active. Frank Solis, who is often referred to as "Pancho," has worked in the pressroom for twenty-eight years. He says every once in awhile when he was by himself down in the pressroom, cleaning up, he would feel something watching him, and he would get chills and goosebumps. Sometimes Solis saw the apparition of a man who seemed to be playing hide-and-go-seek behind the presses. He said that he had only seen the specter in the afternoons, never at night, and always it came to the same area.

The *San Antonio Express News* recently ran an article about their resident ghost in the October 1996 issue of *Enside Source*, the employee publication. This article mentioned the occasion when Solis was in the basement area trying to move a heavy roll of paper. As he struggled, a man's arm appeared next to him and helped him push the cumbersome roll away. Solis said he was so frightened he ran off so fast he forgot to thank the mysterious "helping hand."

Robert Jones, an employee in the pressroom for thirteen years, said he has heard the old cars that used to carry the paper rolls running on their little tracks, and he knew no one was around. Most recently, as Jones was cleaning up the area around the new presses, he saw a white shadow pass by.

I mentioned these strange appearances to my psychic friend Sam Nesmith. He went down and walked all around the *Express News* building, covering the whole block where it is located. He came up with some fascinating tidbits. In fact, Sam told me he had been in contact with the old gentleman, and he seemed to know a great deal about him. How psychics communicate with the dead I do not even begin to comprehend. But Sam has been right on the money so many times before, I just listen to what he tells me and then pass it on to my readers to, as Robert Ripley said, "believe it or not."

After an evening of walking and listening and actually communicating with the spirit of the old man who comes to the *News* building, Sam says the black-clad entity is a man who came to the United States from Ireland as a young man. When he left his homeland, his father, knowing he might never see his son again, gave him a big silver pocket watch as a keepsake. It became the young man's most treasured possession.

Born with one leg slightly shorter than the other, the man always walked with a slight limp. When the Civil War began, because he was living in the North and was a great admirer of Abraham Lincoln, the young man tried to join the Union army. Because of his disability, the army would not accept him. He was an excellent horseman and became a teamster for the U.S. Army, driving supply wagons for the military.

After the war, the young Irishman learned that many of his countrymen were living in San Antonio where they had settled in a district referred to as the Irish Flats. He decided to move south to a more temperate climate. He promptly found employment with a wealthy Irish family, as a coachman and groom for their horses. The large home and adjacent carriage house, where the man lived, were on the block where the second *News* building is now located, at the corner of McCullough and Broadway. This is the old *San Antonio Light* building.

Jerry Salazar later told me the old man's ghost has been seen in both the buildings, which are situated in the Irish Flats section of San Antonio. According to Sam, the old Irishman never married. He did enjoy his work and had many friends. He always wore a high crowned hat and a dark coat with a cape attached. He wore a Lincolnesque beard and sideburns and indeed, greatly resembled the man he admired so much.

In communicating with the spirit, Sam said the man comes around because he is searching for his watch, which was of great sentimental value to him, and which was stolen. He had requested that, when he died, his timepiece be buried with him. The undertaker, deciding it was foolish to place such a fine watch in a casket, decided he would keep the watch. What he did with it is unknown, of course, but Sam believes the watch still exists and is somewhere in San Antonio, possibly in an antique shop.

Sam believes the man's spirit cannot rest until the watch is located, and of course, he is looking in the vicinity of where he used to live and work, long before there was an *Express News*!

After I talked with Sam, I called Jerry to tell him what I had heard, and Jerry, who is also quite sensitive, was not even surprised. He evidently sensed much of what Sam had told me, and he said he had already planned to make a concentrated effort to search the antique shops for the watch, which he also feels exists. Psychics are truly fascinating people!

# A Spirit Glows
# Among the Candles

Vicky Garcia always gets to work early. It's her job. Around 6 a.m. every weekday morning she arrives to turn on the lights and the heat in winter, or to open the windows when the warm weather comes. By the time the other workers in the department where she works arrive, everything is in readiness for another day at the Reed Candle Factory. Nearly every morning Garcia says she feels as if she is not alone. An unseen presence seems to follow her around as she organizes the area for the day's work. Once she felt such an overpowering presence of "something waiting for me" at the head of the stairs, that she turned around and ran down the steps, her heart pounding violently. She wouldn't go back upstairs that morning until she was able to locate another factory employee who agreed to accompany her. Several employees say they have had similar experiences.

The Reed Candle Company is a very old and successful business located at 1531 West Poplar Street. The founder of the company was the late Peter Doan Reed. His son and successor, Peter Nathan Reed, has continued to carry on the family business. It was Peter's wife, Sister, who told me that it was more or less taken for granted that "Papa Reed," as the founder was affectionately known, still comes around, keeping a watchful eye over the business and its employees.

It's an interesting story how the senior Reed came to be involved in the candle-making profession. He was the son of an Irishman, Robert Reed, who came to Texas from Tallahassee County, Mississippi, at the close of the Civil War. The twice-wounded Confederate veteran settled in the small town of Luling with his family. After his wife died, the widowed Reed moved south to Mexico where he eventually met and married a beautiful Mexican woman. Five children, three girls and two boys, were born to that union.

Peter and his brother Henry were of course born in Mexico. There they were educated and married. The Reed brothers started an ice business in Jalisco, which they called "Hielo Cristal" (Ice Crystal). Peter sold his share of the growing business to his brother and settled in San Antonio with his wife and family. He opened a small Red and White grocery store. One of the items he carried was votive candles, which were especially popular with his Hispanic customers. They were shipped from Chicago and were sometimes difficult to obtain. Reed felt he would be much better off if he could manufacture them himself, so he began to experiment with candle making, operating in a small garage behind his home.

As his little business grew, Reed realized he needed to modernize the operation, so he purchased a small building on West Popular. In 1937 he also bought some votive candle-making machines, of which he was quite proud. In those days he ran his little factory with the help of his family and just one paid employee.

According to his daughter-in-law, Sister Schodts Reed, Peter Doan was a friendly and dynamic man. He was proud of his candle business, and he worked at the factory until he was well into his seventies. He was also the founder of the Little League baseball program in San Antonio, and he loved to provide baseball uniforms, caps, and gloves to little under-privileged boys in the West End. Many of today's civic leaders give Reed credit for steering them in the right direction towards becoming responsible citizens. The philanthropic Reed was crowned Rey Feo in 1960 for his altruistic works.

With so much hard work, dedication, and pride placed in his business it is no real wonder that Mr. Reed's spirit would occasionally return to keep an eye on things. Longtime employee Lupe Asebedo has worked at the plant for thirty-one years. She is the supervisor of the decorating department which employs thirty-two workers. Asebedo recalled having lots of visits with "Papa Reed." He often walked through the factory, pointing to some of his special machines, saying, "Just think, these are all mine." She said he wasn't bragging. He was just so obviously proud of the business he had built through so much hard work. He was the kind of employer the workers could talk to and visit with, and they all greatly respected him. Lupe described him as being "tall, slender, always well dressed and mannerly. He was an elegant old gentleman and he never went anywhere without a hat." It was a great loss to the community and his factory employees when he passed away in 1980.

Vicky Garcia is not the only employee who has experienced something rather unusual at the factory. Lupe said once when she was downstairs in an office engaged in a private conversation with an employee, they saw someone pass the open office door. She stopped talking and said, "just a minute," as she went to peer out the door to see who had passed by, since the conversation was private, of a personal nature, and she said she didn't want any eavesdropping. Whoever passed by was nowhere to be seen, and she said there was no place they could have vanished in that particular part of the building. Lupe also remembered being patted on the shoulder while washing her hands up in her department, known as Section 23. She definitely felt somebody give her a friendly pat, but no one was anywhere close around! She also said the whole room suddenly turned cold at that time.

Later I spoke to Victor Gaitan, who came to work at the plant in 1993, so he never knew the elder Reed. But Gaitan has seen the shadowy figure of a man standing more or less in the same area where Lupe was patted on the shoulder. The figure was standing near the wall by the sink, and the workman was working on a labeling machine at the time. Gaitan was quite startled to see the figure which he said was definitely a man, but because the corner of the room was rather dark he couldn't make out any features. He also said a woman who no longer works at the Reed plant told him she once had a glimpse of somebody standing by the door in the same section of the factory.

There's a presence there. That's what a number of workers say. They all believe it is Papa Reed, so nobody is afraid of him. There is practically no turnover in the factory. Some employees have been there over forty years. Peter Nathan Reed, who succeeded his father in running the business, has greatly expanded the operation. It covers a vast area, and I was most impressed as Sister Reed escorted me over the factory explaining what each department does. The plant manufactures over one hundred and fifty different candle products and employs over a hundred workers, shipping its products all over the world.

The factory is a cheerful place. And it's clean, and of course, it smells wonderful, too (they make a lot of scented candles). If Papa Reed still comes around, and there are certainly those who believe that he does, he's a benevolent spirit. He must be proud of his son, Peter Nathan, who has capably filled his shoes, both in heading up the candle factory and carrying on as a benefactor to the youth of the city. The younger Reed was named Rey Feo in 1993, the only son to receive the same honor bestowed upon his father.

Long may the candlelight shine!

# A Spirit at the Soap Works

When I was writing the story about Tracy Hammer's Riverwalk Inn, Hammer mentioned a building the firm founded by his father, Stanley Hammer, now occupies. The Hammer Company has its offices in the old Menger Soap Factory, a historic landmark now completely restored.

The old limestone building at 500 North Santa Rosa was listed on the *National Register of Historic Places* in 1973 and as a Texas Historic Landmark in 1983.

Of course, there's a ghost story attached to the landmark, but first, how about a little background history? It's an interesting story.

Johann Nicholas Simon Menger, who was born in 1807, came to Texas with the Henri Castro Colony. Shortly after his arrival, the German immigrant moved to San Antonio. It wasn't long before he became one of the city's first industrialists! In 1850 he opened a factory that supplied soap for much of the city of San Antonio and southwest Texas. The first structure he built was destroyed in an 1859 flood of the San Pedro Creek, which literally washed the building away. In 1873 Menger built the second structure for his factory, which can still be seen today. It serves as offices and party rooms for the Soap Factory Apartments, owned by the Hammer Company. It looks as sturdy and permanent today as it must have looked when it was first built.

Menger utilized the waters of the nearby San Pedro Creek in his production process, and soon he was producing all types of soap, known by such exotic trade names as Alamo Queen, Dragon Soap, Katy Flyer, Trilby, and German.

Hammer Company (formerly Menger Soap Works)

While the historic plaque mentions Johann Nicholas Simon Menger, there is a large poster advertising the soap products inside the building that refers to him as Simon Menger. Also, an article which appeared in the *Herald* of September 6, 1859, detailed the flood which destroyed the soap factory, to the tune of $1,500 worth of property. Another article from the same paper, dated March 13, 1878, referred to a Mr. S. Menger as being San Antonio's first classroom music teacher. Steve Green, librarian at the Institute of Texan Cultures, was able to clarify for me that this was the same Mr. Menger known as Johann and often called Simon.

The *Herald* article from 1878 speaks at length of the successful little business:

It is across the San Pedro where the celebrated soap factory of S. Menger and Sons is situated, a factory established over 20 years ago and capable of making sixty-nine thousand pounds of soap of all grades, from the finest toilet to the family soaps at one and the same time. This factory is in fact one of the notable institutions of San Antonio and should be visited as such by those coming to our city and seeking to learn of our resources. At present the average sales from this factory amount to twenty-five thousand pounds of soap per month, and when this fact is noted and the large amount of other soaps used here is included, in the consideration of the subject, it will be at once appreciated why it is that San Antonians are so cleanly in their habits and appearance.

For twenty years Mr. S. Menger has been experimenting in the making of various kinds of fancy soaps at his factory and one of the latest results in his experiments is the production of Cotton Seed Oil Soap, a soap which for healing and cleansing properties is not excelled, or indeed equaled, by the celebrated Castile soap. This soap is made in the most careful and cleanly manner; it is invaluable in the sick room as well as in the toilet. For softening the skin it excels glycerin, and for cleansing it is without an equal.

Now, several employees at the Hammer Company have told me that the old building has a lingering spirit which they suppose might be left over from the soap manufacturing days. Linda Vorhees, office manager, often has heard footsteps going down the stairs and across the lower floor entrance foyer, which has a stone floor. Then the steps go back up the stairs again. This is always when she is alone in the building. Cari Faulk, her assistant, has heard the same sounds of footsteps.

Linda told me that once when she was in the ladies' room, where there is a sizable gap between the floor and the door, she saw the distinct shadow of something passing the door of the restroom. A look outside revealed nothing. When she is alone in the building and the old shutters are closed, she often hears footsteps in the building. When she opens the shutters, the noise stops. She says it's as if the spirit, whatever it is, is playing games with her.

Cari once saw the figure of a man standing about ten feet away from where she was standing at the coffee machine. He was just looking at her. She took a second glance, and poof! he was gone! Both Cari and Linda feel strongly there is a friendly, nonthreatening presence in the building, and it is a male presence.

Maybe it's just Simon Menger, wondering why they're not still making soap in his old factory headquarters!

# A Watchful Spirit at the Witte

The Witte Memorial Museum at 3801 Broadway is located on the northeast side of Brackenridge Park. First headed by Ellen Schulz Quillin, who was director and curator for many years, the museum opened in 1926. It was named for stockbroker Alfred G. Witte, who bequeathed a large sum of money to the city with the stipulation a museum for the people be built within the confines of Brackenridge Park.

The museum includes natural history exhibits, a fine American Indian display, the Koehler Gallery of Early American Art, and a fine Texas collection. On the grounds numerous old pioneer homes have been relocated to the banks of the San Antonio River, which runs at the rear of the property. An enjoyable and educational day can be spent at the Witte, and the museum shop is a fine place to buy unusual gift items as well.

I was told by several current employees and docents that a ghost story is attached to the place. I contacted Linda Johnson, the museum director, and she said she had never seen or felt the presence of a ghost there but was aware of the stories that had been circulated. She referred me to an article which ran in the *San Antonio Express News* on July 3, 1988. The article by Ann Cain Tibbets was called "Witte's Ghost." The writer stated nobody she talked to had denied the possibility of there being a ghost in residence at the Witte. Of course, we all should know that a building so filled with artifacts of the past, belongings that once were treasured by persons now long departed, might take on a spooky appearance at night when all the tourists are gone. And, doubtless,

The Witte Museum

a lot of energy from the past may still be going snap! crackle! pop! in the old building as well.

Dr. Bill Green, a former curator at the Witte who went on to become Capitol Historian for the State Preservation Board in Austin, seems to believe there's a ghost at the Witte. He said when he first came to the museum in 1981 he kept locking his door when he left his office, but when he returned it was always unlocked. The burglar alarm went off and he was blamed for it, even when he wasn't there, and no one else, including any intruders, was there either. This kept happening on a regular basis.

One staff member came to work early one morning and entered a vault through a heavy single door. She reached up on a shelf to get an artifact down, and at that moment a cold blast of air hit her and filled the vault. At the same time, off to one side, she saw a figure move out of sight. The employee was quite shaken by the sudden chill and commented to Karen Branson, the secretary seated near the vault, asking her if she'd suddenly moved from her desk. "No," was her reply, and then Branson added, "so you felt it too?"

Ms. Branson also told the *News* writer she had heard sounds in a room across from her desk. It sounded like screening trays were being shaken, she said.

At least four people told the reporter that papers move around on their desks.

The attic, which was formerly used as a library, seems to be the most active portion of the building. A gardener who went up there once on an errand said a bony hand touched his shoulder when he was alone up there, and he refused to go back.

One museum guard, when asked if he had ever encountered a spirit, replied off-handedly, "Sure. Who hasn't?" Then he went on to say it was a lady and she looked "like she always did. It's just Mrs. Quillin."

Another staff member spoke of unexplainable activity in the old library of the building. She said the coffee room was on the floor just below the library at one time, and she recalled when she was there drinking coffee she heard a sound like a wooden chair being scraped on the floor above her and then there were footsteps. The sounds were distinct. She also said she had heard footsteps on the metal stairs that led up to the library on numerous occasions, but when she got up to look to see who it was, no one was ever there.

Ellen Schulz Quillin, who almost single-handedly brought the Witte Museum into being, hung around there almost until she died. Many feel she was so involved and dedicated that even death will not separate her from her beloved museum. Towards the end of her long life she came to work when she was even then very ill and under her doctor's orders to go to the hospital for treatment of her high blood pressure. And ask the employees and docents. They think she's still there, at least much of the time. They take her presence for granted, and she is welcome.

Quillin especially loved the library because research was her big love. She wrote her book *The Story of the Witte Museum*, with Bess Carroll Woolford, there in the library. It is not surprising that it is her favorite spot to come back to for visits.

This remarkable woman was born around 1890. She grew up on a farm in Michigan and craved knowledge from the time she was just a little girl, literally "drinking up books." She went to the University of Michigan when she was only sixteen and majored in science and natural history, which were considered unusual studies for young ladies in those days.

In 1916 Ellen moved to San Antonio. She taught botany at the old Main High School. She loved to take her students on field trips to the woods around San Pedro Park to hunt for "specimens."

She and her students raised money to buy a collection of odds and ends, rocks, minerals, stuffed birds, Indian artifacts, and such from a Houston man named H.P. Attwater. Quillin and her young students begged for contributions on the street corners near the Gunter Hotel. They had bake sales, they sold bunches of bluebonnets for a dollar a bunch. (Now it's illegal to even pick bluebonnets, much less sell them.) At last they were able to raise the $5,000 that Attwater wanted for his collection. These items became the first collection handed over to the Witte Museum when it was built.

Then the feisty schoolmarm begged Mayor John W. Tobin for help until he finally gave her $7,500. A later gift of $75,000 from Alfred G. Witte made the museum a reality, and Quillin, the driving force behind it all, became the first director.

In October of 1960 Mrs. Quillin was forced to retire. She had served the museum for thirty-four years. She was given the title of director emeritus, but she still kept a watchful eye on "her" museum.

Ellen Quillin died at home on May 5, 1970. No one knew her exact age, but she was at least eighty years old at the time of her death. She lived a full and productive life. She was happy with what she had accomplished, which was to establish a fine museum for San Antonio. It was the most important part of her life. And there are those who would say she never left it.

# Ghosts Behind Bars

It was through a chance meeting with a young man named Rudy Ybarra that I began research on this story. It took a long time, but the search for information was both challenging and interesting.

Ybarra, an employee at the new Bexar County Correctional Facility, told me he had heard several stories of a ghost being at the old jail, the one at 218 South Laredo, now maintained as a contract jail by Wackenhut Corrections Corporation. It is called the Central Texas Parole Violator facility.

I spoke with numerous employees at the Bexar County Sheriff's Department before the story finally began to come together. It's the story of a ghost named Hugo, and how he came to be at the old jail in the first place.

Hugo Saenz was a twenty-two-year-old inmate who had been incarcerated and was awaiting trial for the July 1977 murder of a southside woman named Connie Zuniga. The woman's brother, Robert Farias "Comanche" Riojas, was a local underworld character, classified by the police department as a Class I drug dealer. He was a major trafficker in heroin. He was instrumental in orchestrating the revenge killing of Saenz. He provided heroin, money, and the promise of legal assistance to four inmates for their cooperation in ridding the world of one Hugo Saenz.

Saenz was found hanging by a rope made with strips from a mattress cover, in a shower stall in his fourth floor jail cell on September 17, 1977. Investigators first ruled the hanging a suicide, but the medical examiner at the time, Dr. Ruben Santos, later determined Saenz' body had first been beaten and strangled. A small bone in his neck had been broken. The man was killed, then hanged, to make the death appear as a suicide.

From numerous articles obtained from the files of the *San Antonio Express News* with the help of librarian Judy Zipp, I was able to learn the real story behind Saenz' death.

Riojas had "connections" inside the jail. He paid former jail captain Johnnie McRae the sum of $300 after telling him on September 13, 1977, that he wanted Hugo Saenz placed in the same cell block with Jose Luis Maldonado and Juan Rodriguez Salinas, two prisoners whose assistance Riojas said he had enlisted in his plot to have Hugo Saenz killed. According to Riojas, who later plead guilty to plotting Saenz' murder, Captain McRae, had, from time to time, done "special favors" for the drug dealer. This was always in return for money. Riojas said that Sgt. Richard Ramos, another jail employee, also helped him, arranging special visits for him to see certain people, and also delivering dope to prisoners. Riojas saw that Ramos was well paid for his "trouble." Riojas claimed at his trial that he spent between $15,000 and $16,000 to have Saenz killed. He said several people were on his payroll, including McRae, Ramos, former jail administrator Roy Olivarri, and local attorney Alan Brown. Brown is supposed to have been aware of the plot to have Saenz murdered, and he delivered money to those involved in the conspiracy.

It seems that the unsuspecting Saenz was suddenly transferred to a cell block occupied by Maldonado, Salinas, Martin Andrade Reyes, Eddie Rivera, Felix Ricondo, and several others. Ricondo was not involved in the conspiracy. The transfer of Saenz to the cell was arranged by Captain McRae, whom Riojas had bribed.

Sgt. Ramos was not involved in the conspiracy, but he was later charged with obstructing the investigation into Saenz' death by attempting to prevent three other jail guards from testifying.

One inmate, David Villareal, said he was playing cards with Hugo Saenz when suddenly another inmate approached Saenz from the rear. He had a rope which he quickly flung around Saenz' neck and pulled him to the floor. Another inmate put his hands on Saenz' mouth and nose so he couldn't breathe. Two other men held his feet and a fifth held his arms. Another observer, an inmate named Teofilo Tellez, later testified he saw five inmates haul Saenz' lifeless body into a shower, where they hanged him. That was where he was later discovered by guards.

The trial of the conspirators who carried out the murder plot, along with Captain McRae and Sgt. Ramos, began in February of 1980, according to an article which ran in the *San Antonio Express News* dated February 20, 1980. Riojas, who in March of 1979 had been sentenced to twenty years in state prison for murder, attempted murder, and possession of heroin, decided to cooperate with authorities, becoming a government witness in the trial after experiencing "a religious awakening."

So much for the murder of Hugo Saenz and the subsequent trial of his killers. This is the background of why Hugo Saenz' ghost has been reported at the jail.

Bexar County Sheriff's Deputy Gary de Valle has been helpful to me, as has Gene Sanchez, the commander of the criminal division at the Bexar County Correctional Facility. Both men said they'd heard the stories of the jail being haunted but had seen nothing themselves.

Deputy Sheriff Nancy Baeza, who is now in the criminal division's warrant section, said she had a couple of ghostly experiences while working in the "old jail" (now the Wackenhut facility). Baeza told me a strange thing happened in 1984 during her tenure at the prison. That year they were doing a lot of renovating and remodeling, and one portion of the seventh floor on the south left side of the building was completely closed off during this time.

Nancy was in the "cage" monitoring the television screen which gave her an overview of the cellblocks when she suddenly saw the figure of a man appear on the catwalk. This was a walkway between the cell rows and the outside windows. He was clad in a T-shirt and what looked like regular boxer shorts. She watched for a few minutes, and when he didn't go away she called a couple of other guards. Sgt. Pete Olivarez saw the figure on the camera, too. He told Nancy, "But that area's all closed off, no one can get in there." But the figure was plainly visible on the screen for a full five minutes. It was just gazing out the window. One guard was sent back to the area to search, and no one was in the closed-off portion. The sergeant said the figure on the monitor looked exactly like Hugo Saenz to him!

A number of former employees at the old jail who asked not to be named knew of Hugo Saenz' story, and all of them said, "Oh, a lot of people have seen his ghost at the jail." That's about all I could get them to say.

Nancy told me that back in 1983-84 she was assigned to the seventh floor where the female inmates were incarcerated. She had made her rounds, checking the inmates, in the wee hours of the morning. A woman in cell number 12 was awake and Nancy stopped and chatted with her for a few minutes. As the two conversed, Nancy happened to glance towards the corner cell, number 13, which she knew was unoccupied. To her amazement she saw a hand grasping the bars of number 13 as if someone were trying to pull themselves up from a sitting position using the bars as a brace.

Nancy thought, "It's late. Maybe I'm just seeing things." She soon went back to the "cage," which is the area where the guards sit in the center, controlling the electronic locking and unlocking of the cell doors. Another officer came on duty and went out to the south right wing to make another check. She soon returned and asked Nancy, "Who is that girl in number 13?" Nancy told her it was an empty cell. "No, it isn't," said the other guard. Nancy told her to go check again. A few minutes later the other guard returned, utterly baffled. The cell was indeed empty!

I also talked to Mike Phillips, who works at the new Bexar County Jail on Commerce Street. He used to work the "dog watch" or late shift. He said there are "pods" there, big square, almost empty rooms surrounded by cells. There's an electronic panel to lock all the doors to the cells. He told me he heard a door open with a loud click and then close. The closure made a big noise because it echoes. A careful check revealed all the prisoners were asleep and all the doors were locked. This happened to Mike two different times, and he still can't explain it. Looks like there may be a spirit or two floating around the new facility which just opened in 1987!

Lt. Johnny Reyes told me he once saw two eyes glowing in the darkness . . . like animal eyes, but it was in an unoccupied cell!

Apparently, Hugo Saenz' spirit hasn't been seen around the old jail for some time now. After all, Riojas, who planned his murder, and the inmates who carried it out, were all discovered and punished. Although he was far from an exemplary character, Hugo deserved better than what he got. But his killers got their comeuppance too. His spirit doesn't need to hang around the jail anymore.

As for the others, it's anybody's guess who they are and why they are there. As much as they must dislike being behind bars, it looks like a jail would not be a place where a ghost would want to come back. But then who can really explain why ghosts do what they do anyway?

# The Aggie Spirit

Aggie Park, located at the corner of Loop 410 and West Avenue, has been the scene of many barbeques, meetings, parties, dances, Aggie Musters, and various other events over the years. In the past three or four years, numerous staff members at the big complex have reported there might just be something in the building besides the Spirit of Aggieland.

I doubt there are any Texans not aware of the indominable spirit of former students of Texas A&M University. Their fervor for their alma mater, football team, and one another is legendary! In San Antonio the "spirit" reached such a fever peak that a group of Aggies banded together and bought 3.3 acres of land back in the early 1940s on which to build a facility where they could have private Aggie barbecues and gatherings.

A man named Henry Wier owned a large dairy farm at that location when it was still considered to be way out in the country from San Antonio. Every year the local Aggies got together and rented a couple of acres from Wier, having the dairy man mow the tall grass as part of the deal. Then, according to all the stories I've heard, they'd have barbecues, reminisce, down a few beers, discuss the football situation, and generally enjoy some good fellowship together. These were strictly stag parties. Then, when Wier decided to get out of the dairy business and sell his property, ten members of the Aggie group got together, pooling their money, and for $999 were able to buy the three acres. They called this venture Aggie Memorial Park, in honor of several of their number who had passed away. The first thing they did was build a huge

Aggie Park

brick and concrete barbecue pit. Then, in 1953 they constructed a building so they could hold meetings year round. This building, which has been greatly enlarged since that time, was dedicated in 1954.

The San Antonio facility is the only one of its kind in the state. There are A&M Clubs all over the country, but none can boast a park and large meeting facility such as Aggie Park.

I recently learned the multipurpose building is believed to be haunted. I conducted one of my *Spirits of San Antonio* evening ghost tours for members of the Aggie Wives' Club, their husbands, and guests. Several of the group mentioned to me it was certainly a shame I had not included the story about Aggie Park's ghost in any of my books. Although I am a member of the Aggie Wives' Club, I seldom attend meetings because of work conflicts, and so I had not heard of the ghostly presence that is said to lurk around Aggie Park. Linda Turman, who got the group organized for the tour, told me she had recently been told by Kathleen Sheridan, the executive secretary of the San Antonio A&M Club, that the park was haunted.

Telephone conversations with Ms. Sheridan and her assistant, Mildred May, revealed some enlightening information. Both ladies said they had started noticing things happening about two or three years ago. At first it was just lights mysteriously going on and off, then things would get misplaced and later reappear. They have both keenly felt the presence of someone or something in the building with them. This is most noticeable when one or the other of them is alone, working in the building after club members and the custodial staff have departed for the day.

Kathleen told me her ten-year-old daughter was in the building with her one afternoon when the child saw a whitish, misty form, which took on the appearance of a man's figure, in the vicinity of the bar. She actually saw the figure appear, then disappear, twice during the course of the afternoon.

Sheridan told me when work was being done on the building, a decorator was there quite late one evening. Suddenly he felt something holding him tightly to the spot on which he stood. For about sixty seconds he stood rooted to the spot, unable to move in any direction. Then, whatever the force was, it let go of him and he could move about. He says it was an absolutely unforgettable experience! Another man, a painter, came to work in the evenings when he got off his regular day job. He reported seeing strange shadows with human forms moving about in a deserted hallway where he was working. He was very unnerved by this occurrence.

Another worker, a military veteran who is now attending a local university, was so upset by seeing moving shadows and feeling he was not alone in the building, he said he would not come back and work in the building at night anymore.

Ms. Sheridan said one afternoon she was in the building with two ladies who had come to look at the building before they decided to rent it for an upcoming function. Because there are a lot of windows and it was a bright sunny day, Kathleen did not turn on the lights in the building. Then, suddenly, all the lights went on. There was no explanation for this at all.

Both Kathleen Sheridan and Mildred May told me they had never believed in ghosts before, but both women definitely believe the building at Aggie Park is haunted. Sheridan's theory, based on the fact the park is located on the banks of a creek where Indians used to camp and is only a short block away from where a large Indian burial ground was recently discovered, is that the ghost might be the spirit of an Indian hanging around the site of his former camping grounds. She thinks the spirit is an "old soul" that has been around for a long while.

Ms. May told me she has had numerous experiences with things moving around after she has placed them somewhere. Even chairs in the building have been mysteriously moved. These occurrences most often happen near the back of the building, the area closest to the creek.

Two Aggie Wives' Club members, Barbara Roberson and Marilyn Muldowney, who is the club president, told me they also believe there is a spirit in the building. Barbara recently went there to open the building for an evening meeting. The combination for the lock had been given to her by Kathleen Sheridan, who first warned her not to be by herself when she went into the building. When Barbara questioned her as to why she shouldn't be alone, Ms. Sheridan told her she might feel the presence there and be frightened by it as others had been.

Barbara proposed that the spirit might be a former Aggie club member who loved the place so much he just comes back now to keep an eye on things. I have another theory. After the creek flooded and inflicted a lot of damage on the building, the members decided to enlarge as well as repair and renovate the buildings. This was about five years ago. The ghost activity has only taken place in the past four or five years since so much remodeling has been done, and most students of ghost-lore know this often brings the spirits out. Maybe one of the former builders of the original building is the other-worldly visitor!

Many members, now deceased, were intensely loyal both to their alma mater and the local A&M Club. Several former members even requested that their memorial services be held at Aggie Park. At least two wakes have been held there. One was especially memorable. A former member, a prominent veterinarian, made arrangements prior to his death that a wake be held at the park for all of his old Aggie buddies and their wives, as well as his business clientele. Barbara and Ken Roberson attended, and they told me hundreds of people turned out for the party, which included heaping plates of barbecue with all the fixings, kegs of beer, assorted and unlimited libations, a dance band, decorations, and a gala atmosphere. The host also attended, in his closed coffin! Dr. Charles Wiseman, another veterinarian and a friend of the deceased, said a bottle of Jack Daniels was placed right beside the casket!

Every year on April 21 a muster honoring the dead is held at Aggie Park. It is a very moving ceremony, with the lighting of candles and the calling of the roll of deceased Aggies who have died during the previous year. There's seldom a dry eye in the crowd when the last strains of taps echo through the big building. These ceremonies are held all over the world wherever Aggies are able to gather together. Personally, I have attended them in four states and in England and Spain. So fervent is the Spirit of Aggieland that A&M men serving as officers at Corregidor in 1942 held a muster just prior to being captured by the Japanese!

For whatever reason Aggie park is inhabited by a spirit, Kathleen Sheridan and Mildred May are not afraid of it. They have learned to take it for granted. They believe whatever is there is a benevolent spirit, and only there to keep an eye on things. Personally, I think a friendly ghost would never find a more "spirited" place in which to dwell than the meeting place of Texas Aggies!

If you would like information about the available facilities at Aggie Park call (210) 341-1393.

# CHAPTER 4

# SCHOOL SPIRITS: PUBLIC AND PAROCHIAL

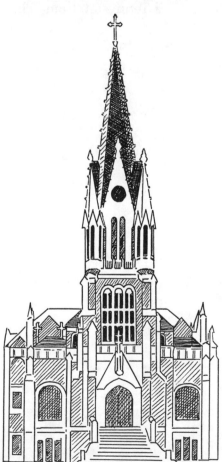

*A footstep, a low throbbing in the walls,*
*A noise of falling weights that never fell*
*Veiled whispers, bells that rang without a hand,*
*Door handles turn'd when none was at the door,*
*And bolted doors that open'd of themselves.*

Alfred Tennyson, from "The Ring"

# Spirits Cling to Schools

For some reason, schools and institutions of higher learning seem to often be haunted by former students, administrators, teachers, and custodians.

Perhaps there is an excess of energy attached to schools where so many young minds have worked at breakneck speed to absorb knowledge. Sometimes when a tragedy is attached to a school as well, due to a death, either by a tragic accident, homicide, or suicide, that aura of sadness clings to the old buildings, too.

Sylvia Sutton, a good friend of mine who spent many years as a teacher and later as a school principal, told me that often, as she worked after hours or on Saturdays, she heard little footsteps, locker doors opening and then slamming shut, and children running and laughing. She knew she was in an empty school building, and yet the sounds were real. She told me that other teachers had spoken to her about having had similar experiences. Like me, Sylvia believes there is so much energy generated around a school that much of it lingers and is capable of manifesting in various ways at certain times. How else can such phenomenon be explained?

There are several interesting stories here about schools in the San Antonio area. Some are public schools. Others are Catholic institutions. There are even a couple of stories by a Catholic sister, whose veracity no one can doubt. All these stories are interesting and thought-provoking.

# Ghosts in the Library

A couple of years ago I was asked to come to Whittier
Middle School to tell ghost stories from one of my books to the
sixth grade English class which my neighbor, Terry Garcia,
taught. Some of the youngsters asked me if I had heard their
school had a ghost. I didn't ask many questions as the students were hurrying to gather up their books and get to their
next class, and I had another appointment to meet as well. At
that particular time I hadn't planned to write another San
Antonio book, so I didn't pay much attention. Now, of course,
I wish I had!

Also, a deceased friend of mine, a former teacher at the old
Edison High School, which is now Whittier Middle School,
had mentioned to me that there was a ghost story connected
to the old school. The building, constructed in 1929, was once
a part of the now defunct Los Angeles Heights School District.

I started to search and inquire about a ghost story, but I
have not been able to find much, only rumors and hearsay. I
did locate one good witness to the fact there are some mighty
strange noises and happenings after school is out and the
place has more or less settled down for the night. I spoke to
Linda Mensar, the librarian at Whittier, and she told me
there's a story around that a young lady was killed on the
staircase leading from the library up to the auditorium and
it's her ghost that still remains at the school. Mrs. Rachel
Martinez, the parent-liaison teacher, told me that teachers
who have worked there late into the evening have heard
books being moved about the shelves in the library, and
they've also heard chairs being moved about. The library, on

the basement level, used to be the location of the school cafeteria.

I asked Mrs. Martinez if she had heard the story about the young girl being killed, and she said once when there had been a reunion of the Edison class of 1953, a couple who were there told her that they knew the story because they were actually there when the accident happened. They said a girl of about fifteen or so years of age had accidentally fallen and was killed on the stairs.

Another story that seems to have been around a long while is that one of the janitors was killed in an accident in the same stairwell area. According to Mrs. Martinez, this area is sometimes used as a makeshift dressing room, as it leads from the stage to Martinez' office.

I could tell that Mrs. Martinez feels there is a presence of something in that basement area where her office is located. She said when she had been working at the school for about two weeks, she stayed late one evening to work at her computer and get all the students and their parents' names entered. She kept hearing books being shifted around the library shelves next door, and she knew no one was in the library! Then the door from the stairwell to her office opened all by itself. It has a knob that has to be turned to open the door. No one was anywhere around. She felt a sudden coldness around the doorway as well, and we all know that cold spots are symptomatic of hauntings.

According to *San Antonio Express News* writer Paula Allen, who also researched the Whittier story, the principal, Raul Prado, has seen no evidence of ghostly presences at his school. I do believe that Mrs. Martinez is sincere in her belief that there is some sort of a presence there. I must say, the spirits must be well read, since the library area seems to be their favorite bailiwick.

# A Spirit in the Science Lab

Soon after the book *Spirits of San Antonio and South Texas*, which I coauthored with Reneta Byrne, came out in 1992, my friend Carolyn Cauley Barry said something to the effect that it "certainly was a shame I didn't include the Kennedy High School ghost story in my book." I sort of filed that remark way back in the far reaches of my memory at that time. When I decided to do a second book on San Antonio's ghosts I recalled Carolyn's remark, and called her. A former faculty member of Kennedy, she said I would do best to get in touch with someone who had taught in the science department if I really wanted to get the correct story. This took a lot of sleuthing. David Ochoa in the South San Antonio District offices was most helpful. He suggested right away that I get in touch with Roberta Smith, a former faculty member at Kennedy. This turned out to be easier said, than done. I finally got one telephone number from another former teacher, Dr. Mary Christopher, but that number turned out not to be a working number. Then I learned that Smith had once taught at Cole High School at Fort Sam Houston, so I contacted the office of Principal Buddy Compton at Cole. His secretary finally located Roberta Smith for me, and Mrs. Smith called me. That's how it's done; lots of calls, inquiries, and sometimes good fortune finally hits, as it did in this case.

Roberta and her husband, David, are both former faculty members at Kennedy High School, which is located at 1922 South General McMullen. Roberta was a wonderful source of information. She knew all about the Kennedy hauntings, and

John F. Kennedy High School

in fact, she felt most of the many manifestations were directed towards her!

Smith and two other teachers had taught science classes together from about 1974. The school district had just established a trimester system, and the trio divided up their classes, with Smith specializing in zoology, another teacher conducting what were called "science basic" classes, and the third instructor, Gus Langley, specializing in botany, the study of plants.

Smith says Langley was a giant of a man, nearly seven feet tall. He had a large frame and was somewhat overweight. The students were both terrified of him and adored him. The blonde, blue-eyed instructor was a tough taskmaster, but he was apparently a good role model, since several of his former students wound up becoming science teachers.

I asked Smith how old Langley was at that time, and she said she didn't really know for sure but would judge him to have been somewhere in his middle forties.

Langley also had a kind and sympathetic side to him. Smith said when she first came to Kennedy she was sometimes a little overwhelmed by her job, and Langley often comforted her, telling her everybody makes mistakes and everybody has to learn.

Langley enjoyed taking his classes on field trips. They often went to Palmetto State Park to collect plant specimens. The science classes took on a special project during those years, Smith recalls. A depression in the ground back of Smith's classroom sometimes collected a good bit of water after a rain. The teachers got permission from the administration to enlarge the depression until it formed quite an attractive little pond. There various plant specimens and interesting creepy-crawlers the students had captured were kept. The pond became home to numerous tadpoles, minnows, crawfish, rice fish, etc. They even had fund-raisers to help raise the money to further enhance the area, and Smith recalled Mr. Langley got a water recycling system set up. All the students enrolled in the biology classes took great pride in their pond project.

Roberta Smith told me that Gus Langley, while a giant figure of a man, was not in good health. He was asthmatic and at one time spent several weeks at the State Chest Hospital. He feared he might be in the beginning stages of tuberculosis, but Smith says she doesn't believe it was ever established that he had the disease. Several times he told Roberta he was so tired of feeling sick and having to frequently go to the doctor for treatment. Although he apparently loved his work and enjoyed his students and fellow teachers, Smith says, looking back, he was probably a lonely and often depressed bachelor.

Smith recalls the Friday afternoon when Langley came to her room. He didn't just wave at her and say "Have yourself a good weekend," as was his usual Friday custom. This time he came into her room and took her hand, looked her square in the eyes, and just said, "Good-bye."

Late the following Sunday night, the principal, Antonio Rodriguez, called the Smith's house. He told them he had just received a strangely disturbing call from Gus Langley's nephew. The young man had not seen his uncle since Friday. He had gone to the house several times and no one answered his knock on the door. He considered this odd because all the lights were on and Langley's car was there. The young man was plainly perplexed, and so he had called Rodriguez. The principal called the Smiths and asked them if they would drive the short distance from their home to Langley's and check up on him. Evidently, Gus' nephew also called the authorities, because by the time the Smiths arrived at the house, an ambulance was already parked in Langley's driveway.

The doors and windows had been nailed shut all over the house. Langley had literally nailed himself into his home. He had apparently taken a shower, dressed in his best pajamas, turned on his television set, and climbed into bed. Then he took a huge overdose of drugs. It was, without a doubt, a carefully orchestrated suicide. Because there was the terrible odor of death permeating the entire house, and the body was bloated almost beyond recognition, the coroner judged that Langley must have taken his life sometime Friday evening. Smith says she will never forget the shocking, gruesome experience of walking into the scene of such a tragic ending to a man's life.

Roberta Smith said the Kennedy students were all shocked and grieved at the loss of the popular teacher. Those students who wanted to attend the funeral were allowed to leave school. Roberta said she elected to stay with the students who didn't go, so that the other faculty members could go to the services. I got the feeling from our conversation that she had been so repulsed and shocked by the appearance of Langley when she and her husband discovered the body that she just couldn't handle the funeral.

Smith recalled that often, when they would just be chatting and visiting after school or between classes, the usually jovial Langley would say, "You know, if I ever die, I'm gonna come back here and haunt this school." Roberta usually replied, "Oh, get outa here. . . . "

In spite of his general fun-loving temperament, Smith said Langley didn't like to be crossed, and as head of the science department, he sometimes displayed quite a fit of temperament or would start to pout if he didn't get his way. So maybe there was a dark side to this lonely giant of a man.

Whether it was that dark side, or just a real regret that he had killed himself, it wasn't long before strange things started to take place at Kennedy High School. The first inkling was at the night school, when someone asked the night school principal, Daryl Ochoa, who the new teacher was. It seems a new faculty member who had not known Langley said he had seen a huge man, nearly seven feet tall, going up the stairs. He noted the man had been carrying a grade book, and while he saw him go up the stairs, he thought it strange that he didn't ever see him come back down again. When the new teacher was shown a photograph of Langley in a school yearbook, he identified the likeness of Langley as being the new teacher he had seen. Imagine his shock upon learning that Langley was dead!

Roberta told me that Langley didn't like having his picture taken, so they just used the same photo in each yearbook, from 1963, when he first arrived, up until the time of his death. She couldn't recall what year that was but believes it was either 1977 or 1978.

Mrs. Smith also told me the janitors got to where they didn't like to clean the end of the science hall unless there was somebody with them. One young custodian, a former student of Langley's, said, "I'm not going down that hall. Mr. Langley's back in his room." Another new janitor got really spooked, according to my friend Carolyn Barry, who recalled the man was cleaning up one evening after the night school and a very large man came up behind him and said, "Be sure you clean room 110 real good." The custodian assured him that he would. The next evening the same thing happened. In fact, the janitor had the same experience for several nights in a row, and he finally mentioned it to his supervisor. When he described his nocturnal visitor, the chief custodian knew the identity of the man the new janitor had been seeing. Sure enough, when the man was shown a yearbook photograph, he identified the demanding gentleman as none other than Gus Langley!

Smith told me the area in the hall just outside Langley's old classroom, which later became her classroom, was always extremely cold. This is a classic condition that exists when there is a haunting.

One night the Smiths, who sponsored the pep squad and the cheerleaders, recalled that the band had given an evening concert. Afterwards the band members were changing their uniforms in room 108, just across the hall from the biology room. Now the room where the students were had a swinging door, not a regular lock-and-key type of a door. They all heard a tremendous noise outside the room and suddenly every single locker up and down the hall opened up and banged hard against the others! For some reason the swinging doors to room 108 would not open. Then, just as suddenly, all the lockers up and down the hall slammed shut with a loud bang, and the swinging doors to room 108 opened up of their own accord. None of the students wanted to go into the hall outside the room. Smith said they were all literally petrified with fear!

While most of the kids believed the place was haunted, the janitors believed Gus Langley was still around, and certainly Roberta Smith acknowledged his presence, the school administrators appeared not to believe the stories. Then, one evening the vice-principal went to the auditorium to see that the doors were all locked, with their night-chains on, when suddenly a door he had just checked and chained started to violently shake while the chains rattled and the doorknob turned. He ran out of there fast! He had suddenly started to believe!

The next year a new principal came to Kennedy. He sometimes stayed late to work on his computer programming. He was working on student attendance records one evening after school hours, when he called the Smiths at home. He said, "I have a little problem over here. I keep hearing a biology lecture coming through the vents in my office." The puzzled principal also called his wife, and she drove over from their nearby apartment. Together, the two went down to the science hall. In front of room 110 they could plainly hear a botany lecture going on. The principal said it was absolutely freezing cold as they stood in the hallway in front of the room. They stepped inside the classroom and turned on the lights. There was silence. No one was there. The principal and his wife didn't know what to think. Smith later assured him that he was just being initiated into life at Kennedy High School. Smith told him, "That's just our ghost, Gus Langley. He's sort of pulling your leg."

A former student of Langley's and Smith's came back to Kennedy several years later as a faculty member. He had the room across the hall from Smith's. Once he came running across the hall, his eyes as big as saucers! As he had been sitting at his desk posting grades, every single poster and picture in the room started floating down off the walls and landed right on his work table! Another time Smith recalled a new work table in the science room that came equipped with a basin and faucet that had not yet been hooked up to the plumbing, started to gush water. Some grade books lying next to the basin were splashed with water.

Smith recalled another day, when her room was full of students who were gathered around a demonstration table, they all heard heavy footsteps coming up behind her. The footsteps squeaked. Smith said Langley's rubber soled shoes always squeaked when he walked. She told the students it was probably just Mr. Langley coming up behind her to check up on things. She explained to the teenagers that he had told her he would come back and haunt the school. Then, she added, "Don't let him get to you. He's just playing tricks." At that, they heard the squeaky footsteps again as they retreated towards the door!

In 1981 both Roberta and her husband David left Kennedy High School to accept positions in another school. From what she has heard, Roberta believes her old colleague Gus Langley must have decided he'd done enough haunting. Since there was no one left to remember him, it wasn't fun playing pranks anymore, so he just left Kennedy High when she did!

# The Swinging Lights

I'd heard vague rumors about the possibility of a ghostly presence at McAllister Auditorium on the campus of San Antonio College for quite some time. Not knowing exactly where to begin, I called my friend John Igo, a well-known poet, writer, playwright, and professor at San Antonio College. John did not laugh at my query. Instead, he referred me to Allan Ross, who is head of the drama department at the college. Igo felt Mr. Ross would be familiar with any happenings of a supernatural sort at the auditorium.

McAllister Auditorium San Antonio College

I was able to contact Mr. Ross, and he said as a matter of fact he had at least one unusual, and therefore memorable, occurrence in the auditorium, but it had been years ago. It was sometime in late March of 1968. Ross and several of his drama students were working late one night, painting a large set for a play which was to open the following week. Incidentally, the play was an original work by John Igo, called *Claudius the Falconer*, and John recalled the opening had been on April 3, 1968.

As they worked, Ross noticed strange shadows on the stage. At first he thought, "It's late, and I'm tired. I must be seeing things." Then he chanced to look out in the auditorium. Two large work lights, suspended by heavy cables from the ceiling were swinging back and forth, in ever-widening arcs until they were covering five or six feet as they moved. The work party all stopped and watched them in utter amazement. Then several of the workers went down and checked the doors. They were all closed. They felt no drafts. The air conditioners were not turned on. Yet the lights continued their strange behavior, swinging in wide arcs, back and forth, back and forth.

Finally, Ross said, "Well, folks, let's get back to work." Then, turning to the culprit lights, he said, "I don't know what's going on here, but we've had enough of that!" Suddenly, the lights stopped swinging!

John had told me that the auditorium was built on the site of two old, large two-story houses. They were demolished to make room for the auditorium. One of the buildings supposedly had an unhappy history, but John couldn't recall just what had occurred there. He did know it had most recently been a private kindergarten for gifted and talented little preschool age children. John and several others had visited the interior of the old house shortly before it was demolished. He said, "You could almost hear the youngsters. Their presence seemed to be all around." There were fingerpaints, little drawings, and crayons still strewn around the place.

Perhaps the playful child-spirit of a former kindergartener had come back to the locale of his former classroom and, not finding it as it had been, took out his frustration on the startled thespians!

# Spirits at Southwest Craft Center

Many years before the fascinating cluster of old buildings located at 300 Augusta Street became home to the Southwest Craft Center, it was a Catholic girls' school known as the Ursuline Academy. Its story is very interesting.

The Ursuline Order was founded in Italy by Saint Angela in 1535 as a teaching order. The Ursulines were the first to educate young women in Europe, Canada, and the United States. Their first school in America was founded in New Orleans in 1727. They brought education for young ladies to Texas when a group of them arrived in Galveston in 1847.

When it was realized that San Antonio had no school for girls, Bishop Odin purchased ten acres of land located on the San Antonio River that had formerly belonged to Erasmo Seguin. The bishop contracted with Francois Giraud, a fine French-trained architect, to design and build a school on the acreage.

There was a shortage of money in those days, so the building project moved along slowly, not really getting started until 1851. By then the main building had been constructed but not completely finished. The north wall was not complete, and some of the windows and frames were not as yet installed.

It was to this unfinished building, windowless, filled with rubble from the construction process, surrounded by high grass and weeds, and infested with all manner of bugs, scorpions, spiders, and snakes that seven sisters, four from New Orleans, and three from Galveston, came. The women were accompanied by a French priest, Father Claude Dubuis, of

Castroville. The group subsisted for the first few months on offerings from the local residents. It was some time before their supplies, cooking utensils, and other essentials would be brought in by stagecoach.

The date the group arrived was September 17, 1851. Father Dubuis and the seven sisters worked almost ceaselessly until November 2, when they were able to open their little school.

The first students were children of German, French, Mexican, and Anglo backgrounds. They spoke different languages, so they had to be seated at dining tables with those who could converse with them as they spoke their mother tongues. Gradually they were taught to speak the languages they did not know. The sisters also taught geography, history, and astronomy. In 1852 two Ursuline sisters from Ireland arrived, and they added art, elocution, and music to the curriculum.

The Ursulines were a cloistered order. They wore unwieldy black habits with large white wimples and winged headdresses. No outsiders were allowed into the school. No men were allowed near the place except their priestly protector, Father Dubuis.

A beautiful Gothic chapel was built in the late 1860s, and a dormitory was built in 1866 to allow the boarding program to be expanded. The original school building was added onto in 1853 and again in 1870. The priest's house was added on in the 1880s.

A papal conference was held in 1900 that decreed the Ursuline order would no longer be cloistered. This influenced many facets of the school. To the original curriculum were added literature, spelling, composition, arithmetic, physiology, and gymnastics. The young ladies were also taught to sew and embroider. And of course, they were taught to be little ladies, minding their manners and respecting their teachers and elders.

Finally, because it had become increasingly difficult to maintain the old buildings, the sisters decided to sell their property and move to new, modern quarters. This was accomplished when they opened their new school on the northwest side of San Antonio, on Vance-Jackson, in 1962. They finally sold the old academy property to the San Antonio Conservation Society in 1965.

The Society did a great deal of restoration and repair work at tremendous expense. A few of the Ursuline sisters lived on there even after the new northside school opened. The last of the sisters moved out in 1965.

Although the order of nuns moved to the northwest side of town, it seems the spirits of some of the founding sisters remained in the old dormitory and classroom buildings where they spent such a great part of their lives.

Al Longoria is now retired, but the former security guard at the Craft Center told me there were many nights when he heard footsteps on the upper floors and stairs of the old dormitory building. As he sat on the first floor, keeping his nightly vigil, he heard little running footsteps, like those of little girls. Then, there would be heavier treads of adults, as the nuns apparently rounded up their small charges and sent them off to bed. Mrs. Longoria, who sometimes came down to sit with her husband and keep him company, told me she also heard the footsteps on numerous occasions.

The former chapel is now used for parties and receptions, and of course it is no longer consecrated. Longoria told me he could recall several times when champagne punch bowls had been turned over just prior to a reception, quite mysteriously. It seems quite apparent that the spirits of the sisters did not approve of alcoholic beverages being served in their former house of worship!

Another story I heard concerned a photography instructor who taught in one of the former classrooms. One evening when he was in his darkroom developing film, he suddenly was pushed quite hard from behind. Then he saw a large, dark, shadowy form fly through the adjoining classroom and out the door. Some months later he experienced another such encounter, except the misty form he saw float across his classroom was white this time! Explanation? Well, the nuns wore black habits during the winter months, changing to cooler appearing white apparel after Easter! Now, since it had been a cloistered order, with no men being allowed inside the buildings except for the priest, it is quite evident that the spirit of a sister who had once taught there did not approve of the presence of a male instructor in her old classroom!

Southwest Craft Center—The Chapel

From all that I have heard and the general atmosphere I sense when I visit the Craft Center, the manifestations that have taken place indicate the sisters were protective of the place they had lived in for so long, and they only return with the most benevolent feelings towards the buildings. There is such a good and happy feeling around the place that I would almost like to think of them in terms of being guardian angels!

In 1970 the Conservation Society invited the Southwest Craft Center, which had been located in La Villita since its founding in 1965, to come and occupy the buildings. The invitation was accepted and the move began in 1971. The former academy again became a beehive of activity. Classes in drawing, sculpture, ceramics, weaving, fibers, paper making, jewelry and metal work, photography, and just about anything else creative and artistic were offered to the community. The buildings and surrounding grounds and gardens are beautifully maintained. Parts of the complex, including the gazebo and the former chapel, are available for parties and receptions. During weekdays, delicious lunches are prepared and served in the delightful Copper Kitchen Restaurant which utilizes the former dining hall.

Does all this sound interesting to you? A call to 224-1848 will bring forth information about classes and other available services at the Craft Center.

Personally, I find it especially wonderful that the buildings that were first used to teach young girls the "three R's" and how to grow up to be proper ladies are still being put to such good use. Almost 150 years from the time the school first opened, the lovely old limestone buildings are being utilized for the benefit of the people of San Antonio in a most productive and gracious manner. I do believe the founding sisters would be well pleased!

# A Sister's Last Request

Some of my stories come to me in strange and rather roundabout fashions. When I did a review of one of my books at St. Peter Prince of Apostles Church for their senior citizens group, one of their number, Robert Nelson, told me a charming little story connected with the University of the Incarnate Word. He told me I had better check it out first, before putting it into print. Armed with just this little bit of information, I called the University to try to learn more. They referred me to the Congregation of the Chapel, where I talked with Sister Evelyn. She referred me to the office of Sister Francisca Eken, the archivist, who in turn referred me to Father Thomas French at the retirement center, who is also an archivist and a respected historian. All of these people are busy and hard to reach. But that is all part of the challenge of putting my stories together, and that's what makes it so fascinating.

The end result was that Father French said the story Robert Nelson had told me was basically quite true, and pretty well known around Incarnate Word. Although not sure just what year it took place, Father French said "fairly recently within the last twenty years at least."

It seems one of the sisters who lived in the Mother House died. She had expressed the wish that, after her death, she would like for her casket to be carried to its final resting place, the little cemetery near the Mother Chapel, on the shoulders of the pallbearers. This had been the custom for many years, but just recently they had changed the procedure, placing the coffin in a hearse, transporting it a short distance to the cemetery, and then conducting a graveside service there.

When the sister died it was decided to remove her casket by hearse. Father French said he was told it was a brand new vehicle, in perfect operating order. But when the sister's coffin was placed inside, the engine just would not start. The casket had to be removed and placed on the shoulders of the funeral directors, to be transported to the gravesite. When the graveside ceremonies were concluded, the hearse started up just fine. The new engine turned over at the first turn of the ignition key!

Later, some of the sisters recalled how their friend had felt about being placed in a hearse. They remembered her request to be carried aloft on the shoulders of the pallbearers to her final resting place. It was as if her spirit had willed the hearse not to start so that her last wishes could be carried out!

May she rest in peace!

# Sister Angelina's Stories

On a bright sunny April afternoon I paid a visit to McCullough Hall, on the campus of Our Lady of the Lake University. This is a cheerful residence nursing home the Catholic Church provides for retired Sisters of the Divine Providence who have become too elderly or too infirm to continue their dedicated duties. Sister Angelina Murphy, whom I had met earlier at one of my lectures, issued the invitation to come and visit the sisters.

After my talk, Rose Teniente, a member of the McCullough Hall staff, took me on a tour to see the chapel, dining facilities (meals catered by the Marriott Hotels, no less!), and the basement level fitness center. Then we visited the storage rooms where trunks and suitcases of many deceased sisters are kept in storage. These contain the few worldly goods the sisters possessed at the time of their passing. There seems to be an aura of sadness and poignancy in this part of the building, and I did not want to remain there for long. Frankly, had the spirit of a long-departed nun suddenly materialized, I would not have been at all surprised.

Sister Angelina had hinted she might have a story or two to share with me. She didn't let me down. A multitalented, eloquent woman, the longtime educator and writer handed me a couple of stories she had written about sisters who once lived at McCullough Hall. It is with her permission that they are quoted here, just as she wrote them.

## Sister Solano Appears
by Sister Angelina Murphy

Helen Molberg, a candidate who slept in the fourth floor dormitory, St. Basil, had several encounters with an unfamiliar sister in the convent dormitory at night. This troubled her so that she reported it to the sisters in charge, Sister Ernestine and Sister Callista. They were concerned and questioned her in great detail.

They showed her a series of pictures of sisters who had died rather recently. Helen was able to select with certainty the one who had appeared to her. They gave her directions on how to handle the situation.

The sister was Sister Solano Basner, who had died in 1927 at the age of 39.

Sister Solano appeared again to Helen, but this time Helen was prepared. As she was about to close the door, Sister Solano placed her hand in such a way as to prevent its closing. "Do you want something?" Helen asked, breaking the rule of silence in the dormitory.

"Yes. I promised to make a novena or prayers for a certain intention, but I never completed it. Will you make it for me?" She explained exactly what the novena consisted of and what the intention was.

"I will certainly do that, so don't worry any more," Helen said. Helen did make the novena, and Sister Solano did not appear again.

Helen Molberg has since passed away.

## Sister Amata's Last Hour
### by Sister Angelina Murphy

Rosa Maria (Rosemary) Quintela, recalls vividly an experience she had as a nurses' aide in McCullough Hall. It was the night that Sister Amata Regan died, November 8, 1982.

Sister Amata had asked that the sisters present not pray aloud. At her bedside were Pat Regan, Sisters Regina Decker, Dorothy Hunter, Tiolinda Maroatta, Barbara Jean Hysak, and Teresa Joseph Powers. All was quiet in the McCullough Hall wing.

Rosemary, who still works in McCullough Hall, as well as others on duty, was going about her business. The resident sisters were all in bed. Silence reigned in the hall.

Suddenly Rosemary began to hear music and singing. It came softly at first but grew in volume as though a choir was coming down the hall. It was not like radio or TV music, but beautiful sacred music. Alarmed, Rosemary asked her sister, Angie Hernandez, if she heard anything. Angie said yes, she did. But the hall was empty. They decided to check all the rooms in case anyone had left a radio or TV on. But all was quiet. The sisters were all asleep.

The music grew stronger as if the choir was approaching the center, but no one was there. This went on for a rather brief period of time while the sisters prayed and the aides watched. Asked recently whether they heard the music and singing, Pat and Sister Regina said no, they had not heard anything. Finally the word came that Sister Amata had died. For a few minutes longer the music continued but became more subdued until it finally ceased.

The celestial choir had come to escort Sister Amata to her heavenly home, and Rosemary will never forget it.

# Haunted Halls at Our Lady of the Lake

Our Lady of the Lake University sits on a beautiful campus located on Southwest 24th Street. I was fortunate to learn from a staff member, Michael Boatner, who is the assistant director for residential life, that there have been some episodes of the supernatural kind at the university from time to time.

Boatner came to Our Lady of the Lake in 1994 from a previous staff position at Iowa State. The summer he arrived in San Antonio, Pacelli Hall was being painted, and Michael was assigned a room in the hall while it underwent its "face-lifting." The hall usually accommodates around two hundred people, but for a few weeks that summer Boatner had it all to himself. Well, almost.

It wasn't long until he began to feel a presence in his room. He said the large double bed was positioned against a wall, so he could only get out of it on one side. He awoke one night to feel, intensely, the presence of someone, or something, staring at him. He got up and got a drink of water to calm himself. Then another night, soon after, he was awakened by feeling the weight of something pressing on top of him, almost stifling him. He didn't get much sleep at all that night.

Boatner mentioned this occurrence, and the general feeling he was coexisting with some sort of a presence, to one of the nuns at the university. The sister said she didn't doubt his word as she had heard similar stories before.

One night, not long before Boatner moved to another residence hall, he had spent a fairly restful night. He awoke early in the morning before the sun had come up. He felt someone nudging him gently, as if trying to get him to move over. For some reason he can't explain, he spoke to it, saying, "Oh, how are you this morning?" He moved over to the far side of the bed, and he actually felt the movement as something, some unknown entity, lay down beside him. He said for some reason he wasn't at all frightened, as he believed the spirit was friendly and just in need of company.

Another former resident of the dorm told Michael he had some similar experiences, and he has learned, since moving to another dormitory, that the current occupant of his old room in Pacelli Hall is experiencing visits from the unseen spirit also.

Currently, Boatner lives in Centennial Hall. And there's a presence there also. He has most often felt it strongly around the love seat in his sitting room. He often senses something is watching him, but he says he is not frightened or intimidated by the presence.

When I questioned Michael to learn if he knew of any other campus hauntings, he told me another staff member, Sandy Alvarado, saw a figure dressed in a dark brown habit, much like the clothing worn by Franciscan friars, in a hallway in Theresian Hall. Alvarado had just closed a door into the hallway and walked away. He heard some movement and turned back in time to see this figure. It was quite solid in appearance, not transparent as some apparitions appear to be. It opened the door which Alvarado knew was locked. Sandy called to the figure and it did not turn around to look at him or respond to his call. It just kept moving down the corridor. He said the strangest thing was the fact the figure opened a locked door without using a key!

Boatner said once, when he had been called out in the middle of the night to handle an emergency, he was being returned to his dormitory residence in the patrol car of one of the campus police officers. It was around 3 a.m. The two men were astonished to see the figure of a nun in a black habit, complete with a white wimple and wide white-winged headpiece, standing in the doorway of a building. The driver said,

"Who is that?" He then backed up the car to shine the headlights directly at the woman, but when they did that, the figure both Boatner and the officer had seen completely disappeared! Boatner later learned that other security guards had reported seeing the dark-clad sister as they made their late-night rounds.

That the old campus with its tower-topped buildings and tree-shaded walkways shelters a lot of spirits, there seems little room for doubt!

Our Lady of the Lake University

# CHAPTER 5

# HAUNTED HOUSES

*All old houses wherein men have lived and died*
*Are haunted houses. Through the open doors*
*The harmless phantoms on their errands glide,*
*With feet that make no sound upon the floors.*

Henry Wadsworth Longfellow

# A Note on Haunted Houses

Numerous psychics have told me that about ten percent of all private residences, old and new, have spirits attached to them. What I've learned from interviewing people who have experienced encounters with supernatural beings, ghost don't stay around all the time. They are able to come and go at will. In many cases, they only return on anniversaries of special events, some tragic and traumatic, and others memorable because they recall happy times in the mortal lives of the spirits. Many people are surprised that even modern homes can be haunted. Many new homeowners sometimes find they have a spirit and are totally baffled by the discovery. But then houses can be built on old homesites, and it is also possible they can be placed over old, unmarked burial places. Or, back when a building site was just countryside, there could have been an Indian massacre, a death of a pioneer going across country on a wagon train, or a hanging that might have taken place from a tree limb on the property. The reasons for a possible haunting are endless!

Naturally, older houses are more likely to be occupied by spirits. After all, more people have lived in or visited homes that have a number of years to their credit. There would have been more deaths, illnesses, arguments, and tragedies. Conversely, there would have been more happy times, anniversaries, celebrations, and special events to commemorate by a return visit from a former resident. All sorts of scenes have been imprinted and recorded on the very walls and ceilings of a building, much as a film in a camera records a photograph for future viewing. Some of them are likely to recur from time to time. We call these repetitive scenes "hauntings."

I've lived in a haunted house. It was in England, back in the 1950s. It was frightening then because I was very young, and I did not understand what a haunting was all about. What frightened me as a young woman, I would only find interesting and fascinating now that I have studied the subject and have entered that time in my life commonly referred to as the "golden years."

A lot of haunted houses were mentioned in Chapter One, which includes hotels and inns. Many of San Antonio's bed and breakfast inns are old residences still lived in by their owners, who rent out a few rooms to paying guests. The houses in this chapter run the gamut from old, deserted houses, to brand new modern houses. Each story is different. Each deals with a variety of ghostly personalities and what makes them come to those particular places. Each spirit seems to add to the character of the households to which they have become attached. And each must certainly add an extra facet to the lives of the owners who find themselves sharing their dwellings with a long-term uninvited guest!

# The House on the Upper Labor Acequia

I first learned about the little stone and stuccoed house at the corner of Euclid and Baltimore Streets through reading one of Paula Allen's interesting articles in the *San Antonio Express News Sunday Images Magazine* on January 1, 1995.

My appetite whetted about the old piece of property, a part of the original Spanish land grant given to the Delgado family of Canary Island settlers, I started to do some serious research.

First, I spoke to Paula Allen, who referred me to Jon Thompson, a local architect who lived in the cottage back in the 1980s. Thompson rented the place, which began as a one-room dwelling, from Emilia Migoni of Austin. He told me it had been enlarged, and around 1950 a wooden floor and indoor plumbing had been installed.

According to Thompson, tax records show the building was constructed around 1830. Just think, it was here during the fight for Texas independence! Thompson suggested I contact Carlos and Connie Flores, a couple who proved to be very helpful. They once lived next door to the structure, which was located on the old upper acequia which brought water over from San Pedro Springs through the Upper Labor. These acequias were built by the Spanish missionaries, with the help of mission-Indian labor.

Connie Flores told me she believed there were about five old houses built around the same time, scattered about the little community which would someday become San Antonio. They were of similar style, thick limestone walls that were covered over with stucco. All were humble dwellings with dirt floors and shuttered windows. One of these look-alikes was the old Judge Roy Bean house at 407 Glenn Avenue, and another was a little house I frequently see when I visit the Spanish Governor's Palace. This house is located on Laredo Street between Commerce and Dolorosa. This wee cottage is all boarded up, as is the house on Euclid Street.

House on Upper Labor Acequia

Today a modern clinic building, which is for sale, stands on the corner of Euclid and Baltimore. You have to turn right onto Baltimore to see the little house behind the clinic to the right of the rear parking lot.

The reason I wanted to do some research on the house was because Allen had mentioned in her 1995 article that the place is, or at least once was, haunted.

Carlos Flores told me he grew up on that piece of property. His father, Carlos Senior, owned a family grocery on the corner of Baltimore and Euclid. Then the family home was next to that, and the little stone house was on the lot adjacent to the Flores' family home. There were three lots in the Flores' property. Since his youth, Carlos had heard stories about the little house, and they were fascinating to him and his brothers because they concerned buried treasure! It was rumored that General Santa Anna had used the place during his 1836 stay in San Antonio prior to the Battle of the Alamo, and some of the riches hidden there had supposedly belonged to the Mexican general. Carlos told me that back in the 1930s a trio of young men came to see his dad with a proposition. They asked if they could live, rent free, in the little house, which was unoccupied, if they would renovate the place, since it was in a bad state of disrepair. The young men had a lot of tools with them. Since the house was vacant anyway, the elder Flores agreed to let them live in the place, rent-free, in exchange for their labor.

The trusting grocer let them move in. The men stayed only a short while. Suddenly, they were gone! They even left their tools lying about on the dirt floor. They also left a deep hole right at the foot of the chimney! What they found was never determined, but doubtless they had heard about a treasure being sequestered in the house. The elder Flores, the rightful owner, was cheated out of whatever the men found buried beneath the hard-packed earthen floor.

As youngsters, Carlos said he and his brothers found lots of arrowheads, cannon balls, and all manner of artifacts around the little house. Being youngsters, they just considered these items playthings, and he now regrets that he doesn't know what happened to any of them.

There was a garage apartment back of the Flores' family home. Sometimes Carlos and his brothers slept there. He told me once when they were teenagers, he and a brother heard the neighbor's dog barking. Then, they spied a figure of a woman in a long, flowing white dress come sort of floating or gliding out of the little house and down the driveway leading to Euclid Street. She looked to be wearing an old-fashioned hooped skirt and was sort of bathed in an unearthly blue glow.

I asked Jon Thompson if he had ever had any ghostly experience in the house. He told me he had not, but sometimes he did feel a little uneasy there.

Connie recalled after she and Carlos were married, they lived for a time in the garage apartment next to the little house. Later, they lived in the Flores' family home. At the time, her little boy was about three years old and the baby was still in the crib when, one night, Carlos had gone to his bowling league. Connie and her young son were watching the ten o'clock news, and the baby was tucked away in his crib, sound asleep. Suddenly, she saw something pass by, clad in a black topcoat. The figure also wore a big black hat. She knew she had locked all the doors. She was just terrified. When her toddler said, "Mommy, who is that man?" she knew she hadn't just been seeing things since her little son had seen the figure also.

I asked her what she did next.

She said after the man passed by the doorway of the living room and she checked to see where he had gone (he had just disappeared!) she just totally lost it! She was so frightened she couldn't even dial the telephone or get up and go anywhere. She just sat in the living room, shaking, for about an hour until Carlos came home. She definitely believed the figure she had seen was a ghost!

Carlos told me right around the time that Connie saw the man in black, his uncle also saw what was apparently the same specter. As he walked along Euclid en route home from the Elk's Club, Carlos' uncle spied a man clad all in black who opened the gate and went up the walk to the deserted little house. He went through his own gate next door. Then he glanced back towards the empty little house and there was not a sign of the man in black. He had totally disappeared and was not seen again. Carlos believes this figure and Connie's nocturnal visitor were one and the same apparition.

Connie told me that one time some gifted psychics were consulted about the place, and several of them were in agreement that around the turn of the century an older man and a much younger woman had lived together in the house for a time. He was very jealous of her and completely dominated her. She wore long white dresses often sprigged with small floral prints, and they could feel her presence all around the place still. They believed she might have been killed by the man, and it may be her spirit that Carlos and his brothers saw wandering on the property.

Today, all you see is a very old and rather forlorn little house, with its windows and doors all boarded up. In view of its antiquity, it seems a shame that someone has not seen fit to restore it and put it to some good use. It so perfectly represents the type of architecture employed by the first settlers in our community back in the days when San Antonio was still just a sleepy little frontier town.

# The Hidden Wedding Gown

An interesting story was told to me by John Leal, historian extraordinaire and for a number of years Bexar County's official archivist. It is about a small house now located in La Villita. The building, which was constructed sometime in the 1860s, was originally located at 141 S Street, in the area where the Hemisfair grounds are now. It was built by an Alsatian immigrant, Cirius Gissi, who purchased the land from Charles Kaiserling for the sum of $36 in March of 1864, according to Bexar County deed records that Mr. Leal located. At the time of the fair, the property was owned by a woman named Rosaura Aldana and her husband. The city purchased the building to make way for the fairgrounds, but fortunately, because of its unique building technique, it was considered of enough historic interest that it was moved to its present location in La Villita.

The house is capped by a low pitched, hipped roof, and is constructed of stucco and plaster over cedar post palings. This was called "pallisado" construction. The house has two front doors which open onto a wide and shady front porch.

Prior to its sale and subsequent relocation, Mrs. Aldana was told that some sort of treasure was rumored to be buried behind her house. She hired a man to come and dig in her backyard. He dug for some time and made a very deep hole. Suddenly he was heard to call out, "Help . . . help . . . help me get out of here!" He had been digging when some sort of strange force started pulling him deeper and deeper down into the hole, sucking him down into the ground. He was absolutely terrified. He hurriedly filled up the hole he had dug and departed, refusing to return. As far as Mr. Leal knows, nothing was ever found there.

Then, not long afterwards, as the Aldana couple was sitting in their living room one evening, a strange thing happened. Rosaura was knitting and her husband was reading. Suddenly, she looked up and saw the figure of a little girl, who appeared to be about five or six years old, materialize out of the fireplace. The child was blonde, very pretty, and dressed all in white. Rosaura was more startled than frightened. But her husband saw nothing. And the child disappeared as Rosaura spoke.

A few days later Rosaura saw the little girl again. She appeared to be laughing. But again, only she saw the figure. Her husband did not see anything at all.

Because she was curious why she was seeing the apparition of the little girl, Mrs. Aldana decided to consult a fortune-teller. The psychic told her there was a treasure hidden in the fireplace. She went on to tell Rosaura that the family who had built the house was French. She was right. The builder was an Alsatian immigrant. They had a beautiful daughter who had lost her sweetheart in the Civil War, and she had bundled up her wedding gown and some of her trousseau items and placed them beneath the brickwork of the fireplace. The psychic warned Rosaura that these things were not meant to belong to her, however, and that she should not try to locate them. The woman told her that someone else would find them later on.

Shortly after this, the city made the Aldanas an offer for the house, and it was sold. Apparently, during the move to the La Villita location, a small bundle containing a yellowed and rotting wedding dress, some money, and small pieces of jewelry was discovered hidden in the brickwork of the old fireplace. Leal said he was unsure what had happened to the items, whether the city got them and had them stored someplace, or whether one of the workmen involved with moving the house took them. No one seems to know their where-

abouts today. And Rosaura Aldana has long since passed
away.

The reconstructed house, located just to the right of the
Nueva Street entrance to La Villita, has a plaque in front
which states it was dedicated on January 25, 1970, as a part
of La Villita.

House in La Villita

The building is currently unoccupied. Until recently it
was leased by the "Blue Lady," a well-known psychic reader.
Whether or not the little girl ghost ever kept her company, I
haven't a clue! Since the hidden "treasure" was found, it is
quite likely the little girl spirit moved on to eternal peace
and rest.

# Spirits at the Old Salinas Homestead

My friend Angela Salinas Fernandez told me that her grandparents, Angela and Octaviano Salinas, used to live in the Elmendorf community near the old Harmony School.

The Salinas family had lived on the corner of Nueva and Villita Streets, in a house that is still standing, but they decided they wanted to be further from the center of town to raise their children in a rural atmosphere. The house which they built in Elmendorf was a wooden structure with a wrap-around porch. It was constructed in 1874. The small but comfortable dwelling had a large living room which was also used for dining, two bedrooms, and a kitchen. There was no running water in the kitchen. Water was supplied by a well on the property.

In the late 1800s Angela's aunt built a house next door to the Salinas homestead. For some reason, soon after she moved in, the aunt discovered her house was haunted. Angela recalled years later that she had attended a party following a wedding in the family. The wedding party had come back to the aunt's house to open their gifts, when suddenly they heard the sounds of all the dishes breaking. A thorough search turned up nothing broken or even out of place! The bride had planned to live in the house, but gave up after about a week because of so many strange things happening there. The aunt who had built the house didn't stay long either. She rented it out to various friends and family members. No one stayed very long, according to Angela.

Angela told me that her mother recalled one time, when she was visiting her in-laws (the Salinas), she'd been washing the dishes in a dishpan in the kitchen. She went out in the backyard to throw out the dishwater because there were no drains in the kitchen. She happened to look towards the house next door and noticed a man and woman walking out of the sleeping porch doorway. They walked towards the outhouse in the backyard and both entered it. She thought they were certainly strange, because of the way they were dressed, and she waited for them to come back out so she could get another good look at them. But although she waited a good long while, they never came out! The man had been wearing a dark, long frock coat, and he had a large sword attached to his belt. The woman with him had been clad in a long, flowing white dress. She was slender, had dark hair, and was most striking. As she later thought about what she'd seen, Angela's mother was sure she had seen a pair of phantoms!

Under the old Salinas house they had discovered a big metal box. It contained an old branding iron, and a sword, much like the one the strange gentleman had been wearing! Angela said the front steps of the house used to sort of move as people would start to walk down them. This gave rise to the belief that there was money or other valuables buried beneath the house, or maybe between her grandparents' house and her aunt's house next door.

Angela told me that once, years ago, the Salinas family decided to have someone come out and dig around to see what might be found. They employed an Indian man who was known to be good at "dowsing," which was the employment of a forked rod, or stick, to find either water or metals. I presume it was the forerunner of the metal detector! However, "dowsers" were supposed to have some special gift. They were most commonly employed to locate a good place to dig a water well. This man located a place where he believed there was something buried. Angela said she was a tiny little girl at the time but recalled the incident. The man dug down quite deep and finally hit a metal box. Quite a crowd of family and interested friends had gathered to watch the operation. The Indian man turned and told the gathering, "This box is full of money, but it will turn to ashes, because someone here is very greedy." When he pried open the box a thick, grey smoke rose up in the air and the box was indeed found to be filled with still-warm ashes!

# A Ghost from the Graveyard

On San Antonio's northeast side, in a fairly new, modern subdivision, we have some friends who until recently lived in a nice Spanish style home that's only a few years old. Nothing about the house or the neighborhood would indicate that the place might be haunted. But Olga Castaneda and her daughter, Roslyn, say it is, or at least, used to be when they occupied the house.

Olga saw the figure of a young woman standing in the doorway of her bedroom on two different occasions. Both times the woman was standing sideways, in profile. She was wearing an ecru-colored Victorian style dress which seemed to be made of either lace or some sheer fabric, like chiffon or organza. Her hair was piled high on her head in the style of the late 1800s.

The first time Olga saw the figure, which disappeared almost as suddenly as it had appeared, she didn't mention what she had seen, or thought she had seen, to either her husband, Robert, or her daughter. She was afraid they would think she had gone a little "strange." Then, one morning not long after Olga first saw the apparition, Ros brought up the subject by asking her mother if she believed in ghosts. She went on to tell Olga she had seen the lady in her room, and she described the same figure that Olga saw just a few days before. And then, a few days after that, Olga saw the figure once more, as she appeared again in the doorway to her bedroom.

A short while later the neighbors told the Castanedas that just over on the other side of the easement behind their house where there is a grassy, overgrown area, there are the remnants of a little country cemetery. Olga is reasonably sure the young woman she and her daughter saw occupies one of those graves. Perhaps the farmhouse where the young woman once lived was on the very site of the house where the Castanedas lived. Or, maybe, the other-worldly visitor just preferred the nice, modern, well-appointed house to the weed-infested graveyard where she was laid to rest. Given a choice, wouldn't you?

# The Beautiful Brooks House

The charming Victorian house on Crofton Street that I wrote about at length in *Spirits of San Antonio and South Texas*, in the story which was given the title "The Ghost That Observed Halloween," has since changed owners. Cynthia and David Wiggins have painstakingly restored and decorated the house that for years was known as the Brooks House. In fact, the fruits of their labor were featured in a color spread in the September 3, 1995 edition of *Sunday Images Magazine*.

Liz Wiggins, the lovely daughter of the retired army officer and his wife, showed me through her parents' home. Later, I was able to visit with Cynthia Wiggins and learned that the house still has a mischievous little spirit hanging around. Several times the Wiggins have been startled to hear a doorbell ringing. A quick trip to the front door always reveals an empty front porch. The most unusual thing about these "visits" is there is NO doorbell!

The house, which was built in 1890, was once owned by Judge Sidney Brooks, father of aviation cadet Sidney Brooks Jr., who was the first San Antonio aviator to die in World War I activities.

According to information I gleaned from a commemorative program that was published November 7, 1992, in observance of the 75th anniversary of Brooks Air Force Base, Sidney Brooks was a handsome young cadet aviator at Kelly Field back in 1917. The military had just begun to train pilots for service in World War I. Brooks was preparing to make a final solo flight before receiving his commission as a first lieutenant. He had some strange misgivings about that flight, which was to be cross-country from San Antonio to Hondo and back. The night before the flight, which was scheduled for November 13, 1917, Brooks visited his friend Stuart McManus, who was working as a night clerk at the Menger Hotel. Brooks told McManus that he had a premonition that he would not solo successfully. McManus told his good friend that he would do just fine and he was just having a case of the "jitters."

Brooks and several other cadet fliers took off and flew to Hondo, about forty miles west of San Antonio. They landed there and had a short rest before taking off for their return flight to San Antonio. Just as Brooks' JN 4A aircraft reached the edge of the runway, it nosed over and crashed. Friends and officials with the American Flying Corps, as the Air Force was then known, speculated that Brooks might have fainted in the cockpit. He had been given an anti-typhoid shot earlier in the day. Little was known at that time about how much stress flying put on the human body. Ironically, the problems attached to flying and the technicalities of space medicine are tackled, and often solved, today in the modern laboratories at Brooks Air Force Base, named for young Sidney Brooks just three months after his tragic death. The base later became the training ground for many aviation greats including Charles Lindbergh and Claire Chennault.

Sidney Brooks had planned to be married after receiving his commission. He was engaged to Lottie Jean Steele. The young woman said she was in the backyard of her Terrill Hills home the afternoon of November 13 when she plainly heard the voice of her fiance. He called out to her, not once, but twice. She later learned that she heard his calls at exactly the moment his plane crashed!

The body of the young aviator lay in state in the front parlor of his parents' home on Crofton Street before being taken to the nearby Alamo Street Methodist Church where the funeral services were conducted.

Sidney Brooks never realized his dreams of becoming a flying officer or of claiming Lottie Steele as his bride. Perhaps he rests in peace knowing an Air Force base was named in his honor and a beautiful marble and granite monument topped by a five-foot bronze eagle has been placed there in his memory.

And how wonderful the Brooks' family home is still being preserved and cherished by its present owners!

# A Sad Little Spirit

The people who own the house in this story don't want their names mentioned. It always makes it harder to write a story when some of the facts must be altered or disguised due to the requests of the persons involved. But I will give this story, which really is unusual, my best shot, anyway.

I first met Mr. and Mrs. Curtis, as I shall call them, on one of my *Spirits of San Antonio* ghost tours. Curious, they had signed up to see what a ghost tour was all about. During the course of the evening they confided to me that they had a resident spirit where they lived.

The house in which the family lives is situated on the northwest side of San Antonio in an affluent neighborhood off De Zavala Road. The couple lives in the attractive one-story brick dwelling with their two daughters, one a high school senior, and the other a young widow with a two-year-old daughter.

The Curtises had only been living in the house a short while when they began to sense the presence of someone or something there with them. The younger daughter, Carrie, once saw someone pass by her as she sat in the family room. And she often senses someone moving behind her. The fiance of the older daughter, Mary, who spends a great deal of time visiting at the house, recently saw the apparition of a young woman walking past the door of the room in which he stood. She was blond, and he noticed she was wearing a white blouse. Also, he says he has heard a female voice call out the name of his fiancee several times. The strong fragrance of a perfume they cannot identify sometimes permeates Mary's room as well.

Curious as to why their home might be haunted, the Curtises decided to check into the former ownership of the house. They learned that the people from whom they had purchased the house had a teenaged son who was a high school senior. His girlfriend had spent a lot of time at his house where she was always welcomed by both his parents, his siblings, and his friends. The girl apparently didn't have a close relationship with her own parents, and so she enjoyed spending time at her boyfriend's house.

Towards the end of their senior year in high school the young couple had some sort of disagreement and broke up. The girl was extremely disturbed over the breakup. And, maybe she was upset about other things; an argument with her parents or a disappointing grade in school. No one seems to know for sure. Anyway, one afternoon just before the senior prom, the girl telephoned the boy and told him if they couldn't get back together she was going to kill herself. He tried to talk her out of it, but suddenly, even as they spoke, he heard a loud report, followed by total silence on the line. Disturbed, he drove to the girl's house as quickly as he could. Sure enough, there all alone in her parents' house, she had placed her father's gun to her temple and pulled the trigger. The boy was devastated. The whole high school was in a state of shock that a popular student would so tragically end her life. The boy's family sent him to stay with relatives in another city for a while, and then they decided to sell the house which held so many memories of the girl for their son.

After learning the background of the young woman's spirit, Mrs. Curtis realized that some photographs of a young teenaged boy and girl she had found on a closet shelf when they moved in must have been photos of the boy and his dead girlfriend. She doesn't remember what happened to them; she thinks she probably just tossed them out since they held no significance to her family. Could it be that the young girl's spirit is searching for them?

The Curtises asked me if it would be possible to bring a psychic out to their house. In April of 1996 I asked Sam Nesmith if he would accompany me. Sam asked if he could bring Robert Thiege along also. So the two men and I drove out one afternoon where the Curtis couple and their younger daughter, Carrie, awaited us. The two men picked up the presence of the young woman almost immediately. They felt her presence near a wedding portrait of Mary, the Curtis' older daughter, which hangs in the living room. They also smelled a strong floral cologne around the photograph.

Sam told us that he had often heard suicides continue to come around a place until they use up the length of time they would have been allotted to live on this earth had they not taken their lives. Therefore, he feels the spirit of the girl may cling to the house, where she had been happy, for some time to come.

Before we left the house, we all gathered in the sunroom which overlooks the patio and swimming pool. I said to Sam and Robert, "So you fellows feel her presence here in the house. Do you really think she's still around?" There was then a distinct "rap!" sound as if someone had sharply rapped their knuckles on the wall right next to me. I said, " Is that you, dear? Are you trying to let us know you are here with us?" Again, there came the unmistakable sharp rap on the wall! No one else in the room could have made the noise.

The Curtises said they had been discussing moving to another state, where Mr. Curtis had a better job offer. Sam said the little spirit had become comfortable around them and was probably distressed they might be leaving, and that is why she seems to be around most of the time now. She just doesn't want to let the family out of her sight.

As we drove home after the visit with the Curtis family and their little spirit, both men were very quiet and thoughtful. All of us felt sad for the little lost spirit of the young girl. Finally, Sam ventured to mention the possibility that perhaps the girl had not just been distraught over the breakup of a teen romance, which was hardly enough to cause her to commit suicide. He theorized, what if she had found out she was pregnant and had no one to turn to? What if the boy had turned his back on her, and she knew she couldn't discuss it with her parents? Wouldn't that have given her a feeling of total desperation and desolation? She could certainly have felt sufficiently rejected and disturbed to have committed suicide under those circumstances. Robert chimed in he had also been thinking along those lines, and then I had to admit the thought had crossed my mind as well. All three of us were very depressed thinking of the senseless loss of one so young.

I spoke on the telephone with Mrs. Curtis shortly after our visit. She told me that Carrie had recently had a couple of strange experiences with the spirit. One night just after she went to bed for the night, the face of the young girl appeared just above her head and then floated upwards to the ceiling where it completely disappeared. Then, a couple of weeks later the face appeared again. This time the daughter was lying on her side and she saw the face at eye level as if the spirit was kneeling by the side of her bed. The face was quite white and Carrie said it had an imploring, seeking look like the spirit wanted to talk. In just a moment the face disappeared. Naturally, Carrie was quite unnerved by the appearance of the wraith on those two different evenings.

Mrs. Curtis says they have been hearing the heavy, thudding sound of something being dropped on the floor. But nothing has been dropped! And several times Mrs. Curtis thinks she hears her younger daughter calling her, but when she checks, she finds that whoever she heard was not her daughter! The same thing has happened to Carrie. She thinks her mother is calling her, and when she goes to see what her mother wants, she finds it was not the voice of her mother she heard!

The Curtises plan to move to another city soon. They sincerely hope the little lost spirit will find some peace and rest and will not follow them when they leave San Antonio.

# The Lara's Likeable Ghost

It was quite by chance that I talked with Anna Lara, wife of Mario Lara. I had called the Lara residence to speak to Mr. Lara about his experiences at the Hertzberg Circus Museum. His wife answered the telephone. She had read a couple of my books, and before she turned the phone over to her husband, she told me about some of her own brushes with the supernatural! Ever since she was a youngster, Anna says, she seems to have had an affinity for dwellers of the spirit world. She recalls most vividly that period of her life when she was in her early teens. She spent much of her time in those days visiting with a young married sister and her husband in an old house they rented. The Spanish type home, with a fountain in the front patio and lots of pretty tile both inside and outside of the house, was located on the south side of San Antonio.

Often when Anna visited she recalled experiencing great gusts of wind blowing down the hallway, even when there was no breeze blowing outside. Doors slammed behind her as she walked, and the winds blew with such force her hair would be mussed up. She just knew there was "something strange going on" in that house. Anna, who was about fourteen years old at that time, told about one summer night when she slept over at her sister's house. A young niece was sleeping with her in a small bed when Anna was suddenly awakened by water pouring onto her face and nightclothes. She woke her niece and also her sister and brother-in-law. They turned on the lights and found no water dripping from the ceiling, yet Anna's face was dripping wet and the sheets and her pajamas were soaked. Strangely enough, this was just on her side of the bed. Her niece had no water on either her person or her bedclothes!

Anna also recalled she had talked with some friends about going swimming the next day. However, after that strange night, she decided that "something" was trying to warn her about water, and she decided not to go swimming after all!

Anna's sister was getting more and more uncomfortable in that house and they decided to move. Just before they left, Anna said she saw an intense flash of white light dance over her. The whole family also heard scratchings under the floor. At first they thought maybe an animal might be under the house. Finally, Anna's father came over and took up the floorboards in three different places. There was just dirt under most of the house but they also discovered a big block of cement in the ground under the place where they had heard most of the scratching noises. Afraid to investigate any further, they replaced the floorboards and left the concrete section under the house undisturbed. Anna firmly believes either something of value was buried beneath the cement or, perish the thought, somebody was buried there! The fear of the latter is what motivated the family to leave the concrete section alone. Anna says that she would not be at all surprised if the slab is still there, undisturbed, beneath the old house.

The day that Anna's sister and brother-in-law moved away from the house, Anna was with them. They all got into the car and just as they drove away from the house for the last time, Anna chanced to look back at the house. She will never forget what she saw! There, standing inside the front window was the figure of a man, dressed, she says, "like a conquistador... a helmet and breastplated armor. He was just looking at us as we drove away."

The following year when she was only fifteen, Anna married her childhood sweetheart, Mario Lara. The couple has now, at this writing, been married twenty-one years. Anna says they've lived in three different houses and have had several supernatural experiences in each place. Today they lease a house on West Mistletoe. They've been there for ten years now, and along with their daughters and a two-year-old grandson, they also share the premises with a ghostly resident, whom they believe is a male spirit.

At this house Anna says they've all seen black shadows take form in the hallway. She has heard a man's voice softly murmur "Anna," right in back of her, but there is never anyone there when she turns around.

Soon after his mother's death, Mario was sad and depressed one evening and he couldn't seem to sleep. As he lay in bed thinking about his mother, he suddenly felt something sit down on the bed beside him, and then a soft hand gently stroked his back as if to comfort him. But there was no one in the room with him. He thinks it might possibly have been his mother's spirit, or else it may have been the spirit in the house who just came to be sympathetic.

Anna's two-year-old grandson has also seen something there. He told the Laras "I saw a man." He also said he had seen a little dog under a chair. Their sixteen-year-old daughter has seen the shadow of a dog on the walls of the house as well.

Anna believes that the household ghost is a loving spirit and it just likes the Lara family. She feels it cares about them, and she is not at all frightened by its presence. She does wish, however, that she knew who it is and why it is there.

# The House in Emerald Valley

I met Alfred and Debby Moreno one January Saturday afternoon when I was at the Bookstop at 281 and Bitters Road to autograph some of my books. The couple confided in me that they believed in ghosts because they'd once lived in a house that certainly seemed to have been haunted. Although they no longer live in the place on Cliff Path in Emerald Valley in the northern section of San Antonio, they vividly recall many of the unexplained things that happened there to make them believe their house had another occupant!

Although the Morenos lived there about ten years, they didn't tell many people about their "problem," because they didn't think anyone would believe them, and they just weren't quite sure what to do about it anyway. Alfred said they just learned to live with it and tried not to let it bother them too much.

The house was fairly new when the Morenos moved in. At first they didn't notice anything out of the ordinary. Then, not long after they'd settled in, Alfred was taking a shower one afternoon when he noticed a female shape standing on the other side of the frosted glass shower door. Thinking it was Debby, he spoke to her, but she didn't reply. A few minutes later she stuck her head in the bathroom and said, "Who were you talking to?" Alfred answered, "You, of course. You were standing right there outside the shower." When Debby told him she wasn't, it made him start to wonder. After that, there were numerous times that he would see the shape just outside the shower door, but a glance outside always revealed no one was there. At the same time, things were moving about the house; items the couple knew had been in one place would suddenly disappear, only to reappear sometime later in a place they knew they had never left them. Debby said plastic dishes left stacked on the kitchen counter fell mysteriously during the night to the floor. This happened several times.

The family pets, a dog and a cat, often seemed to sense the presence of something they didn't understand. The animals would sometimes get up and stare as if they were seeing something, or they would start to follow "it" as the Morenos referred to their unseen presence.

Now that they are no longer living in the Cliff Path house and are enjoying a ghost-free environment, the Morenos said they liked reading about the ghosts in my books, because they know they don't belong to them!

# A Baby Cried

Sheriff's Deputy Nancy Baeza used to live on the south side, near Brooks Air Force Base. The address was 2902 Lasses Boulevard. Nancy had a new baby. It was a good, happy baby, cooing and laughing, and cried very little. Yet, Nancy and her husband constantly heard the sounds of a baby crying. She said it was a "sad, hurting little cry." Once when her baby was only about three weeks old her sister and brother-in-law came over to see the new addition to the family.

Nancy said her brother-in-law said, "Why don't you go see about the baby? It's crying." "No, she's not," Nancy told him. "She's sound asleep." He got up and went to the room where the baby was indeed, sound asleep. His face was pale as a sheet because while he stood gazing at the sleeping baby, he still heard the baby crying!

Nancy learned that just behind her house there once was a state-owned orphanage. Only a few foundation remnants are left now. Nancy asked me if it could be possible that the spirit of a little foundling baby who once lived in the orphanage has come back to the neighborhood?

The neighbors on both sides of the Baezas also had some strange experiences they couldn't explain. One man said he and his wife placed a carton of eggs on the kitchen counter. When they came back to the kitchen they found every single egg was perfectly cracked right around the center of each egg. The cracks were all identical. They were dumfounded by this, because they'd checked the carton before they bought the eggs to see none was cracked.

The neighbors on the other side of the Baeza house said they often heard music playing when they had neither a radio nor a television set turned on.

Nancy says she thinks there are definitely strange vibes in her old neighborhood, and she was glad when they moved away!

# The House on the Bluff

When Harriett and Doug Raney and their children, Jennifer and Lee, moved into their spacious new brick home on the edge of the bluff in the prestigious development known as Bluffview, they had no earthly idea they'd soon be sharing their new address with a spirit from another world!

Only later, after they'd settled in, did the Raneys learn a little of the house's history. Built as a spec house in 1980 or '81, the builders sold it prior to its completion. A couple saw it and fell in love with it and were just waiting until it was completed so they could move in. Unfortunately, the wife died before the house was completed, and so the couple never got to live in the place. Soon after, a wealthy bachelor purchased the house and lived there several years. Then, this gentleman married and moved his new bride to his ranch. That is when the Raneys purchased the house.

At that time, the Raney children were still in school. Lee was an eighth grader and Jennifer was a junior in high school.

Harriett spent most of her time at first unpacking, decorating, and generally getting established in the new house, which is quite large. It wasn't long before she began to wonder if she was alone in the house while she went about her chores. She heard footsteps walking down the upstairs hallways, yet a careful check always revealed no one was there. She said the footsteps were fairly heavy treads and discernible as footsteps and not sounds like a mouse or a squirrel might make scurrying about.

Jennifer's room was upstairs adjacent to her brother's room. From the first day she occupied her new quarters, there was something about the room that troubled her. She felt a presence there, as if she were not alone, and it often made her uncomfortable. Often she got up in the night and moved into a second-floor guest room, where she felt more secure, until finally, she didn't even bother to retire in her own room at all. Later on, she felt so uncomfortable even being upstairs, she moved downstairs to her parents' master bedroom suite! She told me that's where she stayed until she finally went away to college!

Harriett told me one time when they had a houseguest from California to whom the guest room was assigned, Jennifer was forced, however reluctantly, to stay in her own room. The houseguest remarked, after her first night, that she'd heard footsteps in the hallway outside her door, and thinking that young Lee might be sleepwalking, she decided to investigate. When she opened her bedroom door she fully expected to see Lee, or some other member of the Raney household, up walking in the hall. Jennifer remarked to her, "See, I told you there is a ghost upstairs." It was soon after this incident that Jennifer moved downstairs.

In addition to the eerie feeling there was a presence in the house, Harriett said often there was the fragrance of a strong perfume that was always prominent in just one part of the living room. It had a fresh floral bouquet, a pleasant aroma, but strong enough to get everyone's attention!

Once, when the Raneys had guests and everyone was gathered in the family room, Jennifer came in from a date and went straight upstairs to her room. In just a few minutes there was a loud thud, and Jennifer came running down the stairs to report a large mirror had fallen off the wall in her room, a mirror that was attached to two fifty-pound molly bolts. It seems the adults in the den had just been discussing ghosts, and one of the guests, a lady who believed in regression and former lives, had been expounding upon her beliefs just at the time the mirror fell. Jennifer thought the ghost didn't like to be the subject of discussions and that is why she (Jennifer

always thought the entity was a female spirit) would get upset and make her presence known in one way or another.

Harriett told me when the family goes away on trips the
motion detector alarm often goes off, although there are no
cats or dogs left there when they go away. And the toilet
flushes frequently when no one has been near the bathroom.
(I hear this a lot when people talk about their haunted houses!)

Jennifer is grown and married now and doesn't live in the
Bluffview home with her parents any longer. But once, soon
after she married, she and her husband, Dave, visited the
Raneys. Dave's aunt had also come over to the house. As the
discussion got around to the ghost, the aunt, who is psychic,
suggested they go up to visit Jennifer's old room. She and
Dave and Jennifer were in the room and Dave's aunt said,
"Now, let's just sit quietly and see what might happen." Suddenly, Jennifer said, "She's here. I feel her." Dave's aunt
agreed. And just then, a large picture that was hanging over
the bed moved, quite discernibly. Harriett said Dave was out
of the room and down the stairs in record time!

Harriett feels like the spirit is only making infrequent visits now. She still feels uneasy when she is in certain of the
upstairs rooms. She doesn't use her computer much because
it is located in an upstairs loft where she feels uncomfortable.
But she hasn't heard the footsteps for a couple of years, nor
has the fragrance of the perfume been in evidence lately. This
is a great relief to the Raneys.

When I spoke with Jennifer, she said she's glad the spirit
seems to have gone on, or at least settled down, and she is
gladder still she isn't living there anymore.

My personal theory, based on what Harriett and Jennifer
told me, is the woman who loved the house, but who died
before she could live there, might be the returning spirit. She
wanted to spend a little time in the home she'd hoped to live
in before moving on to peace and rest. She knows the Raneys
love the house and are taking good care of it, so her presence
won't be in evidence there much longer.

# A House Amid the Brambles

My friend Jackie Weaverling has had several brushes with the supernatural. She believes there are such things as spirits. Jackie told me that she has a cousin who used to live in a haunted house, and she wanted me to meet her and hear her story. Finally, we were able to get together: Jackie, her vivacious blonde cousin, Edie Dugosh, and I. We met on a hot July afternoon, and Jackie drove us out to the house where Edie and her husband, Eddie, and their four children lived from 1969 to 1976. On the way we stopped to pick up a friend of Jackie's and Edie's, Vicki Rizzo.

Believe it or not, this was the first time that Edie had returned to the old house since she moved away twenty years ago! The place is located on a sizable piece of acreage on the far south side of San Antonio. The address on the gate reads 1166 West Chavaneaux Road.

Located in a veritable thicket of shrubs, tall grass, and brambles, the old rock house is almost invisible from the road. We had to walk across a weedy field of ankle deep grass and cockleburs to reach the place, which is partially surrounded with a wall surmounted by pillars. The wall, which I judged to be about four-and-a-half-feet high, is made of the same native limestone which was used in the construction of the house.

In spite of its totally deserted and neglected condition, one could tell it had once been the proud residence of someone who put a lot of work, money, and careful planning into it. There's an open upstairs porch, or veranda, several attractive curved arches over doors and windows, and skillfully done stone

A House Amid the Brambles

work. There's a bit of Spanish influence in the architectural style.

Edie told me a lot about the house as we drove out. It had been "love at first sight" for Edie, and she was delighted when she and Eddie were able to lease it. She recalled how hard she and Eddie, and even the children, had worked to clean up, fix up, and paint up, all at their own expense, since it was a rental property and the owners didn't seem to care. Later on, when they had the place in really good order, they pleaded with the landlords, a group of Houston physicians, to sell the house to them. The doctors refused to even consider an offer as they were using the property as a tax shelter. Because they wanted to own their own home and not pay rent to someone else forever, after six years the Dugoshes reluctantly moved out, and until our visit, Edie hadn't seen it in over twenty years. I could see she was greatly affected. So was I, and I'd never even been near the place before! It seemed such a sad thing for such a fine home, a mansion almost, to be deserted and neglected. The two-story house, which I would judge by its architectural style of stone construction with a lot of casement windows, probably dates from the 1930s or '40s. The back door stood wide open to the elements. We didn't go upstairs, nor into the basement, but we roamed all over the ground floor, where paint had peeled off walls and ceilings and lay in dry dusty curls upon the rotting floors. The kitchen, where Edie said she'd cooked so many good meals for her family and friends, had an interesting, wrought iron room divider between the cooking area and the breakfast nook. The green painted divider was done in an intricate ivy leaf pattern. There was a spacious dining room, that still bore the mirrored wall which Edie said she had installed, and the living room was really huge, with a beautiful stone fireplace. The house has an interesting floor plan and must have been a fun house in which to live and entertain guests. To think the owners wouldn't sell the property to the Dugoshes, who really wanted it, and preferred to have it sit, vacant and slowly rotting away, is truly deplorable. A home which could have been preserved is now a total derelict. The feeling of decay and moldering is everywhere. Edie said the yard, now a tangle of weeds and underbrush, had also been very lovely, with a beautiful magnolia tree and lots of rose bushes and flower borders.

Neighboring families had told the Dugoshes, just about the time they moved in, that the house was reputed to be haunted. Edie never learned all the facts, but the gist of the story was that an early occupant (she doesn't know if it was the original builder or someone who lived there later on) went berserk and stabbed all of his family to death and then killed himself. They were also told that no one had ever lived in the place for very long. It seemed that all the families who moved in lost a family member shortly after they became occupants of the house. According to what Edie was told, numerous people had died in the house.

Edie said when she and Eddie were young, with a family of little children who needed a country place to grow up in, and there was so much work to do to just get the place where it would be livable, they didn't have time to chase down any "fairy tales." Now, looking back, Edie says she wishes she had learned more about the background of the house.

When I prompted her to come up with specifics, Edie couldn't recall any dates, but she said there were many things that happened "from day one" to convince them that the place was haunted, by probably more than just one ghost. For instance, they had a piano in the living room that many times started to play in the middle of the night, just simple little tunes, and sometimes it sounded as if a student was just practicing scales. All the Dugosh family were sleeping when the unseen musician decided to play these nocturnal concerts.

There was a large billiards table at one end of the big living room. It was visible from the stairs leading to the upper floor. Often, in the middle of the night, Edie heard the sound of the wooden balls being hit by a cue. She said she'd get up and dash down the stairs to see who was playing pool in the middle of the night. No one! She usually got to the stairs just in time to see the balls still rolling about on the table!

Edie often caught glimpses of a shadowy figure passing by her field of peripheral vision. This happened to other family members as well. And, she said the house was always cold, even with the heat turned on and a big fire burning in the fireplace. I noticed it was quite cool inside on the very hot July day when we visited. One would have expected the place to be stifling hot. Of course, we all know that cold spots are often indicative of hauntings.

The Dugoshes all love animals. They all ride and raise horses. They once even owned a pet shop. They had a number of dogs and cats on the place while they lived there. The dogs often gathered in the front yard and barked and barked, the hair bristling at the backs of their necks. It was as if they were surrounding some unseen enemy. They'd sort of form a circle and bark at whatever they sensed was in the middle of the circle. When Edie mentioned this to the neighbors, they were not at all surprised. They said the dogs were seeing the spirit of the man who had killed his family in the house before taking his own life.

A stray cat, oversized, with long white hair, blue eyes, and a cropped tail, appeared at the house and stayed around the property during the entire time the Dugosh family lived there. They fed him, but he usually hissed at them and remained more or less a wild creature. The first time Edie saw him was startling in itself. The first night the family slept in the house, Edie heard what she thought was a little child crying, "mam..ma...mam..ma." She got up and checked the rooms of all four of her children. They were sound asleep. Again she heard the plaintive cries. Then she looked out one of the bedroom windows and saw this huge cat sitting on a back fence pillar howling and yowling. His cries sounded just like a little child crying for its "mam..ma." Edie went on to say the cat did so many strange things she was convinced the animal was "possessed."

Besides the lower floor which we walked through, there is a full basement in the house. This is a rather unusual feature in a South Texas house, since it's hard to build a basement digging down through solid limestone. The basement was fully finished when the Dugoshes moved in. Looking back, Edie says many of the "bad things went on down there." There was a big room with a stone fireplace and a lovely hand carved bar right under the living room. It had probably been used as a den or playroom. Then there was a big utility room, a storage room, and a little apartment that had probably been used as maid's quarters during the occupancy of previous owners. Edie said they didn't use the basement much as it needed a lot of work done to it when they moved in, and it was always very "creepy." To top it off, they had found several snakes down there as well!

For some reason there were thirteen steps leading down to the basement level. Edie said several times her children went down there to play, and when they tried to open the door which closed the area off from the stairs, they found they were locked in. Try as they might, they couldn't open the door. When Edie answered their calls and banging on the door, she always found the door was not locked at all. Yet something was preventing the youngsters from getting out of the basement!

Upstairs, between the master bedroom and one of the children's rooms there was a big bathroom. Several times, Edie recalled, the light would come on and the door would open. The faucet in the basin would start to run. All this was annoying in the middle of the night. One especially cold night, Edie recalled thinking, "It's so cold . . . I hate to get up . . . oh, I do wish somebody would turn off the faucet and turn out the light and close the door." No sooner said, than done! The light went out, the water drip stopped, and the door gently closed. Edie recalled saying "thank you," before she fell asleep!

Later on, after Eddie Dugosh's father died, his mother moved in with the family. She occupied the only bedroom on the ground floor. It was at the back of the house. Edie said her mother-in-law often saw "strange shapes and figures" and just knew that something unexplainable was going on there.

Although Edie firmly believes the house was haunted, she was never particularly afraid. She said this was probably because she loved the house so much. Sometimes she found the various sounds, like the nocturnal piano practice sessions and the billiards games, a little annoying and certainly puzzling. But she said she had put so much work, energy, and love into the place and had made it so attractive and comfortable, that in spite of some of the annoyances associated with living in a haunted house, she really was disappointed when the owners refused to sell the property.

Only after they moved their belongings out and Edie walked through the empty house one more time to see if anything had been forgotten, did she get a really eerie feeling. And so she never went back until the day we visited the place.

Later, Edie called me to say she and Jackie and Vicki had gone back to the house a couple of weeks later. They went upstairs this time, and Edie said the former master bedroom was freezing cold, on a July day when the thermometer was registering 100 degrees Fahrenheit!

I am still saddened by the utter waste of such a lovely house. I wonder if it is even haunted anymore. I don't think even a ghost would be contented in such a depressing atmosphere.

# Haunted Houses Side by Side

I first met Katherine Long at one of the English teas that Victoria's Black Swan Inn sponsors from time to time. She told me that she had a ghost story she would like to share with me for this book, and as soon as we could arrange a time mutually agreeable to our busy schedules, we discussed her very unusual and interesting situation.

Katherine Hinojosa, her former husband, and three children, lived on Windlake Street on the northwest side of San Antonio. Eddie Long and his wife and two boys lived next door. The Hinojosa and Long children played together, and the neighboring families were good friends.

Then, Eddie's wife walked out on the genial metal worker, leaving him and his two teenaged boys in a state of shock. About a year later, Katherine Hinojosa had much the same thing happen to her. She returned from work one day to find a farewell note from her husband! The attractive brunette was left to struggle with the raising of three children, virtually alone.

Because the neighbors were already good friends, Eddie and Katherine naturally sort of gravitated towards one another. They would chat in their yards between the two houses and discuss child-rearing problems. It was sort of a "misery loves company" companionship at first.

Then, in 1975 tragedy struck the Long household. Eddie's young son Bryan, who was fifteen at the time, tragically died in an accident on his motorcycle. It was caused by a drunk driver. Katherine tried to help Eddie deal with the grief, a sorrow that has never really left him, over the death of his son.

In 1978 the couple decided to get married, and I must say they seem extremely compatible.

Now for the ghost story! When Katherine's three children were between nine and thirteen years of age, the family began to feel there was some sort of entity in the house. This was just shortly after Bryan Long was killed. Katherine was the first to feel the presence. Then, she began to hear footsteps, and they sounded as if they were made by small feet wearing tennis shoes! The entity seemed to run in, then out, of the house, slamming doors, dashing down the hallway, etc. It was an active little spirit! Finally, as time went on, the spirit started to actually manifest and the Hinojosa family all saw a small boy of about eight years of age, with sandy hair and fair skin. Glimpses were always fleeting, and the little figure appeared to be rather transparent as well. Often when he dashed out of Katherine's house, she would see the apparition float out towards the Long house next door. It was all very puzzling.

Katherine's children noticed the entity and discussed him quite candidly with their mother. They said, "Oh, he's running down the hall again." At first Katherine thought she heard one of her own children running around the house, and the three siblings at first blamed one another for the noise, slamming doors, etc, but soon they realized none of them was at fault. There was also a big, easy-to-climb mesquite tree right next to the house. Katherine's trio of children had often climbed the tree to gain access to the roof. Sometimes when the whole family was inside the house, the Hinojosas heard something hit the roof and the footsteps were heard to dash back and forth over the gentle slope of the roof on the one-story ranch-style house.

There were little pranks, too. Katherine said things started suddenly disappearing. A letter, placed on the hall table ready to be mailed, turned up missing, Her favorite fountain pen, kept close by the telephone, disappeared. The remote control for the TV set, always kept on the lamp table next to Katherine's recliner, was nowhere to be found. Then, suddenly, the missing objects reappeared in totally unlikely places where Katherine knew they were never kept! At times Katherine thought she might be losing her mind!

All along, unknown to Katherine, next door Eddie Long was coping with much the same sort of thing. He was trying to raise one young son while still in deep mourning for Bryan. Then, suddenly, Eddie started to see a shadowy little figure of a young boy as it would peep around corners at him. This happened most often when he was in the hallway headed for his bedroom or the bathroom. These appearances were extremely unsettling to Eddie.

All the time Ed and Katherine were seeing one another and getting more serious, until they finally married, neither one told the other of the strange little spirit they were encountering. In fact, as we talked, it became clear that Katherine and Ed kept the little visitor a secret from each other even after they were married. Katherine said that she didn't want Ed to think she was strange, and he apparently was thinking the same thing. The couple kept both houses, side by side, and today Katherine's mother lives in her former home and Ed and Katherine reside in the Long house.

Katherine and Eddie both work. Her mother began to come into their house in the mornings to tidy up and put in a load of wash for the Longs. This was a lot of help for Katherine. Then, one day her mother called Katherine and asked her to come next door as she wanted to talk with her. She told Katherine, "I don't want to come next door to that house anymore. I'm sorry I can't help you, but that house is haunted. That little boy ghost keeps running back and forth, and he makes so much noise. I just don't feel comfortable going over there anymore."

Finally, Katherine decided she had to discuss the situation with Eddie. She recalls telling him, "Eddie, you're never going to believe this, but please listen to me anyway. And please, don't think I'm crazy."

When she told Eddie about the little boy spirit, she added, "You can ask Mom. She saw him, too." She felt this statement would add a little credibility to her story.

Imagine her surprise when Eddie said, "Oh, that. I know all about him. He's been peeping around corners at me for years."

The secrets released, the Longs then discussed what they might do. They decided to take a course in Reiki, which is the ancient Tibetan art of healing and cleansing, under the tutelage of Kathleen Bittner, who is a well-known professional psychic in San Antonio. They felt the little spirit needed to be told he didn't need to hang around them anymore. He needed to go on to the light. They had no idea at this point who he was or why he visited the side-by-side houses. The only explanation they could get from Mrs. Bittner was the little spirit was lonely and looking for a playmate, and he moved into a place where there were other children. Of course, now the children have grown up and are no longer playmate material!

Katherine studied hard and finally felt she could perform a cleansing ritual. It employed the ancient Tibetan rites of burning sage to purify the atmosphere. She told the little boy spirit they all loved him but it was really time for him to move on to a better place. She told him, "We release you into God's arms."

The ritual seemed to have worked, because the spirit wasn't seen or heard around anymore. But strangely, Eddie seemed to really miss the little spirit and became quite depressed after the cleansing ritual.

I thought that was about all to the story. Then Katherine called me soon afterwards, quite excited. Accidentally they had met a woman who told them she was a medium. They mentioned Ed's grief over the loss of his son, and she said she was quite sure she could reach him. The medium came to visit the Longs, and the woman told them the little boy spirit who had long bounced back and forth between the two houses was actually Bryan Long. He explained his presence as a younger child because that was his happiest, most carefree time of life.

He went on to say during his early teen years, after his parents divorced, he had been bitter and unhappy. He had felt resentful towards his parents because the family had been broken up.

This would, of course, explain why Ed felt so close to the little boy spirit, as if it was taking the place of his own son. In reality, it apparently was his son, returning at a younger age, not an uncommon thing for spirits to do.

Bryan's spirit knew Eddie was sad that Katherine had asked him to leave. He spoke, through the medium, and told his father he is now at peace and has learned a lot about forgiveness. He has forgiven his mother who left him and his dad and brother, and he has also forgiven the driver whose drunken behavior caused his death. He feels it was really his time to go when he died, and he assured his father he is contented and at peace now. The spirit concluded by telling his father he loves him and says he will come back sometimes to visit, but he is contented now and wants his father to be happy, too.

Now, I don't know a lot about mediums, other than what I have read. But there have been many documented cases of communication with the dead through these gifted people. I believe this woman solved a real dilemma for the Longs. They've weathered a lot of storms together and can look forward to many happy years of contentment, knowing Bryan has moved on to eternal peace.

# The House at Long Acres

I met Craig and Tom Grover at a class I conducted for "Oasis" back in 1995. I had been asked to discuss some of my research of the supernatural and tell some of my stories to a gathering of senior citizens. After my talk, Mrs. Grover came up to me and confided that she believed in ghosts because she had coexisted with one for a time. Later on when I contacted her, she was willing to share this interesting story with me.

The Grovers bought a frame house on a good-sized piece of property which they call Long Acres. It is on Vance Jackson Road, near Mission Trace. Soon after they moved in, they remodeled it, covering the exterior with fine old handmade bricks. The remodeling job was so successful the house was featured in *House Beautiful Magazine*. The Grovers have lived there over forty years and have watched the city gradually move northward until their "country home" is no longer in the country!

Soon after the Grovers moved in, they noticed various things disappearing. Then, they would reappear sometime later. This was both puzzling and annoying, but at first they paid little attention. Just about that time, Craig said she had acquired a Ouija board, which she and a friend sometimes used, "just for fun." They amused themselves by asking it questions. Then, one day she was listening to a popular talk show host, the late Alan Dale, on a local radio station. He mentioned Ouija boards and went on at length to say he thought they were dangerous and harmful and that people who had them should get rid of them. Craig had already decided the thing sort of spooked her, and so she did get rid of the board. Looking back, she believes the manifestations started just about the time she and her friend were "playing around" with the Ouija.

At the time, the couple were having some pretty serious arguments and disagreements, and Craig now believes it was all tied into the presence of a malevolent spirit in the house. She said she was actually considering getting a divorce. She decided to join a Christian discussion group called Inner Peace, which met at various members' homes. The leader was a lady named Virginia Stavinoha, whom Craig says was very sensitive, and also psychic. Craig told Stavinoha about some of the things that were troubling her and how strange happenings were taking place in her house. When I questioned Craig about these happenings she cited several examples.

For instance, Tom had a tie tac which he really liked. It was gold set with a ruby. Although he had bought it at a flea market, he later discovered it was a valuable piece of jewelry, and he enjoyed wearing it often. He always left it on the dresser in the same spot whenever he removed it. One day it turned up missing. The couple searched the whole house, even emptying the vacuum cleaner bag, looking for it. They failed to find the missing item. Then, a couple of weeks later, it reappeared right on the dresser in the same spot where Tom always left it!

Craig also said whenever she went into the master bedroom a sudden cold breeze seemed to envelop her, and this was most disturbing.

The strangest thing of all was the "case of the orange patent pump." Craig had a pair of orange patent-leather pumps, which she kept up on a shelf in the hall closet. One of the shoes started to regularly appear in the bathroom just after her husband had been there at the lavatory, shaving. She asked him why her shoe was there, and he didn't know what she was talking about. One day she'd just realigned the shoes on the shelf in the hall closet and had seen the orange pumps well established in their usual place on the shelf. She went to the back door to call her husband, who was outside in the tool room, and as she came back into the hall, one of the orange pumps was on the floor. The shoe moved several times more, and Craig became more and more disturbed and puzzled.

Another strange thing that happened while the spirit was active in the house occurred right after a good friend from Houston had visited the couple. Just after she departed, Craig went back into the guest room she had occupied and found her friend's hair dryer lying on the dresser. She called her friend after she figured she'd had enough time to get to Houston and told her not to worry about the dryer; they had found it and would mail it to her the next day. Their friend said she hadn't even unpacked her suitcase, so she hadn't missed the dryer.

That same evening, David, the Grover's son, who was home visiting from the University of Texas in Austin, had taken a shower, and when he came out into the bedroom he saw the dryer lying on the dresser. He picked it up and used it. He later remarked to his mother she needed to send it back to her friend, and Craig told him they planned to pack it up and ship it to her the next day.

The next morning when Craig went into the guest room to get the dryer to wrap and mail it to Houston, it had literally disappeared! She and Tom looked everywhere for it, but it was nowhere to be found. Furthermore, they never did find it!

But a short while later, the friend from Houston called to tell them that the dryer they found in the guest room wasn't hers. She had just unpacked her suitcase and it was right there. Talk about strange!

All these things led Craig to ask Virginia Stavinoha if she thought they might have a malevolent spirit in the house. The leader of the spiritual group agreed to come out one afternoon and visit with Craig and Tom. She asked if she could go alone into the master bedroom. After she came back from meditating in the bedroom, she told the couple that she had, indeed, made contact with a female spirit named "Elsie" and she was extremely hostile. This was during daylight hours. Virginia asked the Grovers if she could return and spend a night in that room.

Soon afterwards, Ms. Stavinoha was as good as her word. She came and spent the night in the house. She told Craig that "Elsie" did not like living in the country and had insisted to her husband that he sell the house. According to what Virginia learned from her visit with the spirit, she hated living in the house, which was then pretty far out of town. She also hated her husband, Herman, and another man, named Leonard, a friend of her husband's who often visited him. Strangely enough, Craig told Virginia the previous owner had been Elsie Tammen, who had lived there many years.

Virginia reported all this to Craig and Tom, and in a few minutes they all walked back into the master bedroom where Virginia had her long visit with Elsie's spirit. They were all astounded to find all the bedclothes in great disarray, as if the covers and pillows were hurled from the bed in a fit of rage! Virginia had told Elsie's spirit she no longer belonged there and it was time for her to move on to the light where she would find peace and rest, and that she needed to give Craig and Tom some rest as well. Soon after this overnight visit by Virginia, and her subsequent talk with the spirit, things started to settle down. Craig and her husband started to communicate better, and the problems they had been having were soon resolved. This was many years ago. They are still happily living together!

This just goes to prove that even malevolent spirits can be calmed down by the right person with the right frame of mind!

# The Old Farmhouse

Norma Breedlove used to live out in the country in a place called the old Weiderstein house. It's located south of Randolph Air Force Base off farm to market road 1518. Some of the property is now a part of a par 3 golf course.

In May of 1969, soon after the Breedloves rented the hundred-year-old house from a widow and her family whose name was Benke, some strange things started to happen. The Breedloves had just hired a young woman to come out and do some housework for them. The agreement was that they would come into San Antonio to pick her up; she would cook dinner and spend the night and then clean and cook all the next day. Then they would take her back home. They hoped she would be able to do this on a weekly basis for them. Well, they brought her out to the house. She cooked a very nice dinner for them and then soon retired to her room. When the Breedloves awoke the next morning, the woman was all dressed and announced she wanted them to take her back to San Antonio. She didn't want to stay and work for them after all. When questioned as to why, she said right after she went to bed, an old man came drifting in, right through the window, and stood at the foot of her bed and just stared at her. When the Breedloves checked, they found the window was nailed shut!

Norma went on to tell me the house they rented had been restored, except for one bedroom, which was used as a store-room. The rest of the place was furnished with antiques, which the Benke family had rented out with the house. It seems that Mr. Benke had passed away. Norma believes the man that appeared first to the maid, and later on to other family members and visitors, might have been the ghost of the former owner.

After about three years, the Breedloves moved. After that, the house was greatly remodeled. The old round cupolas in front have been removed, and Norma says the house doesn't look much like it did when she lived there. The beautiful old barn was converted to a garage. Whether or not the ghostly old gentleman still comes around, Norma has no way of knowing.

# A Strange and Shocking Story

The woman who told me this story about her house and its former owner has asked me not to reveal her identity or the street address of her home. Like other sources I have interviewed, she's just not sure how the story would be accepted by her friends and neighbors, and I certainly respect her wishes, although I do not necessarily agree with her. Frankly, I think they would be fascinated by the story!

I shall call the owners of the house Sara and Tom Percy. However, all the rest of the characters are referred to by their real names, and the story is all true and well documented.

I first met Sara Percy when I was invited to speak to a local women's club one fall morning in 1995. After my talk, she told me that she had a story she would like to share with me if I would like to hear it. Of course, I was immediately "all ears," ready to hear what she had to say regarding her own personal experience.

It was some time before our respective busy schedules allowed us time to get together. I finally spent a pleasant afternoon chatting in her cheerful two-story Georgian-style home located on a quiet street in the prestigious Terrill Hills section of San Antonio.

While Sara told me she has had several experiences in the house that convinced her it was haunted, there was no atmosphere of sadness, anger, evil, or depression that I could discern. I found the place very pleasant, and the atmosphere cheerful and friendly. Sara admitted there have been no recent manifestations, but she believes that it was haunted for a time, at least, by the former owner of the house, Dr.

Lloyd Ross, who built it for his wife, Gladys, and daughter, Mary Ann, back in 1941.

And therein lies a most unusual, sad, and shocking story.

Sara loaned me a copy of *Take a Deep Breath*, by Dr. Elmer Cooper, M.D. (Nortex Press, Austin, 1992) in which he begins a most interesting review of his own life, with the opening chapter centered around his old friend Dr. Ross. This chapter, entitled *Murder Under the Oaks*, is beautifully written, and while it describes a most heinous and bloody crime, it also shows the great admiration, respect, and esteem that Dr. Cooper had for Dr. Ross. After a long telephone chat with Dr. Cooper, I drew the conclusion that the passing of many years has not changed his opinion of Ross, and that his friendship has remained steadfast.

It seems that Lloyd Ross and his family arrived in San Antonio in the early 1940s with impressive credentials. He was trained at Boston's Lahey Clinic and Massachusetts General Hospital. Evidently, his surgical skills and judgment became well known right away. The Rosses soon made a place for themselves in San Antonio society. They bought a lovely home in Terrill Hills, joined the San Antonio Country Club, and Gladys Ross soon became a social leader. She helped to found and served as president of one of the city's most prominent garden clubs. The vivacious brunette was a sought-after guest at social gatherings, and her reputation as a gracious and elegant hostess was well known.

Dr. Cooper describes Lloyd Ross in great detail, and I quote a passage from Chapter One of his book:

> A typical "Type A" personality, Lloyd was the greatest perfectionist I have ever known. He was obsessive, comprehensive, compulsive, brilliant, and extremely correct in manner. A quick sense of humor and capacity for camaraderie with his colleagues saved him from being resented. Always meticulously groomed, moderately tall, round faced, with brown hair, steady myopic brown eyes behind thick horn-

rimmed glasses, he looked every inch the imposing doctor-deity as he strode authoritatively through the corridors of the Santa Rosa Medical Center.

Cooper goes on further to say that the Catholic nuns on the nursing staff at Santa Rosa adored him, his patients greatly admired, indeed, almost idolized him, and the whole medical community respected him greatly. He stayed with his patients in the recovery room until he was sure there were no complications, he visited them up to three times daily, and he made each one feel special. Little wonder that patients bragged about "their surgeon" as if having gone under the knife of Dr. Lloyd Ross was some kind of status symbol!

Cooper and Ross seemed to have hit it off well and often referred patients to one another. Cooper is an internist, while Ross was a surgeon. Each had high regard for the other and knew their patients would receive the highest caliber of care when entrusted with one or the other of these physicians. Cooper states:

> Responding to one another's perfectionistic approach to medicine, Lloyd and I soon developed a beautiful reciprocal relationship. When I referred surgical cases to him, I did so knowing my patients would receive treatment as fine as was available anywhere in the country. He had the same admiration for my medical capabilities, and called me as consultant when confronted with internal medical problems. In unusually difficult cases, he always requested I be present during the actual surgical procedure to cope with any medical exigencies that might arise.

It just seemed natural that the two doctors would become friends on a personal level as well, and they did. They often had dinner together and their wives became friends. Dr. Cooper says that the Ross home was flawlessly immaculate. Everything was always perfectly orderly, not a pillow rumpled, or a flower wilted. He said that he and his wife found it hard to believe anybody actually lived in such meticulous order! The Rosses, with their young daughter, who was a gifted pianist and an honor student, seemed to live the perfect life. They were attractive, respected, and admired by all who knew them. And they were comfortably well-off financially as well.

Ross had made a lot of money. But he had little time to check into investment programs. His time was all taken up with being the perfect surgeon.

Enter, one Willard "Mike" York.

York was a bright investment banker who had been a patient of Dr. Ross. The man had an outgoing personality, and the two men soon developed a close personal relationship. Ross started using York's services as an investment counselor, and it wasn't long until he had turned over quite a sum of money to the banker to invest. Ross also recommended York's services to Cooper, who had treated the man for cardiac arrhythmia. Dr. Cooper said that Mike York was a very attractive man who, although he was small of stature, had a commanding presence. He had a boyish, round face, ruddy cheeks, thinning sandy-colored hair, and deep blue eyes. Cooper found him to be quite charming.

Evidently the Yorks and the Rosses became very close, dining in one another's homes, attending concerts together, going to the same church services. Their young daughters were the same age and shared the same interests, so they became good friends as well.

Then one day in 1947 a short article appeared in the *San Antonio Light*. The newspaper reported that the SEC was investigating one Willard York. It seems that the investments banker was speculating on the market with money his friends had entrusted to him, thinking he was purchasing stocks and bonds for their investment portfolios. He had even given them all bogus investment reports showing what their investments were worth. With some of the money, he purchased a 1,600-acre ranch in Comal County, about twenty miles north of San

Antonio. Unfortunately, his speculations did not pay off, and he lost most of the money that had been entrusted to him to invest.

Dr. Cooper told me he lost quite a bit, around $12,000, but more or less wrote it all off to experience and poor judgment on his part, and he just decided there was no use worrying any more about it. He was, of course, shocked at what Mike York had done and was disappointed in the man, whom he had trusted.

Cooper's friend Dr. Ross was literally devastated. He had handed over a sum of money exceeding $100,000 to a man he had trusted as his best friend. Realizing he had been swindled by a con man resulted in a great blow to his self-esteem. He became extremely depressed, indeed, almost paranoid, over what had happened. Dr. Cooper said that he, some other doctors, and Gladys Ross all tried to tell Lloyd Ross that he would soon recoup his losses with his great surgical skills, and they advised him just to write it all off to tough experience. But he just couldn't get it off his mind. He engaged a lawyer to bring suit against York. He turned down surgical cases, stayed home, and brooded in his study.

Finally, he had all the self-recrimination he could stand. He had not been able to pull out of his depressed state. He and Gladys weren't getting along too well of late. He blamed himself for being so stupid and trusting, and now Gladys had started to agree with him. His ego had become just about as flat as the bank account he had entrusted to York.

Finally, something within him snapped. The great mind of this brilliant surgeon was filled with dejection, humiliation, disappointment, and anger at a man he had trusted, a friend he had loved. The pressure must have built up within him like a great pressure cooker, so filled with steam, the lid just had to finally blow off.

The time had come for Lloyd Ross to take care of things in his own way. And he did.

On Saturday night, June 16, 1947, Ross took his wife Gladys out for dinner at the nearby San Antonio Country

Club. After they came home, he sequestered himself in his upstairs study. For the rest of the evening he tore up personal papers and sorted out things in his desk. He was getting ready to do what he had to do.

On Sunday morning, June 17, Dr. Ross didn't go to church as was his custom. He got up early and dressed and got into his car and headed north out of the city.

It didn't take long to arrive at the Comal County location of the York ranch. He parked beneath a tree alongside the rough, isolated, twisting land that led up to the ranch house. He parked his car so that the front protruded into the road, blocking the passage of any car that might approach. He didn't have long to wait.

According to Elmer Cooper's account, this is what happened:

Presently York appeared at the wheel of his new Buick sedan, en route to church. With him were his wife Gertrude, his mother Mary, and his two children, John and Ann. York slowed when he saw the Ross car, stopped, and put his head out the window on the driver's side and greeted Lloyd in a friendly manner. Dr. Ross approached the car slowly, and when he came abreast of the open window, poked in the head of a rifle which he had held hidden behind him, and blasted away. Willard York sustained three bullet holes in his body and died instantly, slumping behind the wheel of his new Buick. Gertrude York's bullet-ridden body was found huddled in a pool of blood in the passenger's side of the front seat. A white hat and her white gloves, intended for church, were found, unstained, on the seat. Their nine-year-old son John had two bullet wounds in his body and was found near the right-hand door, clutching a bouquet of colorful wild flowers, intended for church. York's mother Mary, aged sixty-seven, seated in the back between the two children, was shot five times. Her body lay crumpled on the seat.

Ann York, eleven, the sole survivor of the massacre, jumped from the car when the shooting began, having managed to open the left rear door, and fled for her life through the rock-strewn road into the woods. She was shot in the right hip as she jumped from the car. In the insane melee of the moment, Ross' glasses fell and shattered on the stony road. Being extremely myopic, he was unable to follow Ann as she raced, dripping blood from the hip wound, through the woods to the nearest ranch house approximately a mile away. In partial shock, she weakly pounded on the door, attracted the attention of the startled neighbor, and gasping for breath, blurted incoherent details of the terrible tragedy before collapsing.

No shoot-and-run sort of killer, Dr. Ross managed to drive back to San Antonio even though his glasses were broken. He went straight to the police department, where he told the authorities, "There's a rifle in the trunk of my car and apparently it has been fired." The doctor was taken into custody immediately. Later, he was charged in Comal County with the murders of Willard and Gertrude York, their son, John, and York's mother. He was also charged with wounding little Ann York. The resulting trial was lengthy and sensational, and the final verdict was guilty by reason of insanity. Although Ross escaped the death penalty, he was remanded to the Texas State Hospital for the Criminally Insane in Wharton, Texas. His sister, Renna Ross, a spinster, so loved her brother that she moved from her home in Ohio to Wharton so she could visit him as often as she was allowed.

Dr. Cooper said it took quite a while for him and his wife to get over the terrible shock of what Lloyd Ross had done. It had been so out of character for the kindly man. And the sisters at Santa Rosa mourned him as if he were dead. No one could comprehend what had sent this gentle, kindly, dignified, and dedicated physician over the brink. He just wasn't a classic killer type, and the shock of what he had done was not easy for those who knew and loved him to either accept or forget.

Dr. Cooper said the Santa Rosa sisters visited him at the prison hospital regularly. Cooper said he also visited his old friend. He found Ross to be totally unrepentant, saying that his act was a result of heavenly voices commanding him to eradicate the York family from the face of the earth! Evidently, the verdict of insanity handed down by the jury was a correct one.

All during the time Ross served out his sentence in Wharton, his wife never once visited him. She literally severed all connections with him. It must have been painful and embarrassing for the once prominent social leader and sought-after hostess to fall from the "top of the heap" and become an object of pity, shunned by her former acquaintances. She had been humiliated by the label of "murderer's wife." She cannot completely be faulted for the attitude she adopted towards her husband.

Sadly too, Gladys Ross and her daughter, Mary Ann, somehow became estranged during the young girl's teen years. The girl disowned both of her parents and was last reported married and living somewhere in California.

During all the thirty-five years that Ross was incarcerated, Gladys never divorced him. She lived all those years alone in her immaculate house, a virtual recluse. She had little to do with the outside world until Alzheimer's disease forced her to take in a housekeeper-companion to live with her. Later, her sister from Ohio, Corrinne, came to live with her as well.

When Corrinne decided that Gladys Ross needed constant supervision in a nursing home atmosphere, the house in Terrill Hills was put up for sale. That is when Sara Percy first saw the attractive gray house with its black and white trim. Although Mrs. Ross was not at all receptive towards strangers, she seemed to take a liking to Sara and let her wander through the rooms of the house. Even throughout her illness, Mrs. Ross was still totally obsessed with her home. It had to be immaculately kept all of the time, and absolutely nothing could be the least bit out of place. She even covered all the commodes in the house, except the one in her own private bathroom, with plastic wrap to keep them clean and from being used! Sara admits she is a little that way, a compulsive house cleaner, but certainly not to the extent that Mrs. Ross seemed to be. Sara also told me the house bore strong resemblances to her husband's parents' home in Houston, and that the couple felt at home the minute they walked in the front door. It didn't take the Percys long to decide they wanted to buy the house.

Because the couple had never divorced, the house was in both Dr. Ross's and his wife's names. Sara had to journey to LaGrange to where Dr. Ross had lived since he was freed from prison. He actually had been taken in by the family of Sheriff Prilop there. Ross's trial had been held in LaGrange, on a change of venue, and the sheriff was quite taken with the doctor, realizing that this was no ordinary mass-murderer. When Dr. Ross was released from prison, Gladys Ross would not allow him to come back home. The kindly sheriff and his family took the old doctor into their own home. When Sara met Dr. Ross and had him sign the bill of sale, she said he was getting up in years, probably in his eighties. After all, he had served thirty-five years of his life in prison! She found him to be courtly and polite, a brilliant, articulate conversationalist, and a complete antithesis of what one would expect a murderer to be like. Sara and the old doctor actually became friends, and he telephoned her periodically to see how she was getting along in his old home. Once, she recalls, when she had been ill, he called to inquire about her health and insisted she pay a visit to her doctor. Of course, Sara had the good taste never to discuss his former life with him, either his days in prison, or the terrible tragedy that led to his imprisonment.

Sara and her husband had a great time redecorating the house, changing the color schemes from the almost "hospital green" that Gladys Ross had chosen for the draperies, carpets, and wall coverings, to a more neutral and certainly more restful color scheme. Today it is furnished in a Williamsburg-Georgian style, elegantly understated and in excellent taste.

Not long after the Percys took up residence in their new home, Mrs. Ross and her sister moved back to Ohio. In fact, Sara said she drove them to the airport when they departed. She doesn't recall just when, but she heard that Mrs. Ross passed away soon after she returned to Ohio.

In 1993 Sara and her husband received word that Dr. Ross had died in a LaGrange nursing home. It wasn't long after this that she began to have the feeling that there was a "strong presence" in the house. She began to hear footsteps on the stairs and on the upstairs hardwood floors. Sometimes the unseen walker would pace back and forth, back and forth. Then, she often would feel as if someone was standing right next to her, and several times she felt a hand gently touching her back. It was never a shoving or hostile touch at all. She sometimes smelled cigar or pipe smoke when the "I know I'm not alone in this room" feeling crept over her. She said most of the manifestations happened in the mornings, and only to her. Her husband never experienced or heard anything. But then, he had never met Lloyd Ross, either. The old doctor was Sara's friend. These feelings were strongest between August and October of 1995. Lately Sarah has not felt the unseen presence or heard the footsteps treading on the floorboards.

I would suggest that the spirit of Dr. Lloyd Ross came around for a time to see his old home again. He probably wanted to be assured it was being well looked after. Since he had met and apparently liked Sara Percy, I believe he has quietly gone on to eternal rest, convinced his beloved home is in good hands. After a tragically turbulent life, culminating in thirty-five years at the correctional facility, the one anchor he had held onto was knowing the home he loved and jointly owned with his wife, Gladys, would be there awaiting him upon his release from prison. However, because his wife had turned her back on him, and his daughter had disowned both of her parents, he was never able to see the house again. And so, when he died, his spirit did what he in life could not do. He was free to roam the quiet, tranquil rooms again, his footsteps resounding on the once familiar stair-treads and hardwood floors.

I believe that Dr. Ross's spirit is satisfied that his home is in loving hands. The physician who saved many lives before his troubled and tormented mind snapped, causing him to take four lives and no doubt disrupt many others, paid his debt to society. Now it would seem that at last he deserves to lie down to pleasant dreams.

# The House in Hollywood Park

Donna Keith lives in a pretty house in Hollywood Park, on land that used to be part of the historic old Voigt Ranch. Her story is about a ghost who came and stayed awhile and now seems to have moved on, since she has had no recent manifestations or disturbances.

When Donna and her family moved in, back in October of 1973, her husband was still on active duty with the Army at that time. The house they decided to buy had been unoccupied for about three years. The original owners were Mexican nationals. The custom-built house had especially wide doorways to accommodate the wheelchair that the mother-in-law of the owner had to use. Evidently, the Mexican family didn't pay their property taxes, and there was a foreclosure. The man was allowed to remove his furniture and clothing before the place was padlocked.

Soon after the Keiths settled in, "things" started to happen. They would go out and return to the house to find their belongings piled up on the dresser, drawers messed up, chairs and other things moved around. Careful checks revealed there had been no break-in, and nothing was ever missing. But these experiences continued, much to the consternation of Donna and her husband. They even talked to the poltergeist, telling it to "cut that out," but it did little good.

One afternoon when the Keiths had a group of friends in to watch the Army-Navy football game, they all watched the TV button go off. They and their friends actually saw the button turn. Then they told the spirit to stop that, and soon the set turned back on again, after they told it firmly, "Leave us alone. Can't you see we are trying to have a party?"

After Donna's husband passed away, the spirit seemed to go away for awhile, but then it eventually came back. Donna said she often sensed somebody behind her, but of course, when she turned to look, there was never anyone there. Sometimes the feeling something was there was so strong that she got very angry, and she would literally yell at it to go away. While never malicious, the poltergeist was irritating at times. Donna said several times the neighbors had reported seeing a light, like someone carrying a flashlight, appearing in her backyard at 2 or 3 o'clock in the morning.

Recently, Donna has experienced no manifestations. Perhaps the spirit realizes Donna is there for the long haul, she's taking good care of the house, and she's not about to be scared off! So why bother her any longer? We believe the spirit has probably gone back to the other side of the Rio Grande!

# The Hill Country Haunting

Dorothy Zimmerman and I met quite accidentally. My husband, Roy, and I were with a tour group we were accompanying to Nuevo Laredo on a shopping excursion. Dorothy and a friend were Christmas shopping at the marketplace. She and her friend sat down at a table next to ours to enjoy a cooling drink, when she happened to notice my name tag. She remarked to me that she knew who I was because she was in the process of reading one of my books. She went on to tell me she had once had a resident spirit at her house and would like to tell me her story. Shortly afterwards I called her, arranging to meet with her in her home.

Dorothy has a couple of interesting hobbies. She is a collector of nativity scenes from around the world and has over seven hundred examples, from very large creches, to tiny ones that can fit into the shell of a walnut. There are elegant porcelains, delicate crystals, and primitive folk art sets. Dorothy said she used to put them all away every January and get them out to display every December. Now, with so many in her collection, she just leaves them out year round, and just about every available bookshelf, tabletop, and what-not cabinet is used to display the sets.

And Dorothy also loves violets. Quite by accident she started her violet collection when she purchased a few old postcards which had violet nosegays depicted on them. She mounted these in a glass frame. One thing led to another, and another collection was spawned! She has clustered violet bedecked postal cards and greeting cards in frames all over the house, and there are shelves of violet decorated teapots, cups and saucers, ornamental plates, tea sets, and vases in several of her rooms. Violet embroidered pillows adorn her guest room bed as well. I laughed and told Dorothy that I hoped she never has to move as it would certainly be a chore to pack up all of her collectibles!

The house where these collections are located is one that Dorothy and George Zimmerman purchased in 1961. It is a rambling ranch-style house which was built on a ten-acre tract in Hill Country Village by C.A. Bitters. The house, constructed in 1946, was built as a country retreat for the Bitters family. In those days, Hill Country Village was considered to be way out in the country. The Zimmerman house on Black Hawk Trail is one of the first houses built in the development, which is located on part of what was once known as the old Walker Ranch.

The Bitters sold the place around 1953 to Dr. and Mrs. Nicholas Wertherson. The doctor was one of San Antonio's pioneer heart surgeons. His wife was employed at Southwest Research.

When the Zimmermans bought the house their children were still small, and they felt the country would be a good place for them to grow up. But it wasn't long after they purchased the place that Dorothy started to feel that there was something, or someone, there with her family. The first indication of something strange occurred one evening when she was in the kitchen preparing dinner. Her husband was reading in the living room. Suddenly, a favorite cut glass bowl on the dining room breakfront was hurled across the dining room, landing on the floor where it shattered into a thousand pieces! George yelled at Dorothy, "Why on earth did you do that?" Just as startled as her husband, Dorothy replied, "I thought you did it, George. Can't you see I'm out here in the kitchen?"

Then things started to disappear. The favorite items seemed to be earrings and scissors. Dorothy said sometimes she'd take off her earclips and put them on the coffee table. Then when she went to pick them up, they'd be gone. And she usually kept some needlework on the couch, with her yarns and scissors on a lamp table next to it so she could do a little work at night while she watched television. She said her scissors were constantly disappearing and she never found a single pair! She said she bought a new pair every time she went to the store for anything! She was really upset when her good topaz earrings, a pair she really treasured, turned up missing. Also, one night after the Zimmermans returned from a social function, she removed her black suede opera pumps. That night they totally disappeared and were never seen again!

All these things were very upsetting to Dorothy. And she told me she also felt a cold spot in the entrance to the hallway which ran from the living room to the bedroom wing of the house. This also led Dorothy to believe there was a ghost of some sort in the house. Her husband really didn't believe her until one evening when they had come in from the airport where Dorothy had picked George up after he'd come home from a business trip. When they walked into the house, they found the big goldfish bowl had been hurled across the room from where it usually sat on a glass shelved cabinet, and fish, glass, water, and plants were all over the floor. Where it landed, it could not have just fallen, it was too far from its usual place. Someone or something had thrown it, causing it to land at the other side of the room.

Dorothy told a friend about all these occurrences, and her friend took her to see a well-known local psychic named Joe Holbrook. The minute the women walked into his office he asked Dorothy, "You have an entity in your home, don't you?" She told him she thought she did and went on to tell him some of the things that had happened. Holbrook arranged to come out to visit and see what he could determine. During his visit he told her she did have a resident spirit, and it was a young woman who was murdered around 1918 or 1919. The psychic went on to say she was only about eighteen years old at the time of her death, which was caused by stab wounds inflicted by a drunken man. Holbrook believed she was killed somewhere in the Hill Country Village locale. Because she was so young at the time of her death, her spirit had not been able to accept the fact she was dead. She communicated to the psychic that she liked being around the Zimmerman place because the family seemed to be good to her.

This helped Dorothy understood why the things that disappeared were items a young woman would take. She said she finally started setting an extra plate and silverware at the table for the little spirit who had told Holbrook her name was Lucille. She said she wanted to stay on the spirit's good side, since she was obviously there to stay!

Holbrook went on to tell Dorothy that the whole Hill Country Village area was a haven for various spirits, and not all of them were nice. He said at least one of them was extremely malevolent, but he believed as long as Lucille was making her home with the Zimmermans they would not be troubled with the evil spirit. Dorothy told me that almost everyone she knew who lived in Hill Country Village in her neighborhood there on Black Hawk Trail and surrounding streets had suffered major tragedies. Several families lost loved ones in accidents. Three or four young people committed suicide. One entire family perished in a private plane accident. The daughter of neighbors across the street was killed in an accident. And then tragedy struck at the Zimmerman home, too. Their nine-year-old son was struck and killed by a car as he crossed Bitters Road just a few blocks from his Hill Country home.

I told Dorothy I found her remarkable to have remained there after all these things happened. She told me she did finally decide to do something when things kept disappearing and Lucille's behavior was becoming a bit annoying. She had a group of friends who professed to be able to exorcise spirits. They came out and burned candles, recited prayers, read the Bible, sang hymns, and did all sorts of things, some of which Dorothy could not explain, to try and get Lucille to move on to a place of light. They told her she didn't have to stay there any longer, and it was all right for her to move on. They must have been successful, because Dorothy says she doesn't seem to be around anymore.

Dorothy says sometimes in a way she sort of misses Lucille, as she had grown so accustomed to her presence, but at least now she knows where all her scissors are!

# The Firefighter's
# Haunted House

Larry Casas, a San Antonio firefighter for eighteen years, has an interesting story to tell. About ten years ago he and his sister, Yolanda Casas, a detective with the San Antonio Police Department, purchased a house in Valley Forge as an investment. Yolanda first lived there alone, then when she decided to move, Larry moved in and the single man has made the comfortable brick dwelling his home ever since.

Casas told me the place is close to Comanche Hill, an area once used as a lookout point by Indian tribes in the area. Today it is marked by a nineteenth-century stone tower. The whole area is dotted with small fields and vacant lots. Larry has seen a number of old grave markers here and there, doubtless the final resting places of pioneer settlers to the area.

The Casas's house is about thirty years old. Larry doesn't know much about the previous owners. But he firmly believes there is at least one resident spirit in the house.

Actually, Yolanda first discovered there might be an entity in the place prior to the time Larry moved in. An orderly person, she would be in the midst of tidying up her house, cleaning closets, dusting, and vacuuming the rugs when she began to notice, on a fairly regular basis, her newly vacuumed carpets had little child-sized footprints appearing all over them. She found this to be extremely strange!

Larry definitely believes there is a little boy spirit in the house. He has dug up broken toys in the yard while putting in flower beds, indicating a little boy might once have lived there.

And he thinks the kind of pranks that the spirit pulls are the mischievous sorts of things a little boy would enjoy doing.

Larry says he's a collector of all sorts of things. He likes antique furniture, and he also has a collection of interesting memorabilia and old toys. Some of the toys he says are "collectibles," toys that will appreciate in value if kept in mint condition. In his bedroom Larry has a hutch on which he used to arrange his toys and collectibles. He said there are two ornamental poles that hold up the shelves on the hutch. On one of them, as a note of whimsy, he once attached a Kermit the Frog, one of the originals, which had legs that were held together by Velcro. They were easy to wrap around the little pole and made to look as if Kermit was climbing it.

Well, early one morning Larry had just climbed into bed (remember, he's a firefighter, who often works all night and has to sleep in the daytime). He had not yet drifted off to sleep when he heard a strange noise. Then he realized what it was he was hearing. It was the tearing noise that two pieces of Velcro make when being separated. He opened his eyes just in time to see the Kermit frog toy in mid-air flight, inching its way towards where he lay in bed, as if it was being carried by unseen hands. Larry said he yelled and jumped out of bed; at that moment Kermit fell to the floor just before reaching the edge of the bed. Larry still can't explain it.

Casas went on to say that many times the toys on the hutch would be moved around the house, even though he knew no one had been there, and the burglar alarm, which is always set, had not gone off. Once, when he came home from work, every single lamp in the house was on the floor. None was damaged in any way. They had to have been carefully picked up and removed from their lamp tables and placed on the floor. But by whom?

Larry said a friend gave him a pretty little Oriental doll for his collection. He had just set it down on the couch. He left the room for a few minutes, and when he returned the doll had been moved to the opposite side of the couch.

Other things happened. Once the washer started up and apparently ran by itself even though there were no clothes in it and no one had turned it on. It was going through the wash cycle as Larry arrived home. And often, on cleaning day (Larry says he's not like a lot of bachelors; he actually likes to clean!) when he cleaned his mirrors around the house, no sooner would he have them all shiny and bright when something would come along and mess them up with smears and fingerprints. And he said the curtains would often billow and blow like a terrific breeze was passing through the house. Yet, he said the windows were always closed and locked and he has no explanation for this unusual occurrence. Sometimes Larry finds the towels scattered all over the floors. The television set changes channels all by itself. And frequently, when he picks up the telephone to dial outside, he hears some sort of preaching or religious service going on through the receiver. He can't explain any of these things.

The only time Larry has actually seen a ghost in his house was once, in the early morning hours when he had just come in from work. He had gone to bed, pulling the covers up over his head, as is his practice, in order to keep the daylight out of his eyes. Then he felt a strong presence in the room, right by his bed. He peeked out from under the covers and saw plainly a man standing right beside the bed. He had on a fedora hat and a trench coat. He was dressed in much the fashion that George Raft and Humphrey Bogart used to adopt in their films of the 1940s. Larry said he yelled at the figure, thinking that his home had been broken into, and the figure just sort of "melted down through the floor." Larry says he still hasn't quite recovered from that experience!

When I questioned him further, Larry said he hasn't had too many things happen just lately, except for the towels being scattered around the floors on a fairly regular basis and the telephone picking up religious services which he can't explain. He says he finally packed all the collectible toys away, and he thinks maybe the little boy spirit doesn't find the place as interesting anymore.

Larry kept telling me he thought he was a sensible, rational person, and what has happened in his house can't be reasonably explained, and that really bothers him. I assured him he was not alone and not to think he was strange because he had experienced some of these things. I just told him, this is an old city. It's old land. And there are lots of things out there we just can't understand.

# Is the Portrait Haunted?

George and Gloria Ybarra are a lovely couple who live in the Colonies North area. They once went on one of my *Spirits of San Antonio* tours. The veteran San Antonio firefighter and his wife, who is on the staff at the University of Texas at San Antonio, told me they had a spirit at their house and would be glad to tell me their story. Of course, I was interested!

The twenty-five-year-old brick home in the upper middle-class neighborhood was purchased about eighteen years ago by the Ybarras. They don't know much about the previous owners. George said the first owners divorced, and the next owners, from whom they purchased the house, were a Braniff Airline captain and his wife.

It wasn't long before George began to feel like there was some sort of presence connected to the house. Shortly after they moved in, one morning about 11 a.m., George was going out the front door when something hit him on the top of his head. It hurt! But he looked around, could see nothing or no one, and could find nothing to indicate what had hit him. He knew no object had fallen, and no one was in sight around the porch. It was both a painful and puzzling experience.

A couple of weeks later, one of the Ybarra's daughters was leaving the house, and again it was exactly 11 a.m., as she was headed to church. As she went out the door she felt hands grip her shoulders, hard, and push her. She lost her balance and barely was able to catch herself in order to avoid a bad fall. It was on the exact spot where something had hit her father a few weeks before.

Gloria told me that over the years a number of puzzling things have happened in the house. Once, about eight years ago, when they had house guests from Laredo, one of the guests was in the bathroom. She was startled when two drawers just popped open and then slammed closed by themselves while she was in the room. She said it looked as if someone had done this, but of course she was alone in the bathroom. Or was she?

George told me one morning when he was out mowing the lawn, he distinctly heard sounds of children's voices coming from the direction of the girls' bedroom. He knew Gloria had gone to the store, and he just believed the children were there in their room, playing. Imagine his surprise when a little while later, Gloria drove up into the driveway, and the two little girls got out of the car. They had gone to the store with their mother! George still can't explain how he heard youngsters laughing and playing when no one was in the house.

Doors open and shut and the bathroom faucets turn on by themselves frequently as well. Gloria told me she doesn't know if a painting they have might have something to do with the strange things that have happened in the house, but she did bring it up. She said just before they moved to the Colonies North house, she bought an old oil painting at a garage sale. It is a portrait of a not-very-attractive old man, surrounded by some rather sad, wilted-looking flowers in the background. There is a lot of writing on the paper backing of the picture, but it is in German, and the Ybarras had never had it translated. I managed to get the writing translated, but it only revealed the name of the company which framed the strange work of art. Gloria said when one looks at the painting in a certain light, crosses of varying sizes seem to appear all over it. It is an eerie painting. George says it is just plain ugly. Gloria seems somehow attached to it, so it remains in place on the wall.

I told the Ybarras there is always the possibility the resident spirit in their home is connected to the painting, since I know of other incidences where this has happened. Getting rid of the painting might make life a little more serene at the Ybarra household, and then, maybe not. The Ybarras seem to have no reasonable answer for the various manifestations they have experienced over the years. And neither do I.

# The Spring Branch Ranch

Kim and Scott Knowlton live on a piece of property that was once known as the old Wehe place. The Wehes were a German family who farmed and ranched in the Spring Branch community north of San Antonio in the late 1800s. The house occupied by the Knowltons was built on the property around 1920, but Kim isn't sure of the exact date.

The original stone house, of one-story pier and beam construction, consisted of a living room, two bedrooms, and a very small kitchen. Sometime around 1970, a portion of the wide wrap-around porch was enclosed to form a third bedroom, the kitchen was enlarged, and a bathroom was added to the structure.

The Knowltons say the house has shown signs of being haunted ever since they moved in, but Kim said they are not particularly frightened by the strange things that have occurred. They are just curious.

The living room, which is large, with a vaulted ceiling, has been furnished with Victorian period pieces, including an old church pew. Kim refers to it as her "piano room." The piano, an antique upright, provided the first indication that the house might be haunted. Although it is not a player piano, it plays, by itself, at times. The sounds are usually full chords and scales. The Knowlton's bedroom is separated from the sitting room by just a doorway. They have often heard the instrument strike up a few chords in the middle of the night, and they also hear the voices of men in conversation in the big parlor. When they step inside the room, the voices stop. Although it is quite plain the men are engaged in some sort of conversation, Kim has never been able to make out what they are saying. All three of the Knowltons, Kim, her husband Scott, and their nine-year-old daughter Whitney, have heard the music and the voices.

Just a short time back (January 1997) Kim was awakened by the sounds of a little girl's giggles. Since Whitney is only nine, Kim thought she had slipped into her parents' room. But then Kim noticed a figure bathed in the white glow of moonlight, standing at the foot of her big four-poster bed. The figure was that of a little girl, about six or seven years old, and she was hanging onto the bedpost and laughing as little girls sometimes do. She appeared as a misty, semitransparent form, but Kim says she saw enough to know she was a very beautiful child, with long hair. She was dressed completely in white, and her garment could have been either a dress or a nightgown. After a short time the little figure slowly faded away.

Just a few nights later, in February of 1997, Whitney came and crawled into bed with her parents. She said, "Mommy, who is that man standing in my room?" Kim told her she didn't know, but not to be afraid; just go on to sleep.

Kim told me there are cold spots all over the older part of the house, but not the parts which have been added on. I asked her if she knew if there had been any deaths in the house, and she said she really didn't know.

Recently, the Knowltons found some old leftovers from previous occupants of the property which had been left in the barn. Among other things, there was a portrait of a baby dressed in a long white christening gown. Kim couldn't tell if the infant was a boy or a girl, because it was completely bald headed. The photograph is in an old-fashioned oval frame. Kim wonders if the picture might be an early likeness of the little girl who appeared at the foot of her bed.

The Wehe ranch was once quite large, but has been divided up. Kim says there's an old cemetery where some family members were buried about a mile from her house. She has not done much investigating to see who is buried there, but she does know a Wehe man and his son are among the occupants of the graveyard.

The Knowltons appear to be happy in their country home. They know it's haunted, but except for being curious as to who their visitors are, they are not intimidated by them. They believe the spirits are friendly, and therefore they are welcome in their home.

# CHAPTER 6

# STRANGE
# UNEXPLAINED THINGS

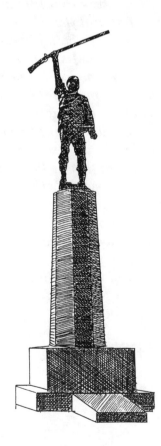

## STRANGE UNEXPLAINED THINGS
Docia Williams

*Strange unexplained things that go "bump in the night"*
*Creatures with features that elucidate fright!*
*Like Converse's wolf-creature that fills us with dread,*
*When the moon rises full and the rivers run red. . . .*
*And the ghost Cadillac that's both big and black,*
*That's roaming the roads to McDona and back.*
*While dancing diablos roam old Milam Square,*
*I've never seen them, but I'm sure they are there!*
*There's a man who dances on strange chicken feet,*
*A devilish man that you don't want to meet!*
*From the depths of the river, the sad mournful cry*
*Of La Llorona is heard, to those who pass by,*
*No one can save her. Forever she's there,*
*Luring her victims, her sorrows to share.*
*When the moon rises full and the night's deathly still*
*And the shadows creep over the woodland and hill,*
*There are "things" so frightening, they'll give you a scare*
*Go search for them. Find them. They're lurking out there.*

# Specters, Spooks, and Legendary Beings

Many of the stories included in this chapter are legends. They have been repeated in this community for a very long time, having been handed down from one generation to the next. Many have their roots in the Hispanic population of South Texas.

Obviously, I have not been able to document many of these frightening tales, as I have done with most of the stories told in preceding chapters. Many of them have been told, changed, and passed down by word of mouth from parent to child. The originators of most of these stories have probably passed away. Some are too utterly preposterous to be believed, yet some people will swear they are true! At any rate, they are the real fright stories, guaranteed to make the heart beat faster and the goosebumps to rise! And some belong uniquely to San Antonio!

Some of the stories in this chapter are about all sorts of strange, unexplainable things that don't quite fit into any of the categories covered in preceding chapters. They were, for the most part, told to me by friends of long standing. These are about real occurrences that real people within my circle of acquaintances have experienced. I found them interesting and I believe you will also.

Don't forget, the strangest things always seem to occur when the moon is full, the night is quiet and still, and the clock strikes the hour of midnight.

# La Llorona

Not only symphonic works feature "variations on a theme." Here's a story with many variations, which has been passed down by word of mouth for generations. It's the story of La Llorona, the weeping woman, who is the grande dame of all South Texas spirits. In spite of the twists and turns of the various versions, there seems to be a common theme, a lesson in morality, that is still used to great advantage by many Hispanic mothers to teach their offspring to follow the straight and narrow pathway.

Nearly every South Texas town, from Corpus Christi to Laredo, Seguin to San Antonio, Del Rio to El Paso, has heard of her. John Igo, greatly respected locally as a poet, playwright, writer, and educator, told me he has long been fascinated with the various stories about La Llorona and offered to share some of them with me. He said these stories go back almost three hundred years and more than likely originated in Mexico.

One of these versions of the weeping woman's background says she was a young woman who was married in a big church in Mexico. As she stood by the altar wearing her beautiful white wedding gown, she promised the priest that she would give her first son to the church to become a priest. However, when she did have children, she decided this really was not what she wanted for her offspring, so she went back on her word, and her first son was not delivered into the priesthood. As a consequence her house caught fire, the children all burned up, and she herself was burned and deformed, her face taking on the characteristics of a donkey, or horse. This "donkey lady" is doomed to search forever for her children.

Her searches are said to center around creeks and rivers. Women are said to have seen her, but men usually just hear her as she cries for help. Some men have drowned trying to reach her. A dim figure in white has been seen near creeks by numerous people, according to Mr. Igo. People living near the confluence of Alazon Creek and Martinez Creek here in San Antonio have reported hearing her mournful cries. She is said to call out, "mi hijo, mi hijo . . . " ("my son, my son") from the depths of a river or stream. Those who would venture to rescue her are often drowned in the attempt. Those who have survived are said to have seen "something white" floating on top of the water. Some people have further stated that she most often makes her appearances on rainy, foggy nights.

Mothers, grandmothers, and aunts of little Hispanic children have long told them to stay clear of rivers and streams and to come in before dark or "La Llorona might get you," so this is a sort of safety lesson for youngsters.

There's another version to the story that says there were two baby girls, twins, born to a family. When they were infants, they were taken to the church for baptism. They were so identical, one of them was apparently baptized twice. The other baby was never baptized. She married and when she was about nineteen she had a son and a daughter. But she did not love them, so she drowned them in an acequia. When she died and went before God, He told her she would have to return to the world and search for her children until the end of time. Then she would be pardoned. They say she appears where there are streams and acequias, canals and ditches, and her weeping and wailing is a terrible thing to hear.

My favorite version of the many I have read, is one I first read about in the October 1983 edition of *Texas Highways Magazine* in an article penned by Corpus Christi psychologist and writer Jane Simon Ammeson.

Ammeson wrote about beautiful Luisa, a peasant girl who was wooed by an aristocratic and wealthy Spaniard, whose name was Don Muno Montes Claro. Now Don Muno loved the girl, but he knew because they were of different classes he could never marry her. So he set her up as his mistress, providing her with a nice little cottage on his estate where he could visit her frequently. While he tended his estate and mingled socially with those of his social status, he spent the nights making love to beautiful Luisa. The couple had three children and Luisa was contented with her lot in life. That is, until Don Muno quit coming around to see her. It had been some time since he last paid her a visit and she was very distressed, so she summoned up all her courage and journeyed some miles to the big estate where her lover made his home. She asked the servants if she could see him, and was told that was an impossibility as he was being married that very day to a woman who was a member of the aristocracy with whom he associated. Heartbroken, Luisa hurried home to her little cottage. In a frenzy of grief and rage, she killed her little children and then threw their bodies into the river. Of course, she was arrested and hauled off to prison. It wasn't long until she lost her mind, and she died, screaming in anguish for the little ones she had killed. Strangely enough, this version of the story has Don Muno, back in his beautiful hacienda with his new bride, dying of some unnamed cause on the same day that Luisa breathed her last. Of course, the story has the soul of little Luisa doomed to search the streams and rivers forever for her dead children, crying out for them to all who would listen.

These are just three examples of the La Llorona story. The weeping woman is well known all over this part of the world. And I actually have spoken to people who say they have seen her!

Jerry Salazar, who is employed at the *San Antonio Express News*, grew up in Laredo. When Jerry was a youngster, he was with a group of other boys standing on the riverbank. They all saw this woman standing on the opposite bank. She wore a long, flowing white gown and had long black hair. She appeared to be very beautiful. She reached out her arms, beckoning to the young boys to come into the river and cross over to where she waited. The youngsters had enough sense to turn and run home as fast as they could go! They knew they had seen La Llorona!

When Gene Sanchez, now the commander of the Criminal Division at the Bexar County Jail, was a youngster, he and his buddies sometimes got into what Gene calls "a little mischief," here and there. He says that he grew up in a rather poor section of San Antonio, near Five Points. There wasn't enough money in the family budget for an allowance for extra spending money, so sometimes Gene and his two best friends, Jesse Bazan and Gilbert Rodriguez, used to go "car prowling." Gene asked me if I knew what that meant, and I had to confess my ignorance. Well, the boys, who were about twelve or thirteen at the time, used to break into parked cars and help themselves to anything lying about on the seats: gloves, cameras, parcels, anything they thought might be of value. Then they'd pawn it when they had an opportunity.

The boys knew if they took their ill-gotten loot home, their parents would "beat the hide off them," so they hid their stolen goods in the ledges underneath the bridge that spanned Camaron Creek. (The creek is underground now, covered with a culvert constructed to prevent flooding.)

One afternoon about dusk the boys went down under the dark bridge. There was quite a bit of water in the creek in those days. Suddenly, they heard something. They turned, and all three of them saw her at once. There was this woman dressed in a long white gown, which looked almost like a nightgown. She had long black hair, and she was combing it with a big Spanish comb like the women wore in their mantillas. She would dip the big comb in the creek water, then run it through her hair as she knelt by the side of the stream. And she was making a moaning, sobbing sound all the while she was combing her hair. Gene said it was weird!

The boys stared at the strange figure for a few minutes, and then she slowly disappeared—just faded away! The boys took off running and didn't stop until they reached their homes. Gene told his mother what he had seen. She asked him, "Son, have you done anything wrong?" He couldn't lie to his mother, and so he told her what he and the other boys had been doing. His mother told him that La Llorona had come to warn them to stop doing bad things. It was, she said, "a sign from God."

Gene said the boys never broke into another car. They all ended up making good records in school and got college educations, becoming solid citizens. Jesse lives in Junction, Kansas, now. Gilbert, now deceased, became an outstanding labor leader at Kelly Field, and Gene, the little boy who once broke into cars ended up being the commander of the Criminal Division of the Bexar County Sheriff's Department!

It's amazing what La Llorona can accomplish!

Just in case you've nothing better to do and want to go looking for her, you might want to know just what La Llorona looks like. There are many descriptions, but in general she is said to be beautiful, until you can see her closely. Then, she either has a totally blank face, or else she has the long distorted face of a donkey or a horse. She dresses in long, flowing robes, which usually are white, and her long, shiny fingernails often look like silvery knives in the starlight.

Whether such a wraith actually exists, or whether she is a figment of many vivid imaginations, La Llorona's legend teaches several good lessons to those who would heed them. Don't be cruel to your children. And to the children themselves: Be good. Stay home. And don't go near the water.

# Woman Hollering Creek

There is a little creek between San Antonio and Seguin that bears an unusual name. It is called Woman Hollering Creek. There are a number of legends about how the creek got its strange name. Visitors to San Antonio often comment on having seen the sign by the bridge which spans the creek on I-10.

My historian friend Sam Nesmith told me he had heard that a pioneer family who lived along the banks of the creek were attacked by Indians. The husband, who was working in the field, was killed and scalped. His wife, knowing what a terrible fate awaited her children at the hands of the Indians, killed her youngsters by drowning them in the creek. Then, she went stark raving mad. The Indians, when they came upon the woman on the banks of the creek, were fearful of her, as they were of all people afflicted with madness, and they let the woman go. She wandered the creek banks sobbing and crying for her lost children, a "woman hollering," and they say her spirit still returns to search for them.

Another explanation for the naming of the stream is that panthers or "wild cats" used to roam the area, and the creek was a favorite watering hole for them. The screams they made, resembling a woman's cries, resulted in the early settlers naming the creek Woman Hollering Creek.

John Igo thinks maybe the creek is just another place where La Llorona searches for her little ones. I don't plan to go out there after dark to find out.

# The Dancing Devil

Now, here's a story that is hard to believe, but those who were there say it is true. There were articles concerning this event in the *Express News* back on October 28, 1979, and still another on October 29, 1989. There's a nightclub called El Camaroncito Nite Club located at 411 Old Highway 90 West. That's where it all took place. There's not much to say about the building. It is a sort of square, windowless, cement-block structure, wedged in among other businesses. But back about Halloween of 1975 a strange event is said to have occurred there that still causes shivers when it is mentioned.

There was a big crowd there that night, lots of couples, lots of pretty ladies, and the place was pretty lively. The little band played some mighty rhythmic conjunto music, rancheritas, and one good cumbia after another. Everybody seemed to be having a great time! Then, in walked a stranger, a handsome Latin-type wearing a white suit, complete with lots of gold chains and a black, open-chested shirt. One of the women who was there that night was quoted in the *Express News* article as saying "He was the most handsome man I have ever seen. I noticed him right away. He was just the type of man you can't take your eyes off of. . . . " The woman, whose name is Rosa Garcia, said he danced with nearly all the women, and he was a wonderful dancer. She said, "Oh, my, he could dance, and he never got tired. He danced with several women. And it's funny, you know, because I don't remember seeing him sit down at a table. He wasn't with a woman. He was just everywhere." And did Rosa dance with him? "Oh, yes, and I wish I could have danced with him all night long. We danced a cumbia and he danced circles around me. Now and then he would grab the hem of my chiffon dress and swing his arm with it. Just his touching my dress, was like he was touching me. I can still remember the chills going up and down my back," she said. "He had some kind of power."

Finally, he asked a young beauty who was rather aloof to dance. Soon he had her on her feet and they began to sway to the music. She became almost entranced as they moved over the floor. The unsuspecting woman rested her cheek on his shoulder. They swayed, but their feet were still.

Then, something really strange happened. For a moment the enchanted woman broke out of her almost hypnotic trance and she glanced to the floor. "Your feet! Your feet!" she screamed, and tore herself from the tight embrace of her partner. Dancers on the floor stood frozen as she shouted and struggled to free herself from the man's clutches.

Then other women began to scream, and some started to mumble prayers. Two ladies actually fainted. The men, less frightened but still not wishing to approach the man, grabbed their partners and retreated to their tables or backed up against the walls.

But their eyes never left the well-dressed man's feet, which had been dancing away in fashionable Stacy Adams shoes. Now, in horror, they watched as four long-nailed stubs stuck out from under both of his trouser cuffs.

They were chicken feet. This was a sign of the devil!

After the commotion subsided, the shoeless stranger ambled off towards the men's room. Rogebo Cruz and three of his friends followed after the man. But Cruz recalls that only a cloud of smoke and the strong smell of sulfur remained in the men's room. The man had gone out the shattered window. Now everybody knows the devil prefers the smell of sulfur to Old Spice!

The devilish stranger never came back to El Camaroncito, but they say he also made a visit to the Rockin' M Club in Lockhart back in the 1970s.

# Milam Square, Where Devils Dance

Milam Square is a tranquil spot between the Santa Rosa Hospital and the lively Market Square, or El Mercado. It has been beautifully landscaped, and recently some fine playground equipment and a number of attractive wrought iron park benches have been added to the area. But once it was the cemetery where all Protestant settlers were buried. Directly across Houston Street, where the Santa Rosa Hospital now stands, was the old Catholic cemetery. The area was designated as a cemetery as early as 1808.

Today the peaceful park is dominated by a beautiful statue of Ben Milam, who fell on December 7, 1835, while fighting Mexican troops commanded by General Cos. The valiant Milam was one of the early leaders in Texas's bid for independence from Mexico. His body was buried there after its removal from the old Veramendi house where he had been mortally wounded. His grave, marked with a simple granite stone, is still there in the park which was named in his honor.

An article in the *San Antonio Express News*, without a byline, dated March 1890, stated that the area was west of San Pedro Creek where nobody lived. It said that there was a graveyard there, however, and the unknown writer mentioned that a curious feature of the graveyard was the piles of human bones and skeletal remains heaped all over the ground. This must have been during the time the bodies were being exhumed for removal to another cemetery, so this area could be converted to a park.

Records show that at least part of the cemetery's ownership was transferred by the Bishop of Galveston to the Sisters of Charity of the Order of the Incarnate Word in 1874. Many of the bodies lying there were later removed to the old San Fernando Cemetery; others were left untouched, and no sign of them remains today. However, local legends say the spirits of the victims of violent deaths appear from time to time, and that any person passing by the area who has evil thoughts just might count on being visited by these specters, whom locals call the "Devils of Milam Square."

# The Black Cadillac Ghost Car

We were first told about this phantom car by Judy Schiebe, who used to be a social worker. Her territory included the area around McDona. She said the people out there were very superstitious about a "ghost car" that was said to appear at dusk and had run many people off the road. They used to warn her to leave that area in plenty of time so she wouldn't run into the big black Cadillac.

I mentioned this to John Tolleson, a longtime resident and local tour guide. He said he had heard of the ghost car's appearance for years He said there was a gang of bank robbers known as the Newton Gang who terrorized folks in these parts for many years. They drove a big black Cadillac. This was around Prohibition time.

The hoodlums used to stay at the old Continental Hotel next to the Spanish Governor's Palace on Military Plaza. It is now a city office building.

The Newtons were afraid to put money in the San Antonio banks since most of their wealth had come from robbing them in the first place, and so they went out west of town and buried their ill-gotten cash, marking the spot with a big rock. They were all pretty drunk at the time. And, it was dark. Well, there are lots of rocks in that territory, and they all look pretty much alike. When they sobered up enough to go and reclaim their treasure, they just couldn't find it. So the story goes that their spirits just keep coming back looking for their stash, and that old black Caddy careening down the back roads is their old getaway car!

# Poor Old Hobo Joe

In the Depression years, many a man seeking employment or free transportation would hitch a ride on a freight train. These people who had fallen on hard times were often referred to as tramps or hoboes. They would travel about the country, working a little here and there to provide some means of survival.

Well, back in 1932 the summer night skies turned blood red when three boxcars on a section of track southeast of San Antonio caught fire. An unfortunate hobo was caught inside one of the cars and was unable to escape. His screams rang out in the night as horrified onlookers and railroad workers tried, in vain, to rescue him.

No one ever knew his name, so the nickname Hobo Joe was given to the unknown unfortunate who perished in the fire. Workers returning the next morning to take his remains for a Christian burial were unable to find anything at all. Yet, someone had burned alive that night. Of that there was little doubt. The screams had been far too real.

There has never been an explanation for the mysterious disappearance of the remnants of "Joe," but there are those who live in the vicinity of where the fire occurred who swear that nearly every night, at 11:45 p.m., the time when the poor man was cremated alive, frightening screams can be heard as Hobo Joe returns to the scene of his death as a sober reminder of his tragic fate.

# The Wolf Creature of Converse

There's been a story around since about 1965, about a San
Antonio version of a werewolf, which is said to roam the hills
and valleys near the community of Converse. It is seen most
often around FM 1518 at a place known as Skull's Crossing.

Supposedly, a retired military man returned to San Antonio to live. He had a thirteen-year-old son who was quite
studious and preferred to read and study rather than pursue
any athletic endeavors. His father was very interested in
hunting. That's why he settled on the eastern edge of the city,
where easy access to acres of hunting land was near at hand.

The former soldier was disappointed that his son did not
display any interest in his favorite pursuit. He felt the boy
displayed "sissy" or unmanly behavior. One night he presented the youngster with a rifle and told him to go out and
not return until he had "shot something."

Just before dark, the boy returned home without any
game. He told his dad a terrifying story about a wolf-like creature which had stalked him through the low cedar breaks.
Thinking the boy was just making excuses, the man sent him
out again into the now darkening hills. But this time the boy
didn't return home. When he was still missing the next day,
his now-concerned father organized a search party to go off on
horseback to look for the boy.

After searching all that afternoon and night, the men
found their way to a low valley near Skull's Crossing, and
their horses refused to go any farther. The men dismounted
and, afoot, began a cautious search of the valley, determined
to locate the boy. They were totally unprepared for what they

would find. Only a few feet into the dark valley, the men came upon a half-man, half-wolf-like creature, feeding on the remains of the boy's torn and bloody body. Startled, the creature disappeared into the trees. The only traces left were the mangled remains of the boy.

The full moon is said to call him out, and legends surrounding the mysterious wolf man claim sheep mysteriously disappear. And they say a nearby creek still runs blood-red on those nights when "something strange" is out there, stalking the eastern hills.

# The Haunted Railroad Tracks

Is it a legend? A made-up story? Or is it really true?

To be perfectly honest, there doesn't seem to be any documentation to substantiate this story. I've tried to find records in the libraries and newspaper files that would give a date and some details about a tragedy that is supposed to have happened a long time ago. The story, which has been a part of San Antonio's lore and legends for many years, concerns a train-school bus accident that is variously described as having happened in the 1930s or 1940s. I talked with a couple of elderly Southern Pacific Railroad men, and they said they vaguely recalled hearing about such an accident but could recall no details. It was a long time ago, and it doesn't look like anyone who might know about it is even alive now. The newspaper librarian has to have the date of such an incident in order to look up any news account in the microfilm files, and I just don't have it. It does seem like an accident of such magnitude would have been widely reported at the time.

So take it for what it is. A good story. A legend. But because it is so well known, it must be included in any ghost story book about San Antonio!

Years ago, the story goes, a school bus taking a group of ten youngsters home from the consolidated county school on the far south side, stalled as it started up over the Southern Pacific Railroad tracks. The driver couldn't get the bus to start. And suddenly, from out of nowhere, or so it seemed, the five o'clock freight train loomed into sight. The train couldn't stop and the school bus wouldn't start, and the result was a tragic accident at the crossing where Shane and Villamain Roads meet.

It is said that all the children and the bus driver were killed. Strangely enough, no mention has ever been made, to my knowledge, as to the fate of the train's engineer and his crew.

All we know, and this is what makes the story so fascinating, is that when a car is parked on Shane Road about thirty or so yards from the tracks, with the gears placed in neutral, and the driver's feet off both the brakes and the accelerator, it will suddenly start to roll towards the railroad tracks, gaining momentum as it progresses. The vehicle will cross the tracks, which are raised, and then come down on the other side, rounding the curve on Villamain Road.

Frequently people dust the trunks and rear bumpers of their vehicles with talcum powder or cornstarch, then when the rear of the vehicle is checked after its crossing over tracks, there always seems to be some small handprints visible in the powder. The oft-repeated story goes that the spirits of the little dead children don't want another bus or car to come to the tragic end that they did, and so they keep watch to insure a safe journey by pushing a vehicle up and over the tracks out of harm's way.

The area, which is pretty spooky anyway, with weed-overgrown stretches along the way, and trash and litter strewn along the roadside, is not a place where one would enjoy a pleasure stroll. Several murder victims have been dumped in the general vicinity of the crossing. One was as recent as August 1995, when the decomposed, blanked-wrapped remains of either a small woman or a young girl was found in a grassy ditch about thirty yards south of the intersection of Villamain and Shane Roads. The skeletal remains were judged to have been there at least two or three weeks when a man out walking his dog in the area discovered them. It's just not a nice place to be in the first place. My psychic friend Sam Nesmith told me there are lots of bad vibes in that general area.

Another friend, Jackie Weaverling, told me one time she was with a group on a trail ride on Shane Road. They were coming into town for the annual stock show and rodeo, and they paused by the side of the road to rest a short while. Jackie had her horse in a trailer. She said he nearly tore up the trailer trying to get out, and he was usually a calm, laid-back animal. She said some of the other trail riders had a lot of trouble getting their horses to go over the tracks. None of the animals were very calm out in that area, and it was only after they finally left that vicinity that they would settle down. I have always heard that horses are very perceptive to scenes of death and tragedy.

Numerous television crews have filmed cars going over the tracks. My husband and I have been interviewed at the crossing by the *Eyes of Texas* series, Fox National TV News, the *American Journal*, and Sci-Fi Channel's *Mysteries, Magic, and Miracles,* as well as numerous local stations. And so many people come out to the famous crossing around Halloween each year, the San Antonio Police Department has to send officers out there to direct traffic! Of course, I always include the strange crossing and tell the oft-repeated legend as the finale to my *Spirits of San Antonio Tours.* My tour participants would probably ask for their money back if I didn't!

# The Night the Rains Came

It was rather late at night as John Igo made his way home. He drove slowly along Hausman Road, which is located between Interstate 10 and John's home on Waller Road. The rain was pelting down in sheets, and it was difficult to see the road ahead. Then, suddenly, in his rearview mirror, John noticed a car closely following him. It seemed to have materialized from nowhere, which he thought rather strange. After about a half mile, the following lights completely disappeared. This troubled Igo because he knew every inch of that stretch of road, and he knew there had been no side roads or driveways into which the car could have turned. Fearful that the car had run off the road in the heavy downpour, John stopped his car. He got out and ran back, looking for the missing automobile. He saw nothing; no lights and no car, and he heard nothing but the falling rain.

Still puzzled, John returned to his car and started up slowly. Suddenly he saw, not more than thirty feet ahead of him, a turbulent flow of water as Leon Creek, which normally was just a narrow little trickle of a stream, had risen over its banks and completely covered the road ahead of him. John says he feels positive that had he not stopped to check on the mysterious "car lights that weren't" he could have driven right into the torrent!

While this isn't a ghost story, it certainly smacks of the supernatural to me. I believe the mysterious tailgaiter was actually a guardian angel that followed and protected John that stormy night.

# The Haunted Family Portrait

My good friend Sylvia Sutton is a most interesting woman. She is a retired school principal and a serious student of history. She's also a direct descendant of the Leal and Carvajal families, who were among the Canary Island settlers of San Antonio.

Sylvia told me a story about a family portrait that is today in the Houston home of her youngest son, James. The picture, one of a pair, is so realistically done, for a long time the family thought it was an old photograph. It was later discovered that it is a finely done charcoal likeness of Sylvia's great-grandmother and her two small children, a boy of four and a little girl about two years old. The little girl was Sylvia's grandmother, who was born in 1894.

Sylvia's older sister, Florence, inherited the picture. It was not long until she began to hear strange noises, a sort of scratching, gnawing sound that came from within the framed picture. It seemed to just occur when Florence was depressed or worried about something. She decided maybe termites or some other insects had gotten inside the frame. She took it to Glassers, a local glass company, and asked if they would open it up and check it out thoroughly. That is when the discovery was made that the picture was a charcoal rendering and not a photograph. Glassers said there was absolutely no infestation of any kind in the picture or the frame. Yet, for some strange reason the scratching continued at times, and finally Florence was so disturbed and puzzled by it she asked Sylvia if she would keep the picture for her. Sylvia took the picture, along with a companion picture of her great-grandfather, and hung them in her dining room. Her younger son, James, especially liked the family portraits.

As long as the pictures were just in Sylvia's dining room, the strange scratching was never heard. But if Florence came over and was worried about something, the noises would begin. Florence took the pictures back a couple of times, but they upset her so much, Sylvia finally agreed to become their permanent caretaker. However, when James, now grown, asked if he could hang the ancestral likenesses in his Houston home, both Sylvia and Florence consented.

Sylvia really believes the picture of her great-grandmother, her grandmother, and great-uncle is haunted. What do you think?

# The Phantom of the Playground

Phil Barragan, the classified credit manager at the *San Antonio Express News*, told me he had an experience as a youngster that he has never forgotten. I asked him if he would share it with my readers and he very kindly sent me this account, which I quote in his own words:

This is a story of something that happened to me when I was about ten years old back in 1949. I lived at the Alazan Apache Courts and my house was located in front of the playground. At one end of the playground was a telephone pole with a light on top. The sidewalk between some houses led to the street on the other side. At night, that area was very dark because the playground light was the only light there. It was summer. It was hot, and there was no air-conditioning. The neighborhood kids would always sit outside until late. Being that my house was in the middle of the playground, we all sat in my front yard. There was myself, a boy we called "El Huero," who I recall later played basketball for Lanier High School, Chale, Joe, Mando, Porky, Larry, Sally, Jo Ann, and Tommie. One evening, as we sat around there telling stories, someone noticed a man leaning on the telephone post. He wore a white long sleeved shirt, a black hat, and black trousers. He stood there looking our way, but saying nothing. After a while we looked back there and he was not there, and no one had seen him leave. The second night when he appeared we started walking towards him, but he ran down the sidewalk and was gone. The following night we hung out closer to the post and waited. When he appeared we ran to catch him, but he ran down the sidewalk and disappeared. We were determined to find out who he was and what he was doing in our neighborhood. We all decided to jump him when he showed up. El Huero, being the biggest, was closest to the post. It was eleven o'clock when the man showed up. This time we heard his footsteps coming up the sidewalk. We waited for him to reach the post and lean against it. The post was the only thing between us and him. El Huero sneaked up on him and threw his arms around the post to catch him, but no one was there! No one saw him leave even though we were all around him. I think that was the first time I ever knew the feeling of cold fear. As long as I lived in that neighborhood, he was never seen again.

# The Ghost Riders

Several years ago, my friend Sylvia Sutton bought a ninety-acre piece of property in Attascosa County. There was an old fence completely circling the acreage, and Sylvia had to have a couple of openings cut in the fence and gates installed to gain access to her property.

There's no house on the land, but it is quite close to a new housing development, so it is no longer a lonely stretch of land far from civilization. Sylvia has a camper situated there and says she enjoys going for an occasional weekend to get a few days of peace and rest.

It wasn't long after she bought the property that Sylvia went out one day just to roam around. She took a few snapshots of her new acquisition to send to her sons. When one of the photos was developed, the images of three men on horseback could be plainly seen. One was wearing a wide-brimmed hat that Sylvia says was the type worn by early vaqueros, not a "western" type hat, and yet not the very broad brimmed hat worn by the colorful Mexican charros. She took the photos to a professional photographer friend and asked him what he made of the figures. He enlarged the photo, and the figures were even more visible. The only explanation that can be made is the sensitive film picked up the images of a trio of ghost riders!

Not only home to cowboy spirits, the ranch property also seems to be the locale for ghost lights. Generally, they appear to follow the line of the old fence on the side where Sylvia had the openings made. Usually the light, or lights, as sometimes there are two or three, are of a yellowish cast, like the color of a lantern's glow. At other times, the light takes on a bluish cast. When one walks towards the light, as Sylvia has often done (she's a brave one, that Sylvia!), it moves back and forth, will stop and start again, moving up and down like a lantern when it is being carried. Then, they eventually disappear. Sylvia has had several hunters on the place and they have also mentioned seeing the strange lights.

Sylvia's former husband, Jim Sutton, a well-known historian, thinks the land may be a portion of the once large spread owned by early Texas patriot Jose Antonio Navarro. Maybe some of his vaqueros never left!

# The Highway Warrior

Veteran Kerrville bus driver Clarence Skloss told me about an unusual experience he had in August of 1996. He'd had plenty of rest and was wide awake and alert. He enjoyed his wee-hours-of-the-morning scheduled run to West Texas. Usually congested Highway I-10 West was pretty quiet at this hour, and Skloss was making good time coming out of San Antonio. He'd gotten just past the exit to Fiesta Texas Six Flags when suddenly, seemingly from out of nowhere, a figure dashed across the three-lane highway in front of the coach.

Clarence isn't one to tell tall tales. Actually, he's usually a man of few words. But he shared this story with me because he says he's willing to swear the figure he saw materialize suddenly on I-10 was an Indian brave! The man had long black hair and was wearing what Clarence described as "antiquated Indian clothing." He was unable to see the face, as the figure never turned towards the oncoming traffic to see if it was safe to cross or not—another strange thing. It was as if he didn't even know the motorized vehicles existed. He just crossed over and then completely disappeared when he got to the median divider!

In his rearview mirror, Skloss saw the eighteen wheeler that was following along behind the motorcoach hit his brakes. The driver must also have seen the Indian warrior figure. Clarence told me several of his passengers sitting in the front of the coach who were still awake also saw the Indian.

Clarence has no explanation, save one. He thinks he saw the ghost of an Indian brave crossing the interstate highway.

Not so strange, really. Just a little over a century ago that area out west of San Antonio was Comanche and Apache territory. I'm inclined to think Clarence is right!

# Epilogue

Along the quiet thoroughfare, as darkness cloaks the city,
What is that we see?
A torn sheet of newspaper being hurled along the street,
Propelled along its way by gusts of wind?
As it tosses and tumbles along, do our eyes deceive us?
Are we seeing just an old discarded scrap of yesterday's
news,
Or are we glimpsing something far more remarkable?
Could it be possible we are seeing into the mysterious
realm of the unknown,
As spirits, long slumbering in their dank and lonely graves
Return for a little while, to roam the quiet streets
And twisted little alleyways of a slumbering city,
Seeking out the places they once knew so well?
Their substance takes on a misty whiteness in the glow
of moon beams
Filtering down from a cloudless sky.
That wind-tossed wisp of white. Where did it go?
No newspaper that.
Only a soul intent on visiting a familiar place once more,
A respite from the grave. When darkness falls.

Docia Schultz Williams

# Sources

**Newspapers**:
*San Antonio Light*
　Feb. 23, 1980
*San Antonio Express News*
　March 1890; Oct. 28, 1979; Feb. 17, 1980; Feb. 20, 1980;
　Feb. 26; 1980; Oct 30, 1983; July 3, 1988; Oct. 29, 1989;
　Nov. 20, 1994
*San Antonio Herald*
　*Sept 6, 1859; March 13, 1878*

**Magazines and Periodicals**:
*San Antonio Monthly Magazine*
　October 1981
*San Antonio Express News Magazine*
　October 1989
*Texas Highways Magazine*
　October 1983
*Current Magazine*
　Feb. 17, 1994
*San Antonio Express News Images Magazine*
　Jan. 1, 1995; Sept. 3, 1995
*Enside Source*
　Company Newsletter, *San Antonio Express News* Vol. 1,
　No. 5, Oct. 1996

**Stories**:
"Sister Solano Appears" by Sister Angelina Murphy
"Sister Amato's Last Hour" by Sister Angelina Murphy

**Books**:
*Spirits of San Antonio and South Texas* by Docia Schultz
    Williams and Reneta Byrne
    Published by Wordware Publishing Inc, 1993
*Bird's Eye View* by Augustus Koch, 1873
*Take a Deep Breath,* by Elmer E. Cooper M.D.
    Published by Nortex Press, Austin, Texas, 1992

**Personal Interviews**:
I wish to thank the following individuals who gave me leads
to stories that I otherwise would not have been aware of,
and those people who shared their stories and information
with me through personal or telephone interviews, or
through correspondence:
Dan Abram, painting contractor, New Braunfels
Paula Allen, columnist, *Images Magazine, San Antonio
    Express News*
Jane Simon Ammeson, writer, *Texas Highways Magazine*
Warren Andrews, bellman, St. Anthony Hotel
Lupe Asebedo, employee, Reed Candle Company
Nell Baeten, owner, Grey Moss Inn
Nancy Baeza, Bexar County Sheriff's Deputy, Warrants
    Division
Sue Baker, former sales director, St. Anthony Hotel
Lorenzo Banda Jr., security guard, Cadillac Bar
Carolyn Cauley Barry, former teacher, Kennedy High School
Scott Becker, owner-operator, Cafe Camille
Tracy Becker, wife of Scott Becker
Libby Bishop, Possum Flats Haberdashery
Kathleen Bittner, San Antonio psychic
Karen Blakeman, manager, Faust Hotel, New Braunfels
Mike Boatner, staff, Our Lady of the Lake University
Charles Booker, writer, *San Antonio Express News*
Allison Boone, 1996 president, San Antonio Junior League
Bud Bradford, homeowner
Lenore Bradford, homeowner
June Bratcher, owner, Conventions San Antonio/Daisy Tours

Sue Burkhalter, Southwest Craft Center
Larry Casas, San Antonio firefighter
Olga Castaneda, schoolteacher
Roslyn, daughter of Olga Castaneda
Barbara Celitans, curator, Hertzberg Circus Museum
Buddy Compton, principal, Cole High School
Dr. Elmer Cooper, author of *Take a Deep Breath*
Brenda Cordoway, employee, Cadillac Bar
Alma Cross, owner, Bullis House Inn
Jennifer Raney Curren, former resident, Raney house
Brandy Davis, Bed and Breakfast Hosts of San Antonio and
    South Texas
Gary DeValle, Bexar County Sheriff's Deputy
Cathy Diaz, co-owner, Linden House Bed and Breakfast Inn
Carla Dillard, housekeeper, Faust Hotel, New Braunfels
Edie Dugosh, former resident, haunted house
Mark Eakin, bellman, St. Anthony Hotel
Sister Francesca Eden, archivist, University of the
    Incarnate Word
Manuela Espinosa, housekeeper, St. Anthony Hotel
Sam Davidson Faires, staff, Victoria's Black Swan Inn
Cari Faulk, employee, Hammer Company
Angela Salinas Fernandez, story source
Lydia Fischer, former sales manager, Chamberley Gunter
    Hotel
Linda Frazier, employee, Cadillac Bar
Father Thomas French, archivist, Retirement Center,
    University of the Incarnate Word
Deborah Fresco, employee, Cadillac Bar
Carlos Flores, homeowner
Connie Flores, homeowner
Jet Garcia, staff member, St. Anthony Hotel
Terry Garcia, former teacher, Whittier Middle School
Victor Gaitan, employee, Reed Candle Company
Betty Gatlin, owner, Gatlin Gasthaus Bed and Breakfast Inn
Steve Green, librarian, Institute of Texan Cultures
Rick Grimm, faculty, San Antonio College

Craig Grover, homeowner
Tom Grover, homeowner
Nancy Haley, co-owner, Terrell Castle Bed and Breakfast Inn
Johnny Halpenny, manager, Riverwalk Inn
Tracy Hammer, owner, Riverwalk Inn
Arthur Howell Jr., source
John Igo, poet, professor, playwright, faculty, San Antonio
    College
Peter James, psychic, *Sightings* television series, Sci-Fi
    Channel
Tana Jaroski, firefighter, San Antonio Station 12
Linda Johnson, director, Witte Museum
Anita Jounes, executive secretary to general manager,
    Menger Hotel
Donna Keith, homeowner
Johnny Keith, Kerrville Bus Company
Captain Ben Jack Kinney, USN Retd., co-owner, Karbach
    Haus, New Braunfels
Kathy Karbach Kinney, Phd., co-owner, Karabach Haus,
    New Braunfels
Mary Kathryn Knowlton, owner, Exclusively Victorian
    Boutique
Kim Knowlton, homeowner
Mary Krzywosinski, staff, Our Lady of the Lake University
Al Langston, security guard, St. Anthony Hotel
Anna Lara, homeowner
Mario Lara, custodian, Hertzberg Circus Museum
Marcia Larsen, owner, Alamo Street Restaurant
Deborah Latham, playwright, director, Alamo Street
    Restaurant-Theatre
John Leal, historian, former Bexar County archivist
Ed Long, homeowner
Katherine Long, homeowner
Terri Long, front desk, Crockett Hotel
Al Longoria, former security guard, Southwest Craft Center
Gil Lopez, general manager, Camberley Gunter Hotel
Sharrie Magatagen, owner, Oge House Inn

Ernest Malacara, assistant manager, Menger Hotel
Rachel Martinez, faculty, Whittier Middle School
Mildred May, staff, Aggie Park
Chris McKinney, charter manager, Conventions San Antonio
Jessie Medina, manager, Cadillac Bar
Linda Mensar, librarian, Whittier Middle School
Rodney Miller, hotel staff, Menger Hotel
Peggy Moneyhun, sales manager, Crockett Hotel
Dave Mora, reservations manager, Crockett Hotel
Carmen Morales, manager, Prince Solms Inn, New Braunfels
Alfred Moreno, homeowner
Debby Moreno, homeowner
Marilyn Muldowney, president, San Antonio Aggie Wives Club
Marjorie Mungia, volunteer, National Parks Service
Sister Angelina Murphy, Sisters of Divine Providence, Our
    Lady of the Lake
Gil Navarro, assistant manager, Menger Hotel
Robert Nelson, story lead
Nancy Nesmith
Sam Nesmith, historian, psychic
Ann Norris, front desk, Crockett Hotel
Liz Null, psychic
David Ochoa, staff, South San Antonio School District
Dr. Robert O'Connor, director, Hertzberg Circus Museum
Barbara Perkins, former manager, Bright Shawl Tearoom
Maria Watson Pfiefer, historian
Mike Phillips, Bexar County Sheriff's Deputy
Katherine Poulis, co-owner, Terrell Castle Bed and
    Breakfast Inn
Harriet Raney, homeowner
Sister Schodts Reed, owner, Chabot-Reed House
Jo Ann Rivera, owner, Victoria's Black Swan Inn
Vicki Rizzo
Barbara Roberson, member, Aggie Wives Club
Allen Ross, drama department, San Antonio College
Franklin Rowe, Conventions San Antonio/Daisy Tours
Jerry Salazar, telemarketer, *San Antonio Express News*

Gene Sanchez, commander, Criminal Division, Bexar
    County Sheriff's Dept.
Judy Schiebe, former social worker
Becky Whetstone Schmidt, columnist, *San Antonio Express
    News*
Kathleen Sheridan, exective secretary, San Antonio A&M
    Club
Cindy Shiolena, guest, Menger Hotel
Chris Silva, firefighter, Station 12
Curt Skredergard, co-owner, Royal Swan Inn
Helen Skredergard, co-owner, Royal Swan Inn
John Slate
Roberta Smith, former faculty member, Kennedy High School
Thomas Smith, former custodian, Hertzberg Circus Museum
Cecilia Steinfeldt, curator emeritus, Witte Museum
Barbara Strackbein, former employee, Country Cottage Inn,
    Fredericksburg
George Stumberg III, owner, Cadillac Bar
Justin Stutz, owner, Possum Flats Haberdashery
Sylvia Sutton, educator, historian
Michael Tease, manager, Bullis House Inn
Rose Teniente, staff, McCullough Hall, Our Lady of the
    Lake University
Susan Terry, source
Joie Thiege, psychic
Robert Thiege, psychic
Lynna Thomas, owner, Weinert House Bed and Breakfast
    Inn, Seguin
Jon Thompson, architect
Shari Thorn, executive secretary to general manger,
    Crowne Plaza St. Anthony
Cliff Tice, owner, Yellow Rose Bed and Breakfast Inn
John Tolleson, San Antonio city guide
Roland Trevino, San Antonio firefighter, Station 12
Linda Turman, member, Aggie Wives Club
Hector Venegas, general manager, Menger Hotel
Jane Vivian, docent, Witte Museum

Linda Vorhees, office manager, Hammer Company
Cindy Waters, former staff member, St. Anthony Hotel
Jackie Weaverling, story source
Donna West, former owner, Royal Swan Inn
Cynthia Wiggins, owner, Brooks House
Liz Wiggins, former KENS -TV anchorwoman
Dr. Charles Wiseman, veterinarian
Bitsy Gorman Wright, owner, Mariposa Bed and Breakfast
    Inn
George Ybarra, San Antonio firefighter
Gloria Ybarra, homeowner, wife of George
Rudy Ybarra, employee, Bexar County Correctional Facility
Linda Young, bookkeeper-secretary, Grey Moss Inn
Vivienne Zamora, manager, Travis Convention Center
Dorothy Zimmerman, homeowner
Judy Zipp, librarian, *San Antonio Express News*

All photographs by Roy and Docia Williams with the exception of the photograph of the Camberley Gunter Hotel, courtesy of the hotel files.

# Index

# Other Books from Republic of Texas Press

100 Days in Texas: The Alamo Letters
by Wallace O. Chariton

Alamo Movies
by Frank Thompson

At Least 1836 Things You Ought to Know About Texas but Probably Don't
by Doris L. Miller

Civil War Recollections of James Lemuel Clark and the Great Hanging at Gainesville, Texas in October 1862
by L.D. Clark

Cow Pasture Pool: Golf on the Muni-tour
by Joe E. Winter

A Cowboy of the Pecos
by Patrick Dearen

Cripple Creek Bonanza
by Chet Cunningham

Daughter of Fortune: The Bettie Brown Story
by Sherrie S. McLeRoy

Defense of a Legend: Crockett and the de la Peña Diary
by Bill Groneman

Don't Throw Feathers at Chickens: A Collection of Texas Political Humor
by Charles Herring Jr. and Walter Richter

Eight Bright Candles: Courageous Women of Mexico
by Doris E. Perlin

Etta Place: Her Life and Times with Butch Cassidy and the Sundance Kid
by Gail Drago

Exiled: The Tigua Indians of Ysleta del Sur
by Randy Lee Eickhoff

Exploring Dallas with Children: A Guide for Family Activities
by Kay McCasland Threadgill

Exploring the Alamo Legends
by Wallace O. Chariton

Eyewitness to the Alamo
by Bill Groneman

From an Outhouse to the White House
by Wallace O. Chariton

The Funny Side of Texas
by Ellis Posey and John Johnson

Ghosts Along the Texas Coast
by Docia Schultz Williams

The Great Texas Airship Mystery
by Wallace O. Chariton

Henry Ossian Flipper, West Point's First Black Graduate
by Jane Eppinga

Horses and Horse Sense: The Practical Science of Horse Husbandry
by James "Doc" Blakely

How the Cimarron River Got Its Name and Other Stories About Coffee
by Ernestine Sewell Linck

The Last Great Days of Radio
by Lynn Woolley

Letters Home: A Soldier's Legacy
by Roger L. Shaffer

More Wild Camp Tales
by Mike Blakely

Noble Brutes: Camels on the American Frontier
by Eva Jolene Boyd

Outlaws in Petticoats and Other Notorious Texas Women
by Gail Drago and Ann Ruff

Phantoms of the Plains: Tales of West Texas Ghosts
by Docia Schultz Williams

Rainy Days in Texas Funbook
by Wallace O. Chariton

Red River Women
by Sherrie S. McLeRoy

Santa Fe Trail
by James A. Crutchfield

Slitherin' 'Round Texas
by Jim Dunlap

Spindletop Unwound
by Roger L. Shaffer

Spirits of San Antonio and South Texas
by Docia Schultz Williams and Reneta Byrne

Star Film Ranch: Texas' First Picture Show
by Frank Thompson

Tales of the Guadalupe Mountains
by W.C. Jameson

Call Wordware Publishing, Inc. for names of the bookstores in your area: (972) 423-0090

Texas Highway Humor
by Wallace O. Chariton
Texas Politics in My Rearview
Mirror
by Waggoner Carr and Byron Varner
Texas Ranger Tales
by Mike Cox
Texas Tales Your Teacher Never
Told You
by Charles F. Eckhardt
Texas Wit and Wisdom
by Wallace O. Chariton
That Cat Won't Flush
by Wallace O. Chariton
That Old Overland Stagecoaching
by Eva Jolene Boyd
This Dog'll Hunt
by Wallace O. Chariton
To The Tyrants Never Yield: A
Texas Civil War Sampler
by Kevin R. Young

Tragedy at Taos: The Revolt of
1847
by James A. Crutchfield
A Trail Rider's Guide to Texas
by Mary Elizabeth Sue Goldman
A Treasury of Texas Trivia
by Bill Cannon
Unsolved Texas Mysteries
by Wallace O. Chariton
Wagon Tongues and the North
Star: Tales of the Cattle Trails
by Eva Jolene Boyd
Western Horse Tales
Edited by Don Worcester
When Darkness Falls: Tales of
San Antonio Ghosts and
Hauntings
by Docia Schultz Williams
Wild Camp Tales
by Mike Blakely

## Seaside Press

The Bible for Busy People
Book 1: The Old Testament
by Mark Berrier Sr.
Critter Chronicles
by Jim Dunlap
Dallas Uncovered
by Larenda Lyles Roberts
Dirty Dining: A Cookbook, and
More, for Lovers
by Ginnie Siena Bivona
Exotic Pets: A Veterinary Guide
for Owners
by Shawn Messonnier, D.V.M.
I Never Wanted to Set the World
on Fire, but Now That I'm 50,
Maybe It's a Good Idea
by Bob Basso, Ph.D.
Jackson Hole Uncovered
by Sierra Sterling Adare
Just Passing Through
by Beth Beggs
Lives and Works of the Apostles
by Russell A. Stultz
Los Angeles Uncovered
by Frank Thompson
Only: The Last Dinosaur
by Jim Dunlap

Pete the Python: The Further
Adventures of Mark and Deke
by Jim Dunlap
Salt Lake City Uncovered
by Sierra Adare and Candy Moulton
San Antonio Uncovered
by Mark Louis Rybczyk
San Francisco Uncovered
by Larenda Lyles Roberts
Seattle Uncovered
by JoAnn Roe
A Sure Reward
by B.J. Smagula
Survival Kit for Today's Family
by Bill R. Swetmon
They Don't Have to Die (2nd Ed.)
by Jim Dunlap
Tucson Uncovered
by John and Donna Kamper
Twin Cities Uncovered
by The Arthurs
Unlocking Mysteries of God's
Word
by Bill Swetmon
Your Kitten's First Year
by Shawn Messonnier, D.V.M.
Your Puppy's First Year
by Shawn Messonnier, D.V.M.

Call Wordware Publishing, Inc. for names of the
bookstores in your area: (972) 423-0090